AN UNREMARKABLE BODY

Elisa Lodato grew up in London and read English at Pembroke College, Cambridge. After graduating she went to live in Japan, where she spent a year teaching, travelling and learning to speak the language. On returning to the UK she spent many happy years working for Google before training to become an English teacher. Helping pupils to search for meaning in a text inspired Elisa to take up the pen and write her own. *An Unremarkable Body* is her first novel and was longlisted for the Bath Novel Award 2016. Elisa lives in Surrey with her husband and two children.

AN
UNREMARKABLE
BODY

Elisa Lodato

WEIDENFELD & NICOLSON

First published in Great Britain in 2017
by Weidenfeld & Nicolson
an imprint of the Orion Publishing Group Ltd
Carmelite House, 50 Victoria Embankment
London EC4Y 0DZ

An Hachette UK Company

1 3 5 7 9 10 8 6 4 2

A CIP catalogue record for this book is
available from the British Library.

ISBN (Hardback) 978 1 4746 0633 2
ISBN (Export Trade Paperback) 978 1 4746 0634 9
ISBN (eBook) 978 1 4746 0636 3

Typeset by Input Data Services Ltd, Somerset

Printed in Great Britain by Clays Ltd, St Ives plc

MIX
Paper from
responsible sources
FSC www.fsc.org FSC® C104740

www.orionbooks.co.uk

In memory of Margaret Hegarty, née Farrelly

Part One

External Examination

On Tuesday 14 February 2012 I carried out a post-mortem examination on the body of Katharine Rowan of 121 Crane View Road, Surbiton, at the instance of Dr Brian Steadings, Coroner. The body was that of a 51-year-old female, 5ft 7in in height and of moderate obese build. There was a small scar on the right side of the neck. Both earlobes had been pierced, the left torn.

I remember how my mother got that scar. She was attacked in the school playground. It happened as we waited for the bell to signal the beginning of the school day. I was about six years old, in Ms Graham's class – 2B. My baby brother Christopher was snotty and cold in his pushchair, the front wheels positioned on the 2 and 3 of the hopscotch grid. I remember this because my mother was standing on the 7, making it an impossibly long leap from where I was, at number 1.

Her hair was pulled back, quickly and quietly, by Sue Warren. Sue lived a few doors down from us with her daughter Jenny and son Sam. I had sat in her car and at her table before, but whatever instinct led her to grab my mother's hair – and entangled earring – back in this strangely intimate way, and stare down into my mother's pained face, made her strange and ugly to me.

Remembering that morning, as an adult, I find myself wondering at my failure to cry. Christopher also failed in this basic requirement of the young and immobile whose lot it is to watch their mother plucked from them. But Christopher didn't cry because his pushchair was positioned away from the shuffling feet, from what looked like a rather undignified fight for square number 10. I didn't cry because it simply wasn't an anatomical possibility. I was too astonished by what the woman who looked like Sue was doing to my mother.

And I wasn't the only one frozen by events. The mothers of my friends and classmates also looked on, stupefied. The incongruous hush of a playground before the bell was broken only by my mother's croaky grunts, uncertain but persevering.

Sue spoke first. 'I need to talk to you. About Jenny.' She said it almost calmly, as though my mother needn't rush. As if she'd tapped my mother gently on the arm instead of grabbing her hair up in an angry fist. My mother tried to nod. It made her strained face look even more stretched as she tried to bring her chin down in assent.

The other women approached cautiously when Sue had let go of my mother's hair, their resolve to intervene stiffened by the absence of any requirement to do so.

'How could you let it happen?' Sue's voice was hoarse and dry – I could tell she needed to swallow. 'Allow Richard to put his filthy hands on my Jenny? She's a child. Just a child.'

I saw the looks of concern turn to confusion. They were wondering if my mother had it coming. Finally, one of them broke ranks and stepped forward. 'Are you all right, Kath?' Careful not to look at Sue with anything that might be construed as reproach. At that moment, Ms Graham came out of her classroom and rang the bell vigorously, joyful in her oblivion. Sue stepped away from my mother, her palms out and open in the universal gesture of *it wasn't me* or, even if it was, the preamble to a pretty robust explanation.

My mother put her hand up to her left ear, stroked the earlobe gently and then smelt her fingers. As she looked at me in horror, I began to cry. She was smelling the blood that was running down her neck.

My mother's torn earlobe was just one scar on her corpse among many. The others were more difficult to discern, buried so deep they would only show themselves to the pathologist's scalpel. It was, of course, the most obvious physical assault on her body in the wake of my father's affair, but seeing it recorded so clinically reminds me how public her humiliation was. Not just that day in the playground or even the years afterwards, but now, in her death. Her earlobe, like so much other tissue weighed and fingered, dispassionately reported in those pages, bears witness to all her body suffered. Did the earlobe give the pathologist pause? Did he crouch down and peer closely at the injury and wonder who might have pulled that earring down and away from her body?

'Oh, Christ. You're bleeding. Your earring.' And then, as if we were looking for a set of keys, everybody's eyes slid to the grey surface of the playground and the blue lines of the hopscotch grid. I continued crying until Christopher, jutting his jaw forward for more snot, opened his mouth and joined me in my howl.

It was then I felt Ms Graham's fingers on my shoulders as she gently turned me in the direction of her classroom. 'Come on, Laura. Come with me.' But instead of going through the door to 2B's room, we went down the dark red corridor that led to the school office. She kept her hand on my shoulder the whole time, reassuring me, 'Your mother and brother are coming. They're with Mr Lewis,' when, in

5

truth, I was relieved to be walking away from them with their too-much blood and snot. And sure enough, when I turned round, my chin brushing Ms Graham's calloused fingers, I saw my mother was walking alongside the deputy head with a clump of bloodstained tissue held to her ear. Mr Lewis was pushing Christopher – the too-low pushchair handles forcing him to a stoop.

Ms Graham steered me towards one of the burgundy chairs, their colour deepening the red of the walls and giving the overriding impression of being stuck inside a hideous body passage. The chairs were lined up against the wall outside the school office, reserved for naughty pupils or anxious parents. Except I was the anxious pupil, swinging my legs, waiting for the naughty parent who had been taken into the school office for fighting. Mr Lewis pushed Christopher into the space at the end of the row of chairs and – rather expertly – applied the brake. He turned and knelt down in front of me, his breath heavy and wet with the smell of coffee: 'You sit here, Laura. Mum will be out in a bit. We're just going to have a little chat and see if we can't find a plaster for her ear, OK?' I nodded and looked up to see Ms Graham coming out of the office, shaking her head with disapproval, wearing the kind of obvious disappointment usually reserved for serious misdemeanours: spitting, biting, swearing, punching. Sue's action in the playground and my mother's consequent injury had served as a bloody demonstration of why dangly earrings should not be worn to school.

Mr Lewis stood up and steered Ms Graham away down the corridor. He kept his back to me as he tried to whisper, but I was able to make out the word *fuck*, which I knew to be a very serious swear word. But instead of looking at him with disappointment, Ms Graham just mouthed the words *no idea* and shook her head again. She looked up at me and noticed how closely I was watching them. Placing her hand gently on Mr Lewis's elbow, she moved him aside, walked towards me and sat down in the chair next to mine. Taking my hand in hers, she began patting the back of it with her free hand. I stared down at our conjoined hands for a long time, noting she had blue chalk on her thumb and index finger. She must have changed the date on the blackboard before coming outside to ring the bell.

'Your mummy's going to be fine, Laura. It's just a scratch.'

I nodded my agreement that her bleeding ear, violently torn by Sue, was probably just a scratch.

'Laura, do you know why Mrs Warren was so angry this morning?' Mr Lewis moved a little closer to us but did not sit down. Ms Graham continued: 'Have your mummy and Mrs Warren had a falling-out?'

Even my six-year-old self knew this was an occasion ripe for sarcasm. A perfect opportunity to raise my eyebrows, tilt my head condescendingly and agree: 'Yes, I think so. I think they might not be the best of friends at the moment.' But Ms Graham was a nice person; she was stroking my hand, if not gently, then at least with the good intention of reassuring me while extracting pertinent information. I looked down at our intertwined fingers, wondered who was taking 2B's register and started to cry again.

Many years have passed since that day in 1987. I tried to forget about it. My simple strategy was to pretend that it never happened, and my mother was happy to help me succeed in forgetting. She never tried to coax any fragment of it from me. Neither of us foresaw this, her post-mortem report, politely typed up with her torn earlobe as a matter of reported fact. An invitation to explain. As we both set about pretending Sue's assault on her had never happened, neither of us thought about the possibility that an account would one day be required, or that the day in question would come after her death and removal. When I was alone. A motherless daughter, with no hope of ever seeing her emerge – whole – again.

When she came out of the school office, her earlobe inexpertly taped up with plasters, she walked purposefully towards Christopher's pushchair, released the brake, took the handle with one hand and extended the other to me. I was relieved to emerge from all that red into the bright light of the playground and the promise of a day at home. We crossed the playground, walked over the hopscotch grid without so much as a downward glance and went out of the school gates.

I lay on the sofa for most of the afternoon, my mother happy for me to self-soothe with television. Christopher's cold and traumatic morning extended his usual forty-five-minute nap to just over two hours. The hours of quiet afforded my mother the opportunity to bathe and ice her ear and re-dress the wound. By the time my father came home that evening, she had changed out of her blood-soaked top, and the only evidence of Sue's assault was a subtle flesh-coloured plaster over her earlobe.

My father worked in a bank. In the years after my birth he had been slowly promoted to branch manager, an elevation in duties that kept him away from home for many hours and early evenings. But this was an evening at the end of the strangest of days.

Christopher and I were in bed by the time he came home but I was still awake, trying to piece together what had happened in the playground and wondering how my mother would ever wear an earring in her left ear again. I knew all about clip-on clasps, but couldn't work out what skin it could possibly pinch now that hers was so irreparably torn. The insoluble nature of my mother's injury led me back to her attacker: Sue was Jenny's mother, and Jenny was our babysitter. She came over to help my mother around the house on Tuesday and Thursday afternoons.

The sleepy escapism of the sofa had given way to a racing mind in bed; I was still wired and awake when my father came home and asked my mother what was wrong.

'Kath, come on. You're obviously not fine.'

'Of course I'm not fine. Look what she did to my ear!'

'The woman's a lunatic.'

'Laura saw it all,' she moaned.

'Jesus.'

'This is your fault.'

'I think Sue's the one at fault, don't you?'

'Don't give me that.' Her voice had hardened. 'It was because of you and Jenny. She came to accuse you – but decided to send her message through me, in front of our children!' I heard my mother sniff and walk down the hallway into the kitchen. This was followed by the *spink-spink* of the gas lighter used to ignite the stove. I waited for my father to follow her into the kitchen, but the silence testified to his inaction.

And then, from the living room, his voice loud: 'Give me a reason to stop and I'll stop.'

I moved to the landing and heard my mother exhale loudly. I could see the top of my father's head; he was standing on the threshold of the hallway, hovering uncertainly between the two rooms.

The answer came from the kitchen. It was spoken in a quiet and firm voice: 'Never in the house.'

He put his hands in his trouser pockets and hung his head.

As if something amused him. And then he turned on his heel and walked back into the living room.

I needed to wee and decided I'd use the downstairs toilet. I wanted in on this argument and – though I didn't understand the significance of what she'd just said to my father – I felt an urgency, deep down in my body, to show my mother I was still alive to the morning's events. My father might be sipping a gin and tonic in front of the fire, but I was still awake and straining to hear every movement and sound. I wanted to show her she wasn't alone but I didn't have the emotional vocabulary to explain any of this. All I could do was present myself, at the bottom of the stairs, in my pyjamas and peer through the open doorway of the kitchen. What I saw has stayed with me as an abiding and curious vision: my mother leaning on the work surface with a lit cigarette in her right hand. I had never, in my life, seen her smoke. Until that day. The day Sue ripped her ear apart.

On 12 February 2012 I drove the short distance to Surbiton to have lunch with my mother who, like me, lived alone. When she failed to answer the door, I let myself in. And there at the bottom of the stairs lay her body.

Her death changed everything. But not the spoken or written fact of it, the many euphemisms used to convey a difficult truth. *She passed away. She's gone. She's no longer with us.* It was her physical absence that I couldn't settle on. There had been a body. A body I knew well. It looked like her and it felt like her, but when I touched it, the warmth had gone. And because she was so cold and so dead, someone had driven her away and opened her up. And then into this appalling nothing came a typed report from someone who'd weighed and categorised all of her constituent parts and, in the process, come to a conclusion about how her absence came to be.

Grief rose like a haze of heat, distant and distorted by absolute bewilderment that she was dead. And the unrelenting truth of it, the fact that day after day she was always nowhere, altered the landscape of my life; it drained the colour from what I could see had been a pretty pallid canvas. My small, two-bedroom flat in Balham, once a triumphantly independent purchase, immediately revealed itself as a small, cramped and tatty dwelling. And as I slowed and sank under what was now a certainty, life piled up around me. Dishes soaked in the sink for days, the bin overflowed, the phone rang and still I sat there, on the cold, thin carpet with only her post-mortem report for company. The closest thing I had to her body, I found myself searching for her in the lines that claimed to account for everything she was. They were all there – her lungs, brain, heart – the organs of function, and yet I couldn't be satisfied. My own lungs heaved to the pain of her inexistence, my brain crawled over an absence that would never end: days that would never contain her again. And my heart. My heart was not broken. It was defiant and beating; pumping blood to meet the rising rhythm of my sobs.

I am a freelance writer and journalist, used to working alone and intensely on something, but I exhausted myself looking for meaning. I had never known such loneliness. I closed my eyes and tried to remember her face, the soft white fuzz that skirted her jawbone, but the image skipped away before I could reach out for it. When I opened my eyes again, to the crumbs on the work surface and the damaged sealant around the splashback tiles, I saw what a disappointing life mine was. And would be without her.

*

One evening towards the end of February, as the flat began to darken with the waning day, I felt a sudden urge to seize some of the light I'd ignored all day. I put down my cup of tea and grabbed my keys, my shoes and my coat and almost ran to the front door. I didn't want to talk myself out of it. The air outside was clean and unaffected by my mother's death. There was no time or consideration for her on Balham High Road; no one cared that she'd died with her tongue caught between her teeth. They were just getting on with their Thursday evening and, for a brief moment, I was happy to join them in their act of forgetting. With my head down and my hands in my pockets.

I passed an off-licence and, on a whim, went inside. I felt unexpectedly inspired by the bottles of alcohol, of uncorking oblivion. The carpet beneath my feet was red and garish, the shopkeeper too friendly. I bought a bottle of cheap red and walked home.

Despite the fresh air and change of scenery, I exhaled with deep relief when I got back to the shared hallway of my Victorian conversion. I made my way past the bicycles and pushchairs left there by tenants who had shrugged at the lack of storage space in their flats. My own flat is on the first floor and, once inside, I went straight to the kitchen and, without taking my coat off, poured myself a glass of wine. I gulped it down quickly and then poured another. I felt relieved and relaxed enough to take off my coat and shoes, switch on the lamps in the living room and light the fire. With glass in hand I sat down at the table and began reading the report again, carefully. As the wine spread its warmth through my stomach, I read of the coldness of hers. And then I grabbed for my work bag, thrown down in the hallway on the last Friday of my old life. I pulled at the Velcro strap that held my laptop secure in its sleeve and, with a sudden and urgent need to bear witness, I began reaching within myself for the story of her torn earlobe.

My editor, Andy, called one Friday afternoon around the middle of March. I was absorbed in my writing, the laptop screen providing the only light in the dimming living room. My phone was on the table beside me, on silent so that I would not be disturbed. But the unexpected vibration was enough to jolt my attention and force me to notice that it was almost time to go and buy another bottle of wine. And answer the phone. I accepted the call with a renewed and short-lived interest. One that waned after *hello*.

'Laura? How're you doing?'

'Hi Andy. I'm OK, thanks. How are you?'

'All good here. Listen, say if you think it's too soon, but I wondered if you fancied having lunch one day next week? It's been a while since we spoke and, you know, we're all missing you here.'

'Thank you. And yes, I'd like that.'

'Great. How about Wednesday or Thursday next week?'

'Thursday's good.'

'Thursday, then. Meet in The Goat for 1 p.m.?'

'Perfect. See you then.'

I put my phone down and walked into the kitchen. With nothing to do, I opened the fridge and noticed a yogurt, untouched, on the top shelf at the back. I tiptoed to reach it, feeling pleased it was still in date, but as I peeled the lid off I looked down at the bin. I'd taken the rubbish out that morning and hadn't replaced the bin bag. I put my yogurt down and searched in the cupboard under the sink, and that's when I remembered why I hadn't replaced the bin bag. I'd run out. I threw the yogurt lid in the uncovered bin, knowing not only that I'd have to fish it out later, but that I couldn't go on, holed up and grieving, in a dirty flat indefinitely. Life, with all its humdrum self-importance, was beckoning.

Andy gave me my first job in journalism, writing for the life-style section of a free London newspaper – the kind handed out aggressively at tube stations – in December 2006. I came to his attention because of *Lost Angel*, a blog I began in May 2005. I lived in Angel, Islington at the time, renting a room in a large house. Every week I identified a small historical fact about the area that I extrapolated, however tenuously, to my own life as a twenty-something professional trying to make my way in the bewildering metropolis. Angel was a very exciting place to live in 2005 – its transformation well under way; the bars and coffee shops continued to proliferate, and as more and more young people flocked to the area and its environs, I began to see that I'd hit upon something. My blog became a kind of imperfect diary composed of sporadic reflections, peppered by my own frustrations and insecurities. I began receiving emails from a small number of readers and they helped me to see that there was an appetite for modern reflections on an old path – that however contemporary we might feel, it is comforting to know we are treading lightly on walkways already laid down for us.

My most successful post was a parody of Dante's *Divina Commedia* set in Angel tube station. The twisted sculpture of Kevin Boys's angel in the ticket hall, poised to run down to the trains, gave me the idea to write of my own long descent, down an escalator of record-breaking length, to the hellish pit below, where the scurrying commuters are forced to choose between Morden or High Barnet. I described myself being held in purgatorial sway on the platforms, watching the dark hole that yawned for all of us, and the enduring torment even after boarding a tube – of trying to remain stable as bodies, weaker than your own, jostled and jolted; the search for meaning in the advertisements above the heads of the fortunate few to be seated. It was overwritten but well received; people shared it, and my readership continued to grow.

When I'd exhausted Angel, I moved on to other parts of London, working late into the evening and getting up early in the morning to complete my research. I began receiving enquiries from editors of various London publications interested in serialising my posts, and in 2006, *Lost in London* was commissioned to appear weekly in a newspaper with a readership of just under two million. I began by reprising some of my more popular posts, edited to appeal to Londoners in general and summarised to just five hundred words. Readers were invited to email comments or suggestions, and I spun their ideas into my own fabricated travails.

My mother was proud of me. She used to walk up to Surbiton station every Friday morning to get her copy of the newspaper, handed out at the station entrance. When my column first appeared, she even took her copy and boarded a commuter train heading towards Waterloo. I laughed when she told me and asked her why. She saw nothing strange in it, simply remarking that she wanted to read my column like everybody else. On a busy train. And because she had no reason to be in London, she simply remained on the train and waited for the driver to walk to the other end and take her back to Surbiton.

She never expressed surprise at my ambition to write, but when my work was finally printed for all to see, her pride was indomitable and personal. My achievement became her own. One she could share, happily, with Surbiton's commuters.

I began writing as a journalist in November 2008, just as the term 'credit crunch' firmly embedded itself in the nation's vernacular. The business editor of the newspaper had emailed Andy to ask if he knew anyone who would be interested in covering some of the human stories behind the rising numbers of evictions in the capital. *Lost in London* was still very much my bread and butter, but I was keen to broaden my horizons, so I went to talk to tenants who were on the brink of eviction and what I found surprised me. There were a handful of landlords who, despite their tenants being several months in arrears, had opted not to evict. I managed to interview four – three of whom cited the vulnerability of their tenants as their most compelling reason for declining to evict. The fourth landlord simply didn't have the time or money to commence legal proceedings, but I had enough to shape a story and offer up a positive – albeit minor – rejoinder to the bleak and implacable headlines at the time. I tentatively offered my copy on the rise of the philanthropic landlord in some of London's poorest boroughs to Andy, who passed it to the paper's business editor. It was printed, and so began my career as a London-centric journalist.

The following Thursday I took the tube to Marble Arch, leaving myself enough time to walk across Hyde Park before my lunch with Andy. It was mid-March, and the trees had begun to bud with timid green leaves. I felt just as tight and nervous. It was a beautifully sunny day, not particularly warm, but bright enough to make me regret wearing a jacket. I wanted to take it off and spread it on the short, soft grass. To sit among and away from other people; but I knew that if

I did, I wouldn't want to get up again. Andy and my old life were waiting for me, so I walked across the park to see about rejoining it.

He was at the bar when I walked in, sweating in my too-many layers, all of which had felt essential that morning as I'd shivered in my underwear. The pub was warm and close, surrounding its drinkers with a forced affection. I took my jacket off and folded it over my handbag as I walked towards the bar.

'Hello stranger,' I said, tapping him gently on the arm.

'Laura!' he said, putting his arm across my shoulders and waving a twenty-pound note like a flag at the retreating barmaid. 'I'm just ordering. What can I get you?'

'Oh . . . to eat? What do they have?'

'No, just drinks. We can look at the menu in a minute. If you're hungry, that is.'

'I'll have an orange juice, please.'

'Orange juice. I'm at that table over there in the corner. Go and grab a seat. I'll bring the drinks over.'

I did as I was told and sat down opposite Andy's chair, claimed by his jumper folded over the back of it. And as I sat there, pulling the layers of clothing from myself, I felt a kind of weary awe for the motions that had delivered me to a pub in Kensington. The tube I'd taken; the barmaid pouring my drink; the editor who wanted me to work again. They were all part of a wider and insensible existence. One I could rejoin or withdraw from at a moment's notice.

Andy returned to the table with a pint of lager and my orange juice. He had two menus tucked under his right arm. He sat down and passed me my drink, offering his own up in salutation: 'Cheers.'

'Cheers.' I smiled.

Andy studied my face for a few seconds as he sipped his lager. When he put it down again, his expression had changed to one of sympathetic understanding.

'I'm so sorry, Laura. If it's any consolation, my dad died five years ago. Parkinson's. So I know what it's like to lose a parent.'

I stared down at my orange juice. 'I'm sorry to hear that.'

He shook his head. 'Don't be. I'm just trying to say that I know how shit it can be.'

'It was very . . . unexpected. As I think you know.'

'Yeah. I sometimes catch myself thinking, would that be easier?'

'Would what be easier?'

'You know, someone important in your life dying suddenly rather than a long-drawn-out performance in a hospice.'

I took a sip of my drink. 'I don't know.'

'How was the funeral?'

'Sad. Really sad.'

He reached across the table and grabbed the fingers of my left hand. I could tell he didn't know how long or tightly he should hold them.

'Did you bury her?' he asked, pulling his hand away. As though I might still have some of the dirt under my fingernails.

'No, cremated.'

'Are you going to scatter her somewhere?'

'Not sure,' I answered, sipping more of my drink. 'She's currently on my kitchen windowsill. I need to find her a more permanent resting place,' I said, smiling.

Andy was relieved by the banter. 'Listen, the way to get through something like this is to keep yourself busy. From my own experience, it's the only thing that works.'

I nodded my head and looked behind him to the bar, where the barmaid was holding a glass to one of the spirit optics on the wall, scrutinising herself in the mirrored glass. She looked bored.

'And I've got something just perfect for you.'

'Oh yes?' I said, refocusing on him.

'We're looking to do a series of articles on what the Olympics will mean for east London,' he continued. 'You know – in real terms, not just the landlords and homeowners but minority groups, elderly residents, disadvantaged kids. That sort of thing.'

I heard his words, numbered the community groups, pre-empted the 'issues' and felt suddenly exhausted. I looked down at my orange juice, the ice cubes smaller than they had been. Less willing to clink. 'I'm not sure.'

'What are you not sure about?'

'That I can take something that big on at the moment. And do it justice.'

'OK. Look. Forget the series. Just try one article. I wouldn't ask if I didn't think you were the right person.'

'Can I have a think about it?'

'Of course. And listen, like I said on the phone, we all miss having you around. Have a think and let me know by Monday. OK?'

'OK. Will do,' I said, swallowing. 'So, how are you? And how are the kids?'

'Really good,' he said with a smile. 'Freya's getting on well in Reception, and Jacob loves Year Three.' He picked up his phone and began searching for a recent picture. It took a few seconds but eventually he found one: a young boy with front teeth that were too big for his smile. Beside him was a pretty, diffident little girl.

'They're beautiful,' I said.

He drank his pint quickly and opened one of the menus. 'Did you want to eat something?'

'No, not if you don't.'

'I can grab a sandwich on the way back to the office if you don't feel like it.'

I pulled one of the menus across to me and glanced at the mains. They were all heavy with calories and written conspicuously to appeal.

'I'm OK. I'll get something later on.'

He finished the last of his pint and began pulling his jumper from the back of the chair. 'I've got to get back. Listen, Laura, it was great to see you.'

We stood for an awkward hug across the table. All arms and faces. I waited for ten minutes before following him out of the door in search of a bench and fresh air. I didn't want to risk running into him again.

It felt easy to be outside, neither too hot nor too cold. I knew I'd have to return to work eventually. And the articles Andy had offered me were a gift for anyone in my position. But my mind returned, as it always did, to my mother's post-mortem report and the stark account I'd written of her torn earlobe.

I couldn't go home and face all the things that needed doing there, so I took my phone out of my bag and stared at the screen, willing a reason not to go home to appear. When nothing materialised, I decided to phone Andrea. She answered quickly. And apparently out of breath.

'Laura. Finally. Where have you been?'

'Hi Andrea. I know, I'm sorry.'

'I must have phoned you ten times in the last three weeks.'

'I know. It's been tough.' I swallowed heavily. 'I'm sorry.

What about you? Are you OK? You sound like you've been running.'

'I was. Ran back to my desk from the photocopier when I heard my phone ring.'

'Jesus, Andrea. That's about three yards away.'

'I know, but I didn't want to miss your call. Where are you?'

'Hyde Park, actually. Just had a meeting with my editor. Do you fancy joining me for a drink?'

'You're drinking in Hyde Park? It's two o'clock in the afternoon.'

'No, you div. I'm not *drinking* in Hyde Park. But I would like to go for a drink. With you.'

'I've already had lunch, but it's pretty quiet here. Can you come to Clerkenwell?'

'Yes, definitely. I'll start walking and text you when I'm outside.'

We met in The Betsey Trotwood on Farringdon Road. It was our go-to pub of choice when we worked together. Andrea and I became friends when I got a job as a personal assistant to the Head of Marketing at a small internet service provider based in Clerkenwell in December 2003. She was personal assistant to the CEO, and though the people we assisted were several organisational levels apart, our desks were side by side.

Her face lit up when she saw me sitting at a table in the corner. She put her arms out to embrace me too many metres away. I stood up, awkwardly awaiting her affection. She pulled me to her, crushing my shoulders against her chest.

'I'm so pleased to see you. Let me get a drink, though,' she said, looking at my glass of wine.

'I wasn't sure if you wanted a *drink* drink. Sorry.'

'You're grieving, Laura. Not insane. Of course I want a drink.'

She returned to her seat full of admiration for her large glass of white wine and my face behind it.

'So, bloody hell. Tell me everything. I didn't feel I could ask you at the funeral, what with everything going on, but . . . did you shag him?' She was referring to the night before my mother died. I'd met up with an ex-boyfriend and, rather predictably, we'd ended up in bed together.

'Yes.'

'And?'

'And what? We had full penetrative sex and then he went home to his wife.'

Her shoulders slumped with theatrical commiseration. She sipped her wine, gleefully. 'Shit. Were you careful?'

'I wouldn't call sleeping with a married man particularly careful, but we used a condom and I'm definitely not pregnant.'

'And what now? Have you told him about your mum?'

'No. There's no point. It won't change anything.'

'Do you want things to change?'

'Not really. They've got a little girl together. The whole thing is fucked up.'

'I'm so sorry.'

She watched me as the seconds passed, waiting for something – a sneak peek at my grief. I felt momentary relief as I said, quickly and quietly, 'She was all alone, Andrea. I was too late to help her.' I swallowed the painful dryness that always presaged tears.

'Oh, Laura.'

'Don't worry. I'm OK.'

'I don't think you are.'

I put my hands up to my face and began to cry. Andrea reached across the table and pulled my left hand away. As though she wanted me to confront the thing I was looking away from. She gripped my reluctant fingers and pulled them towards her chest.

'I'm sorry,' I mumbled as I tried to take my hand back. But she wouldn't let go.

'Don't say that,' she said fiercely. 'You don't have to be sorry with me. Let me help you.'

'I know. And thank you. It's just all up here in my head. I can't stop seeing her like that. The way I found her. It's the last thing I think about before I go to sleep. If I sleep.'

'OK, listen to me. Work through what you need to, take all the time you need, but let's arrange to meet again – a fixed date in the diary. You know, a sort of deadline.'

'Excuse me?'

'Eric's always on at me to set targets and agree deadlines. I've got to get his presentation notes typed up this afternoon, actually,' she said, inexplicably turning round and looking at the door, as if he might march in and order her back to her desk. 'So what I'm saying is, we need a plan. It's your birthday next month. Let me come over and cook you dinner. How does that sound?'

'That sounds nice. Thank you. And thanks for project-managing my grief.'

'You're welcome.'

There was lividity on the back of the body. The limbs were still rigid.

My mother was a relatively tall woman. At five feet seven inches, she had long, strong legs that were often prickly. She shaved them in the summer months and allowed the hair to grow, dark and wiry, from September until the first warm day of April or May. Around the time of my birthday, more of my mother's body would start to appear, smooth and white.

In 1987, my sixth birthday fell on Easter Monday. Christopher was just seven months old. My mother baked a cake, covered it in pink icing and arranged for three of my school friends to come over for a birthday tea party. Jenny was there too, alternating between holding Christopher and washing up, while my mother fussed around me and my guests, pouring cups of orange squash and handing out small triangular sandwiches. It was the first bright, sunny day of the year and after tea we were allowed to go and play in the garden. My mother, wearing shorts and a yellow T-shirt, took Christopher silently from Jenny and, tucking a folded picnic blanket under her arm, followed us out. She put Christopher down on the grass, and with her long back to the house, she shook the blanket open to the skies. I watched as she sat down and folded her shiny, shaved legs under her and pulled Christopher into the crook of her lap. He was sucking his fists contentedly, his small round head bobbing backwards against her breasts. My mother smiled, first at me and then up at the sky.

'Are you having a nice time, Laura?' she asked the clouds.

I went and sat next to her and Christopher and took one of his fat hands. It was covered in slobber. 'Yuck!' I exclaimed, wiping it on my mother's leg. I got up to rejoin my friends, who were busy blowing bubbles to send floating over the weeds. As I stood up and turned round, I saw the shadow of Jenny standing inside the kitchen, diffident and awkward, staring out at us from the open French doors. And then came the figure of my father, whom I hadn't realised was even in the house, so curiously absent had he been from the party earlier. He joined her at the doorway and stood still beside her. They didn't touch, but were united in the act of watching the happy scene from a distance: my mother with her children.

The following day, a Tuesday, Jenny came over as usual in the afternoon to look after Christopher and me. I was in the upstairs bathroom, wiping myself after a wee. I heard Jenny's feet pad up the stairs as she went into Christopher's room to lift him from his cot. Her duties began as soon as he woke from his lunchtime sleep. She would change his nappy and take him downstairs so my mother could feed him. But as she began opening his little sleepsuit, I heard my mother's heavier step follow her up and into his room.

'I'll do that.'

Jenny was surprised and a little defensive. 'OK.'

'He's just been a bit fraught recently. I'll keep him with me this afternoon.'

'Shall I do something with Laura?'

'No, don't worry about Laura. I'll take them both to the

swings. You can stay here and hang out that washing.'

'Are you sure?'

'Of course. I think we could all do with some fresh air. Come on you,' she said to Christopher, 'let's get you some milk and into the pushchair.' And with that, she walked out of the room and back down the stairs.

Our house was within walking distance of a small playground with a slide, a set of swings and a rather jaded roundabout. It was where I spent most afternoons during the school holidays – a good place for my mother to sit with Christopher while I played, sometimes with other children but more often on my own. I used to pretend Christopher was my baby, that I was leaving him with a childminder all day and then disappear off down the slide, which doubled as my train to work. My mother would often join in, shouting at me to 'have a good day!' as I hurried away. Sometimes I had to rush down the slide in order to make a flight I'd booked on the swings. At which point my mother would stand up from the bench and, holding my baby up in her arms so I could see him and her from my bobbing window seat, would reassure me with the words: 'Don't worry! I'll look after him.'

On the morning of her cremation, Christopher met me at the funeral home I'd selected in Kingston. He'd arrived on a flight from Sydney the evening before and spent the night in a local hotel. I remember it vividly: he was sitting in the reception area waiting for me, wielding a cup of coffee like a weapon, to hack at the jet lag and grief. She'd left him all alone.

I decided to Skype Christopher. He lives in a large house on the outskirts of Melbourne with his girlfriend Steph. A house they bought together and proceeded to fill with dogs. It was just after seven one bright morning at the end of March, and I was having breakfast at my laptop. He was nine hours ahead and well into his afternoon. I tried him a few times and after the fourth attempt, just as I was giving up and going to make myself another cup of tea in the kitchen, he called back.

'Laura? Are you there?'

'Yep, here. Hang on a sec.' I turned the camera off. 'Trust me, I'm doing you a favour – you don't want to see this face.'

'How are things?' He looked tired.

'OK. Just getting on, you know. I'm working again, trying to get into the habit of running. All that kind of stuff. How about you?'

'Good. Yeah, all good,' he said, nodding. 'Steph's outside, fixing one of the fences. Ruby managed to dig her way under it last night.'

I rolled my eyes, thankful I'd remembered to turn the camera off. Christopher had never so much as stroked a dog before he met Steph, and now they were all he could talk about. They met in 2007 while travelling in South East Asia. He was sufficiently smitten with her to feign an interest in the abiding love of her life. They continued travelling together and then, several weeks before he was due to fly home, he phoned my mother and told her he was going to live in Australia – that he and Steph had plans to marry. Five years on they were still, as far as I knew, unmarried, but heavily committed to a raucous and unruly pack of dogs.

'Have you got any plans for your birthday?'

'No, but Andrea has. She wants to cook for me here. I think she's worried I'm going to become some sort of recluse. You know, the kind who hoards newspapers and plastic bottles and names the rats.'

Christopher folded his arms across his chest and smiled. 'Or obsessive-compulsive? You know, cleaning the toilet seat five times a day. All I'm saying is, think about the kind of recluse you want to be. Don't let Andrea pigeonhole you.'

'Pigeons. I could feed pigeons – like the old lady in *Mary Poppins*.'

Christopher leant down to stroke one of the dogs.

'But anyway, I'll be sure to let you know what form of deranged outcast I become when I phone you from the secure unit.'

'I look forward to it. So what's up? What did you want to talk about?'

'I've been going over some stuff in my head. You know, to do with Mum and Dad. And Jenny.'

'Go on.'

'I'm sorry, it's not exactly uplifting.'

He paused. 'Go on.'

'Well, you were very young at the time, but Mum's earlobe was torn by a woman called Sue.'

'Jenny's mum, I know.'

'Right. And that night, when Dad came home, Mum said something to him about "never in the house". I mean, that's weird, isn't it? Condoning an affair between your husband and a seventeen-year-old girl.'

He looked down at his lap.

'But I don't just mean Jenny's age. Or Dad's age, for that matter. I mean the fact that she – Mum – allowed it.'

Christopher sighed and looked around the immediate radius of his desk for the dog he'd just been stroking. Perhaps he was hoping Ruby would come and dig him out of this conversation. And then he surprised me. 'We're conditioned to think things like that are wrong.'

'Are we?'

'Do you remember Coco?'

'No. Who's Coco?'

'Steph's terrier. Her parents looked after him while we went travelling. No? Anyway, Coco was pretty old by the time we moved here, and he was just tired. You know?'

'Not really.'

'Well, he was. And when we got Ruby, everybody said they'd make great puppies. But Coco wasn't interested. Ruby would back up all the time, trying to get herself all up in his nose, that sort of thing.'

'Please get to the point.'

'Well, then we got Buster, and he was all young and yappy and before long he was mounting her day and night. You could hear the howls for miles.'

'That's a very beautiful story. But what's your point?'

'I'm just saying, you're overthinking things. Jenny was a young piece of ass and Mum was tired. It's really not that complicated.'

We were children from a broken home. According to a recent study, Christopher and I were five times more likely to suffer from emotional and mental problems, problems that often manifest themselves in poor attainment at school. But in my case, academic achievement and going to university were a means of escape.

In 1999, I left home to read English at Cambridge. My mother didn't drive, so the big journeys back to college at the beginning of every term were always expedited by my father. She would sit in the passenger seat – in Jenny's seat

– and stare straight ahead at the road. Uncomfortably still in my father's car. They rarely spoke, connected only by my presence on the back seat and my belongings in the boot. But the moment they drove away, on that first morning of my first term, in silent pursuit of the M11, I remember standing on the street and craning my neck to look up at the grinning gargoyles above; they were smug and superior, their laughter fed by the timid undergraduate. It was the first time I truly understood the effect of my parents' separation on me, as a young person. I looked closely at the red brick of my new college and knew I had no option but to go inside and make this place my home. Because they could offer no alternative. I knew my parents loved me: my father loved me enough to fill the car with petrol and put one of the seats down so all my belongings would fit. My mother loved me enough to sit silently beside him and point in the right direction as we came off the motorway. But they didn't love each other. And the real truth of that fact meant I was on my own.

The first person I met was a girl called Sarah. Pinned on the noticeboard in my room was an invitation to tea in the Old Library where we could 'meet other undergraduates and bid farewell to parents'. In their haste to get going, my mother and father hadn't considered the possibility that they may have neglected a social ritual. But then neither had I; so after a momentary gulp, I felt relieved that in our ignorance we'd avoided an uncomfortable situation.

Sarah was standing at the back of the room, stirring a cup of tea. She had shoulder-length, light brown hair and large oval glasses. Her features were small and sharp, alert like a little mouse. Beside her was a tall, balding man in his fifties. He had his hand on her shoulder and was leaning down to say something pointed and only for her. She nodded as he spoke, glancing self-consciously at me as I walked over to a nearby table and poured myself the first cup of coffee I'd ever drunk. In my haste to join in I neglected to add sugar. I was still wincing at the bitterness when he reached across his daughter's shoulder and introduced himself: 'Michael Fisher,' he said. 'Pleased to meet you. This is my daughter Sarah,' he said, pushing her gently towards me, 'and this,' he reached behind him and tapped a blonde woman with her back to us on the shoulder, 'is my wife Jan.' Jan lifted her right hand in a wave and turned back to the small group of timid under-graduates before her.

'I'm Laura,' I said, shaking his big, hairy hand.

'Have your parents gone?' Sarah asked, her voice – when it came – surprisingly loud.

'Yes. I saw the note too late,' I said, sipping the acrid coffee.

'What are you reading?'

'English. You?'

'Arch and Anth.'

I nodded as though I understood. This was the first of many linguistic landmines I stepped on in Cambridge. 'Have you met any other architects?'

She smiled kindly and said, as though it was her mistake, 'No, sorry – Archaeology and Anthropology.'

'Oh, I see. Right. What A levels did you do?' The fail-safe question.

'Sarah did English, History, German and Politics,' Michael interrupted. 'I'm a science man myself, but she wouldn't be persuaded.' He smiled down at his daughter.

Sarah's mouth twitched, as though she wanted to smile but couldn't. 'How about you?' she asked, looking back at me.

'English, History and Psychology. Oh, and General Stud-ies, but that doesn't really count, does it?'

'It does. It does,' she said, nodding her head with authority and looking around for her father. He'd returned to Jan, whose group had been joined by the Senior Tutor. 'I'd better go,' she said, finding herself all alone with me.

'OK. I'm going to try and find some sugar. See you later.'

I chatted to several people before finally meeting a small group of fellow English students, and we promptly settled into conversation about how little of the recommended reading list sent to us over the summer we'd covered. Another first – the attempt to belie effort and hard work – an accepted deception among undergraduates at Cambridge. I looked around for Sarah, wondering how she was getting on, and saw she was talking to a tall, slightly scruffy guy. Her parents were standing nearby, sipping their coffees and watching. Her companion was wearing the kind of jeans that are designed to fit badly, just loose enough to maintain an air of sartorial indifference but not enough for them to fall down around the knees. And watching him smile and run his hand through his hair, I found myself wondering what his knees looked like. I must have been staring, because Sarah looked over at me and smiled from behind her glasses. It was quiet and subtle, intended not to interrupt the flow of her conversation. I turned back to the English students, all of us bound together by a new sense of belonging.

'That's David over there,' a girl who'd just introduced herself as Jess told me, indicating the scruffy guy. 'He's also English.'

'Have you already chatted to him?'

'Yeah, he's nice. Lives in the staircase next to mine.'

'OK. I'll go over and say hello in a bit.'

Sarah's eyes narrowed almost imperceptibly as I approached

in their direction. David turned immediately and put his hand out.

'Hiya. I'm David. And this is . . .?' He inclined his head towards Sarah, willing her to provide the name he had already forgotten.

'Sarah,' she said, smiling and tucking more of her hair behind her ear.

'We've met,' I said, ignoring Sarah and shaking his hand. 'I'm Laura. Nice to meet you. I hear you're reading English too.'

'Yeah! There's quite a few of us. I've just met someone called Jess? She's over there somewhere,' he said, looking over the sea of bobbing, keen heads.

'Oh, cool. Yes, I've met Jess too.' I looked at Sarah, whose cheeks were red. 'Anyway, I just thought I'd come and say hello. You're welcome to come over and talk *Piers Plowman* with us.'

'Shit.' He ran his hand through his greasy hair. 'Did you read that? I tried, but it was fucking boring.'

I laughed. 'I don't think any of us have. That's what we're talking about, actually. How the entire reading list made us dangerously drowsy.'

'Yeah, like don't-operate-any-heavy-machinery boring. I'll be over in a sec.'

'OK, and Sarah, you're very welcome too. Sorry – didn't mean to be exclusive.'

'That's OK. I'll go and find some architects to talk to.' Her smile had gone, and so too had her parents. She went off to look for them.

I don't know how she did it, but Sarah managed to pull David a few nights later at a fresher's bop. I hadn't seen it coming at all: he was effortlessly charismatic and she was horribly contained. I was sitting at a table in the college bar talking to a small group of girls when one of them raised an eyebrow in the direction of the Junior Parlour, a large sitting room adjoining the bar. Sitting on an armchair with his long legs stretched out in front of him was David, and on his lap – in a side-saddle position – was Sarah. She had her arms around his neck, her hair covering his face in the manner of a bland curtain. There was much speculation about how she'd managed to win such a prize. But what became quickly apparent was that she had no plans to ever let go.

While Sarah and David became the couple that cooked together, I got on with the business of being Laura at Cambridge. Like a road that's been built too quickly, I constructed a version of myself that was still very much in progress. And there were plenty of people I met who simply ran out of road. Guys I slept with in my first year who were happy to go to bed with a carefree and insouciant undergraduate found themselves waking up next to an eighteen-year-old agonising over what it meant the next morning. I clawed at life by smoking weed and listening to jazz, consciously pulling experience to me. Though David was often absent – he'd moved his single bed into Sarah's room so they could assume marital sleeping arrangements towards the end of our second term – the Director of Studies for English dealt Sarah a heavy blow: David and I were designated supervision partners for the Renaissance paper. We were expected to attend a one-hour supervision together every week and began studying, side by side, in the English faculty library. The library, too subject-specific for Sarah, meant we were finally free to get to know each other.

And what I got to know was pretty harrowing. We'd fallen into a set rhythm of smoking every forty-five minutes. One cigarette often became two, followed by a coffee in the canteen – anything to avoid returning to Edmund Spenser and Sir Philip Sidney.

Like me, David had a younger brother. And like me, David's family had been fractured by circumstances. When he was just six years old he'd watched his American-born mother pack bag after bag while he was cared for by their live-in nanny. Her suitcases mounted by the front door until David, suddenly frantic that he might be left behind with a woman paid to know him, went to his bedroom and found a little Team USA rucksack his maternal grandmother had given him on her last visit to London. He knew he had to hurry, that his mother had a flight to catch, so he grabbed a small stuffed elephant from under his pillow and a watch that was lying on his desk. He hadn't yet learnt to tell the time but he knew he'd need it in America: time was different over there – they ate breakfast when he was having dinner. But when he went downstairs, the suitcases had gone. The front door was ajar and his nanny was standing in the opening with her right arm raised. As he heard the tyres manoeuvring on the gritty road, he tried to pull the door wider but his nanny clamped it to her hip. He tried to push her from behind, to force her out so he could get closer to his mother.

'I knew some decision had been made. That they'd agreed it would be better if she didn't say goodbye.'

'I can't even process this,' I said, shaking my head in my hands. The lit cigarette sticking out between my fingers like a candle that's been blown out. The wish already made.

'I know. Seriously fucked-up.'

'What did you do?'

'I tried to get out. I thought if I could just stand on the

road and let her see my face, I thought …' His voice had started to tremble. I put my hand on his arm. 'I thought, if she saw me.'

'She wouldn't go?'

He nodded and lifted the cigarette to his lips, the pain of that morning red and raised again. He inhaled deeply, closing his eyes to the smoke that had pencilled up and away from him. As he exhaled he jammed the heel of his right hand, the one still holding the cigarette, into his eye, rubbing away the moisture there.

'Did you ever see her again?' I asked, looking down at my feet.

'No.'

'Is she dead?'

'No. I hear she lives in Connecticut now. So she may as well be,' he said with a little smile.

'I'm just so sorry. Where was your dad when all this was going on?'

'In the middle of East-fucking-Nowhere on business. He only found out she'd left me the following day when the nanny phoned to ask when he was planning to return.'

'That's just so unbelievable.'

'Yep.'

'Did she ever try to get in touch?'

'She phoned a few times and tried to explain. Said she loved me, that her and my dad were trying to work things out. Bullshit like that.'

'And did they?'

'Did they fuck. My dad wouldn't go with me to the States, and she was adamant she wouldn't set foot in the UK again. It went on for a long time, and I just grew up. Life happened, and she wasn't a part of it. And then, when I was about nine or ten, my dad told me she'd remarried and moved house. She said she'd write with her contact details but never did.'

I hung my head.

'That was the end for me. She hadn't taken me with her, didn't want to come and collect me and then just forgot about me.'

I took a deep breath. 'And James? When was he born?'

'In 1993. I was eleven. And you know, Monica's nice. She's more suited to my dad than my mum ever was. And by that I mean she's more suited to being alone.'

I'd met Monica once or twice. She came up at the beginning and end of term, collecting David and his things. She was glamorous in an effortlessly Mediterranean way, suffering her own youth and beauty as she inspected the time-worn buildings. 'I can't imagine life without a mother,' I said, as much to myself as to him.

'It's pretty fucked-up,' he agreed, dropping his cigarette to the ground and stepping on it. Quietly and firmly.

I remember one warm afternoon towards the end of the Lent term in particular. We were reading Milton – lots of it – in preparation for a supervision at the end of the week. I had been reading the same five lines of *Samson Agonistes* for well over an hour. The words had become inscrutable, blurring and dancing before my slow-blinking eyelids. My head kept pitching forward, my mouth open in pre-sleep surrender until I felt the book pulled gently from beneath my fingertips.

'What are you doing?'

'You look like you're having a stroke. You know you're dribbling, don't you?'

I put my fingers to the corner of my mouth, defensive. 'No I'm not.'

'Well, you were about to. All over this book. You were literally drooling over Milton. That's embarrassing.'

I stood up and stretched my arms above my head. I saw his eyes shift to my exposed midriff. 'How am I going to write about Milton if I can't stay awake to read him?'

'You need some fresh air,' he said, rifling through his pockets for cigarettes and a lighter.

We found a bench in the sunshine and sat down. He pulled two cigarettes from the packet and put them between his lips. He lit them both in a swaying motion and, passing one to me, he said, 'He was blind, you know.'

'Who was?'

'Milton.'

'Yes, I know. I plan to crowbar that into my essay somehow.'

'But even as he was writing, he was going blind. Imagine knowing that the thing you're doing is the thing that's going to destroy you. But you do it anyway.'

I watched him lift the cigarette to his willing lips and considered voicing the irony of what he'd just said, but I didn't want to interrupt his flow; smoking always made David earnest, whereas my reaction was more physical. It made my bowel twist. I clenched my arse cheeks together and tried to hold the bad air in. 'As in, you keep going because you believe in a higher purpose?'

'No. You keep going because you don't know anything else. Even if it means losing something you love. I'm not explaining myself very well.'

'You are. Go on.'

'It wasn't good for me. To just pretend my mum never existed. It was a kind of blindness.'

'And now?'

'Now I have you. And Sarah.' He smiled.

I inhaled too deeply, right at the end of the cigarette. My lower incisors felt hot and uncomfortable as I pulled the caustic flavour into my mouth. The cramps were lower now. I saw the goosebumps rise up on my arm as I thought of the toilet. Any toilet.

'What's the matter with you? Where are you going?'

'I've got to go.'

'Go where?'

'To the loo.'

'Right.' He forced a laugh and pulled another cigarette from the packet. 'Don't let me keep you.'

As the weeks ticked away, we grew closer. By the time the summer term presented itself as an indisputable fact, we found ourselves revising side by side in the library out of habit. If I got up from my seat to go and find a book somewhere in the stacks, I'd invariably return to find a giant cock and balls had been drawn on my notebook. He lent me CDs, books; sketched portraits of me in biro on the back of postcards and pinned them to my door.

During the long vacation we wrote to one another. He went on his much-anticipated two-week break to Italy and, though he was careful to write about other things, I sensed his eagerness to return to Cambridge. I was at home in Surbiton, with my mother and Christopher, delighted every time a letter landed on the mat. My mother asked, only once, who was writing to me.

'Just a friend from college,' I replied with deliberate nonchalance, running upstairs to devour the ink on the paper he'd been the last one to touch.

*

In the end it wasn't the supervisions or the long library sessions or even the camaraderie of escaping with a cigarette that revealed the strength of the attachment. It was much simpler than that. One bright morning in September 2000, before many of the other undergraduates had returned from the long vacation, I saw him standing outside the Porter's Lodge, tall and tanned. He'd returned to Cambridge earlier than planned and was checking his pigeonhole. I was wheeling my bike back into college, the chain clicking over the cobblestones, and stopped still the moment I saw him. The cessation of sound made him look up and his visible elation was unmistakable. That our friendship had been weighed down by deep attachment was clear. To both of us.

But there was still the small matter of Sarah. Three years of undergraduate study were, for her at least, an inconvenient hiatus separating them from department stores and estate agents. I tolerated her because I loved her boyfriend. And I spent the first term of my second year waiting for him to break up with her.

David's room in the second year was at the top of one of the oldest staircases in college. He had little to do with the people he shared it with, and used their eccentricities as a well from which to draw amusing anecdotes he could deliver up to his parched friends. Sarah indulged him as a mother would a precocious toddler, smiling at his perspicacity but never laughing at his humour. He told me about Christina the vet who really cared about bowel movements. She commented on David's irregularity one memorable morning as he emerged from their shared lavatory: 'How are you doing, Dave? Eating enough fibre?'

'Morning,' and then, considering the matter, 'I think so. Yes. Yes, I am, Christina.'

'Just been in there a while, that's all. I've got some insane laxatives if you need them.'

'Why?'

'Why what?'

'Why have you got *insane* laxatives?'

'To relieve constipation. In horses.'

'And what the fucking hell would they do to me?'

'I'm only trying to help, Dave.'

'And I'm only trying to make sure I don't shit myself away tomorrow morning. But thank you anyway.'

Then there was Jonathan the natural scientist. He was fiercely Christian, academic and – according to David – sinfully boring. Jonathan was the son of a rector from a small North Yorkshire village, had never been away from home prior to university and thought David, who was from London, unnervingly cosmopolitan. He once asked him what people *do* in London. David, who had been making a cup of tea in the kitchen at the time, replied warily: 'How do you mean?'

'I just mean, do you go out a lot?'

'Me personally? Yes. I go out.'

'And what about everybody else?'

'What? Sorry – are you asking about everyone else *in London*?'

Jonathan's face flushed as he realised his mistake. 'I just mean, there must be something for everyone. I'd like to go one day.'

'Yeah, you should definitely come. On a Wednesday we go to Buckingham Palace for a pub quiz and get shit-faced. All seven million of us.'

I loved him. And that feeling only intensified the more time we spent together.

One Tuesday evening in November, we arranged to meet

in the courtyard just before ascending the cold stone steps to our supervisor's room at the top of the tower. It was dark outside, and the college was preparing itself for evening; gowns began to appear in the cloisters, broad and black on busy shoulders hurrying along the ancient walkways.

David and I had an hour on Robert Browning ahead of us. When we arrived at the appointed room it was clear the supervision before ours had overrun: we could still hear convivial laughter and the rustling of papers within. I turned to David and noticed the dark circles under his eyes. 'What's the matter with you? You look like shit.'

'Thank you. Just having a few problems with Sarah, that's all.' I said nothing. And my silence encouraged him. 'She wants to get married.'

'What the fuck? Now? You're not even old enough.'

'No, not now. But soon. Laura, how *old* do you think you have to be?'

'OK, I know legally you can. But Jesus, you're not even twenty yet. What's the rush?'

'Her parents have offered to buy us a house. Here in Cambridge. And from their point of view, it would be better if we were married.'

'That's outrageous! You're getting married because they want to invest in property? You can't be serious.'

'It's not like that. They're good, kind people, and they're trying to help us out.'

'Help you out how? By anchoring you to a county fifty miles from London where you can live in sleepy seclusion with their daughter?'

He looked at me in surprise. Daring me to continue.

'How can you even consider marrying her? She's so boring. I wish you could see it.'

'What, because she's not cutting or witty? I know all that. But I also know that she's a very nice person.'

'*I'm* a nice person!' I shouted, my mouth firing flecks of saliva into the air.

He looked down at his trainers and clenched his jaw. As if I'd said something he was dreading. But the door opened and our professor's busy and apologetic welcome made any more shouting impossible. We took our seats on the sofa, at opposite ends, and began pulling papers from our bags. Because of the hour, the darkness and the fire burning in the grate we were offered a glass of sherry and invited to unwind to the lines of 'My Last Duchess'. I carried the discussion until we came to the lines, '"Paint/Must never hope to reproduce the faint/Half-flush that dies along her throat."'.

We waited for David to say something, but his silence appeared resolute.

'I think the narrator glories too much in the sudden and violent nature of her death. It makes it impossible for the reader to believe he ever really loved her,' I said, nervously looking over at David.

'David?' our professor said in polite encouragement.

'With all due respect, Laura, that's a totally moronic thing to say. Of course he loves her – throat flush and all – he just can't *control* her in life, so it makes sense to kill her.'

'I'm sorry, David, but that was unacceptably rude. Please apologise to Laura.'

'No, please. Don't worry. It's fine,' I mumbled, mortified.

'Sorry,' he whispered, and stood up. He left the room, and his bag agape on the floor. It was such an impulsive and unexpected departure that we couldn't piece the discussion back together. We agreed to reschedule for the following week, and that I would take David's things back to his room.

43

I picked up his bag and trudged across college and up the several flights of stairs to his room. When I got there the door was ajar and he was sitting on his bed, smoking a cigarette. I went in and dropped his bag on the carpet. 'We've rescheduled for next Thursday.'

'And? Is that it?'

'And you're a fucking dick.' I turned to go.

'I'm sorry. I'm sorry I need her as much as I do.'

I stopped, but didn't turn back to him. 'You don't need her. You only think you do.' And then I heard him stand up and walk over to me. I felt his fingers on my right shoulder. He'd never touched me, deliberately, before. He pulled me gently to face him. It was the most arousing moment of my life. I thought he was going to kiss me; my mouth braced for the impact of a longed-for act. But he didn't. He leant in and pushed his body against mine, hard and heavy as though he were trying to knock me over. And then I felt the door slam shut behind me as he pushed my body up against it. He looked furious, his breath hot and rapid on my face. I kissed him gently on his cheek, provoking him. A teasing gesture of peace designed to open hostilities. After that there was no more distance, no more talking – he was on top of me. Pulling and pushing at me. Our frenzy made us ineffective, almost clumsy. The bed was too far and domestic for what we had to do. He lifted me off my feet and we fucked standing up, my body rocking the door in its aperture to the prevailing rhythm of his thrusts. We were without care, locked in a physical indulgence that hadn't felt possible a year, a month or an hour earlier. Even as it happened I couldn't believe he was inside me. I understood Sarah's blind possession as I felt my own body cleave to his. And as I thought of her I became more reckless. I pulled at his hair, dug my nails into his neck

44

and made him look at me. He flinched once but I grabbed his face and forced him to meet my eyes, just before he conceded.

The pleasure we uncovered that evening was too primitive, too good to abandon. We continued seeing each other; our lack of discretion, coupled with the fact that none of David's housemates liked him, meant our secret was soon discovered. Sarah was understandably hurt, but not enough to withdraw the promise of a life with her. She gave David a way out: stop sleeping with me and they could try again. But he wasn't ready to go back. Our relationship felt like a destructive act from the beginning; for him, it was an attempt to disown encroaching security. But for me, I realise now, that because I'd grown up among shifting allegiances, I saw relationships as being more fluid than was perhaps normal.

At the end of June, as the long vacation opened up again, David and I clung to one another with promises to meet up. He was meeting his dad, Monica and James in the South of France for a couple of weeks and promised to call me as soon as he got back.

And he did. His voice was tight and cold, suggesting we meet at Embankment tube station. I was there early, nervous and excited. I'd managed to persuade myself that he'd probably been in the company of others when he called. That we'd find our way back to one another as soon as we were together again. But he was there even earlier than me, and didn't take my hand when I approached him. He asked if I'd like to take a walk in the Victoria Embankment Gardens. I followed him, muted by the formality of his invitation and his unwillingness to touch me.

'Would you like a coffee?' I shook my head miserably. I knew something was wrong. We sat down on a patch of grass near the entrance. 'There's something I have to tell you.'

'Go on.'

'I don't know how to say this . . .'

'Christ. Just say it. What's happened?'

'I met up with Sarah.'

'Where? How?'

'She drove up from Italy. We had lunch in Avignon.'

'How splendid for you both!'

'Please don't.' He hung his head.

'Please don't what? Express surprise that you met up with your ex-girlfriend?'

He looked at me for too long. Gently challenging what I'd said.

'And what? Are you back together now?'

'We just talked through a lot of stuff. I think I've been afraid.'

'Afraid of what? A life with someone you don't love?'

'That's not true. I do love Sarah. And I get on really well with her family.'

'Why are you always talking about her family? What have they offered to buy you this time? A chateau? A royal title?'

'Stop it.'

'No, you stop it. Stop being such a fucking twat.'

He put his head in his hands. I pulled his hand away – our first physical contact in nearly three weeks.

'They've made me feel like one of them.' He lifted his head and looked at me, suddenly angry. 'And maybe, deep down, that's all I've ever wanted.'

'Do me a favour.'

'I was six, Laura! Six years old when I was left with a nanny whose name I can't even remember.'

'We all have our problems, OK? You're not the only one to have had a difficult childhood.'

'Yeah, and most kids have the other parent to fall back on. My dad's solution was to give me some bullshit replacement and go back on his merry way.'

I was determined not to feel sorry for him. 'So Sarah's parents are your adopted family now?'

'In a way, yes.'

'And they're prepared to forgive you, are they? For cheating on their daughter?'

'They don't know about you. Sarah hasn't told them.'

I looked at the tourists milling around the gardens, taking photographs, walking slowly among the pigeons, some with their arms around each other.

'Did you fuck her?' I shouted at him with tears in my throat, garbling my question. He looked at me with eyes that were trying to cry.

'I'm sorry, Laura. I don't know what to say. It just felt right – being together again. And we . . . I want to make a go of it this time.'

'What a joke.' I sniffed at the snot that threatened to meet my tears.

'I'm so sorry.'

'Don't be sorry. You're a coward. I knew it all along – I just didn't expect you to run back to her so quickly.' And then, as my fury gained momentum, I turned to him in mock sympathy and said, 'Was she very understanding of your need to fuck other women?' I reached out to stroke his arm, but the feel of his hair, standing on end, reminded me his arm was not mine to touch. I pulled back and stood up.

'I know this is shitty. I feel very shitty.'

'Now it's my turn to say sorry, is it? I wish you weren't feeling so down about this? What can I do to make this easier?'

'Stop it, Laura. I feel bad enough.'

'Do you? Oh God, I'm sorry. Have you just been told by the person you love,' my voice trembled on the ruined hopes of that word, 'that they'd rather be with a deaf fucking dodo?' He stood up now, too, confused by the words I'd used.

'Deaf? What does that mean?'

'*Dead*, Dave!' We were shouting at each other now. 'I mean dead! Because she's got the charisma of a corpse. Oh, fuck this. Be with her. Enjoy your life together. I hope you'll be very happy. But don't ever speak to me again.'

I walked away and back into the tube station I'd only just emerged from. I looked behind me as I descended on the escalator, keeping right in the hope that David would follow me, urgent and certain. I was waiting for the implausibility of romantic comedy to blanket my anguish. For him to catch up with me just as the tube door was closing and mouth the words *I love you* before I was pulled, inexorably, down the tunnel and away to Waterloo. He didn't, of course. I travelled home to Surbiton, alone and utterly rejected.

We ignored each other for the entire duration of my third year. He and Sarah moved out of college and rented privately, so, in fact, he was absent most of the time. At dinners, balls and supervisions we maintained a working distance and, in this bitter and painful silence, our university experience concluded. My parents and Christopher came to attend my graduation in 2002 and help me pack my things. As we stood uncomfortably together on the college lawn, I looked over at David, standing with Sarah and her large extended family. They were posing for photographs. I stared hard at his happiness until he felt the dark shadow of my glare and noticed me. He stopped smiling then and held my gaze. It was intense and meaningful – the same look he'd given me as we fucked against his door. Sarah saw me and nudged him hard in the side, forcing him to click back into photo-mode.

Two years later I saw a note in the college newsletter that David and Sarah had married in a stately home in North-amptonshire, near her parents' house. Twelve months on, another update appeared announcing the birth of their daughter, Beatrice Rose. I had no doubt these notices were intended for me. Sarah had got what she wanted, papering over the cracks of a flimsy commitment with marriage and birth certificates.

Her eyes were pale in colour. The pupils were equal. The face was pale, as were the conjunctivae.

The only evidence of my parents' physical affection for one another was me and Christopher. An examination of how their marriage failed always gave way to a more lurid narrative – an older, married man having sex with a seventeen-year-old girl – but I was more interested in why he took that first step away from my mother. Because I know he loved her, and not just enough to marry her and father two children: he loved her enough to smile as he watched her move around the kitchen, to laugh at her little impressions of me. He loved her enough to hire Jenny when she was finding it difficult to cope at home. He was responsive and considerate in the most obvious way.

It was around the time of my fifth birthday that I began to understand my mother was pregnant. She didn't tell me and neither did my father, but I sensed the change in her body: her breath became sour, her armpits more sweaty and her breasts were full and loose in a way that I knew was significant. And my grandmother began to visit more frequently.

Jean Lambton, my maternal grandmother, lived with my grandfather, Paul, a few roads away from us. They got married in 1957, when my grandmother was thirty-two. I remember my mother relaying this detail to me when I was about sixteen or seventeen, that 'Granny was quite *old* by the time she got married', raising her eyebrow as though I should understand the meaning of this. When I didn't, she elaborated.

'Not by today's standards, but back then thirty-two was quite late to get married and have children.' I agreed. At the time, I thought anyone over thirty was old.

My mother was their only child. They had wanted more, but by the time she was born, in 1961, my grandmother was already thirty-six and her (as it turned out) patchy fertility was fading fast. In many ways, my grandmother was quite a modern woman – her career as an English teacher was well established by the time she finally got pregnant, and she re-turned to teaching when my mother went to school in 1965. But she was also painfully old-fashioned in her approach to marriage, and viewed the disorder in our house as a failing on my mother's part.

In May 1986, as my mother's abdomen began to round into unmistakable pregnancy, my grandmother started dropping in on us mid-morning. Usually just as my mother was on her knees, dressing me or brushing my hair for the day. She had her own key and simply let herself in, closing the front door behind her and making her way quickly into the kitchen. Within minutes of her arrival, the sound of water sloshing over our breakfast dishes would drift up the stairs and my mother would brush at my hair faster. And harder.

My grandmother was a tall woman, like my mother, but of much slimmer build. Her shins were thin and straight, held in place by ankles that were always anticipating a sudden jump. She was the kind of woman who would, without warning, leap up from her seat to grab a more suitable dish, or turn the oven off. She was exhausting to be around.

My mother and I resented my grandmother's presence.

We wanted only to be left alone. We never talked about the pregnancy; I'm sure that most mothers today prepare for the birth of a sibling with picture books and patient explanations, but my mother never felt the need to do any of that. It simply became a more glaring part of our lives. Of her body. But the sudden and indomitable company of my grandmother interrupted the silent understanding between us.

It was early summer, the mornings bright and warm. I wasn't at school, so it must have been during the May half-term. My grandmother let herself in every day and made us feel as though we should be busier; asking my mother what she planned to do with me that day, when the truth was our plan was always the same. In the morning my mother would open the French doors so I could play in the garden while she put some washing out. I used to water the plants or pick the prettiest camellias to make a bunch of flowers that always surprised and delighted her. As she bent down to pick another item of clothing from the basket, I watched her torso press the steadfast mound that would become my brother onto her thighs and then back upright again. I wondered what the baby made of all the movement.

We ate lunch early and the afternoons were spent lying supine on the sofa – she would fall asleep with her arms around me as I watched cartoons, her unstoppable stomach beginning to push me further from her body.

But my grandmother had none of my mother's gentle energy. She fussed around us, tidying and cooking un-necessarily. She suggested trips to the library, shopping in Kingston, anything to get us off the sofa and out of the house. Our happy indolence frustrated her. And when I returned to school for the summer term, she suggested my mother get rid of Jenny.

'I'll pick Laura up.'

'Jenny doesn't pick her up. I do that.'

'So what does she do? What are you paying her for?'

'Just to be here. To help out.'

'I'll help out. I can come over in the afternoons, if that's what you want.'

'No. Thanks, Mum. But no.'

'Kathy, I'm your mother. I *want* to help.'

'We're fine. Laura and I are fine.'

So my grandmother took no for an answer, but continued trying to push Jenny out. She began to appear – always on a Tuesday or Thursday – with an elaborate savoury meal covered in pastry and topped with kitchen foil, just ready for the oven.

One afternoon in particular, still in my school uniform, I walked into the kitchen to find my grandmother's bottom elevated and swaying as she poked around in a cupboard trying to find a suitable saucepan. My mother was standing over by the sink watching her, sullen.

'Potatoes. That's what we need,' she said happily to herself as she put a saucepan down on the stove. Jenny, who arrived at around two-thirty in the afternoon, awaited my mother's instruction; she was perplexed by how busy my grandmother was. She didn't understand that my grandmother was trying to make her redundant. But my mother did. So she tried again.

'Mum, I told you. Jenny's doing dinner tonight.' Jenny was holding my hand – we were standing together in the kitchen, watching this domestic drama play out. My grandmother had a meat pie balanced deftly on her left hand, her ankles exerting themselves under the strain of her bent knees as she opened the oven door and peered inside.

'Kathy, I'm here to help you. That's all. This is just a spare,' she said, indicating the pie still hovering before the flames. 'I made it with the leftovers from last night's dinner. Richard will enjoy it. All men love a meat pie.' She nodded to herself, confirming her own incontrovertible truth.

'Jenny, could you take Laura into the living room and read with her, please?' I didn't see Jenny nod, but I felt her hand pull me away. As we walked into the hallway, I told her I wanted to go upstairs and change out of my uniform first. Jenny went into the living room while I went and sat on the stairs and heard my mother's tone change: 'What's that supposed to mean?'

'A wife is supposed to cook for her husband. Not hire a young girl to come into the house and ... flirt around the kitchen.'

'The only person flirting around this kitchen is you!'

'Kathy, a man's head can be easily turned.'

'But if I cook him a meat pie that won't happen?'

'You're pregnant, you have Laura, the house is a mess. I understand why you've asked her to help, but I don't think it's a good idea.'

'This is none of your business! I know you're trying to help, but I don't need it.'

My grandmother must have put the pie in the oven because, though quieter, her voice was nearer my mother and more audible to me on the stairs. I moved my face close to the banister and saw my grandmother put her hands on my mother's arms, as though to hold her in place. Her nose was just a few inches from my mother's. 'It's not a good idea to let another woman fulfil your duties at home. But if that's what you need to do, at least let that woman be your mother.'

'What do you call this?' she said, tearfully indicating

54

her small bump. 'Isn't this *fulfilling my duties*?'

'Don't get upset. I'm only trying to help. I'll call in tomorrow and see how you are.' And with that, she walked into the hallway, poked her head round the living room door and said – with implausible brightness – 'Bye, Jenny!' and let herself out. She hadn't seen me sitting on the stairs.

My mother didn't move. She just stood where my grandmother had positioned her, her head bowed and her hands by her side. I pulled myself up from where I'd been sitting and stepped, with deliberate care, down to the hallway. Jenny was sitting on the sofa, waiting for me, but I walked past the living room and back into the kitchen. As I rounded my mother's statue, I put my hand in the crook of her slackened fingers. It returned her to life immediately: she gripped my small hand and, bending down, she lifted me up and against her. I wrapped my arms and legs around her body, in the manner of a small chimp. She carried the burden of my five-year-old body over to the work surface where she could sit me down and hold me comfortably. It was only as she pulled her face away and smoothed my hair down over my ears that I saw the standing water in her pale eyes. Her corneas were buried beneath a sudden and unexpected deluge. I watched as the salty fluid overflowed her lids and dropped down onto her cheeks, and for that brief moment, I was completely absorbed by the intricate mechanism – how her body sought to service emotion with water. She saw my eyes follow a tear down to the outer reaches of her mouth. She smiled it away and leant in to kiss me gently on my cheek. I felt the water break between us.

One warm evening in the middle of July, my mother and grandmother had a huge falling-out. Over me.

It was the beginning of the summer holidays, I'd broken up from school and my mother's pregnancy was well advanced. She was hot, uncomfortable and almost always tired. Her ankles were thick and swollen. Jenny had come over with her younger brother Sam, who was ten, and the three of us spent the afternoon playing in the garden, splashing water at each other. My mother sat on a lounger, her feet elevated, watching us and laughing. Jenny occasionally declared herself out so she could go and check on dinner.

And then, like a dark cloud smiling, came my grandmother. She had let herself in and walked through to the back of the house, full of false cheer. My mother, whose lounger was facing away from the French doors, had no need to turn round. She merely hung her head and looked down at the cup of tea Jenny had just placed in her hands.

'Hello, darling,' my grandmother said to me, and held out her arms. I put the measuring jug that I'd been using to launch water at Sam down on the grass and walked over to her, reluctantly. 'What's all this?' she said, giving my back a light tap. 'You're wetter than an otter's pocket!' I didn't know what an otter was. But I knew something happy had been totally eclipsed by her arrival. And that we couldn't get it back as long as she was there.

Perhaps my grandmother knew she wasn't wanted, because she bustled her way back into the kitchen and began interfering with dinner. At around 5 p.m., she came back into the garden with a towel for me. 'Laura! Come and get dry. Let's have a quick bath before dinner.'

My mother turned round. 'Mum, she doesn't need a bath. She can just dry off and get into her pyjamas.'

'It's no trouble. I've already run her a small one. Come on, Laura.' I looked at my mother for the next move. Holding her hand up to the sun so she could better see them, my mother said to Jenny and Sam, 'You two had better get home. Your mum will be wondering where you are.'

Despite the warm water, my grandmother's hands were cold and efficient. As my mother said goodbye to Jenny and Sam and tidied up the kitchen, my grandmother sloshed water up my back and used her fingernails to dig around in my ears and between my toes.

'Doesn't your mother clean you?' she mumbled to herself, as she extracted another particle of grey grime from a remote part of my body. I felt affronted by my grandmother's exacting approach to what was mine, and decided to pre-empt any attempt she might make to clean my private parts by doing them myself. I put my hand down between my legs and, using my fingers, began rubbing myself. Perhaps it went on for too long; perhaps I looked as though I was enjoying it, I don't know. But when she saw what I was doing she stood up and stared at me.

'What on earth are you doing?'

'I'm cleaning myself. The way Mummy taught me.'

'Get your hand away right now! That's dirty. And *not* how you clean yourself.'

I lifted my hand up out of the water and then, in sudden surprise at being told off, began to cry. My mother, drawn by my cries, came up the stairs and walked into the bathroom.

'What's going on here? Laura, why are you crying?'

'Granny told me off,' I spluttered between sobs.

'Mum?'

'Kathy, she was *touching* herself. Down there.'

'I was cleaning myself. Cleaning my moo-moo. Like you told me.'

'Laura, you clean yourself with a flannel or a sponge.

Not your fingers,' my grandmother admonished before my mother could say anything.

My mother turned to my grandmother and, straining to keep her voice under control, said, 'I want to talk to you outside.' They walked away from the bathroom onto the landing and tried to keep their conversation confined to the hallway, but it quickly ballooned up and away from them.

'Kathy, it's not a good idea to encourage that sort of thing.'

'Laura is free to clean herself, touch herself, however she likes.'

'I'm trying to help you understand—'

'Oh, I understand.' My mother's whisper was long gone. 'I *understand* that you're trying to make her feel ashamed of her own body.'

'Kathy!'

'Don't "Kathy" me. I won't let you do it. I won't let you come in here and tell us what to do, how to live and how to be thoroughly miserable!'

'What's this all about?'

'You. Making my daughter feel dirty and wrong. Assigning shame to things.'

'Don't be ridiculous! I'm just trying to show—'

'I'll finish Laura's bath. I think you should leave.'

'You're tired.'

'Yes, I'm tired. Tired of being told what to do. Please go.'

I heard the sound of footsteps going down the stairs. My mother came back into the bathroom. She was swaying on her feet in exhaustion. I looked at the grey deposits under my fingernails where I'd scraped at my skin. When I pressed my finger pad up against the nail, the dirt popped out. I put my hands back under the water and sat on them.

*

I agreed to write the articles on the Olympics for Andy, and on 21 April, my thirty-first birthday, I sent him the second in a series of five. Entitled *East of Eden: In the Shadows of the Olympics*, I'd written about how great swathes of east London were still decrepit and largely ignored. I felt pleased with it: precise, evocative and honest, it was all the things that had made my blog a success. I emailed the copy to Andy and walked into the kitchen, where I pulled a half-empty bottle of wine from the fridge. I poured myself a large glass and resisted the urge to light a cigarette as well. The first sips of wine quickly translated my elation into settled conceit. I heard the intercom buzz, and pressing the button in the hallway, admitted Andrea's crackly voice.

'Laura? Let me in.'

Andrea and I were very different: she was happy to be a personal assistant – and, when she wanted to be, she was a very good one – but I had hated it. After graduating from Cambridge, I spent six months looking for a job that would allow me to rent a room in London, work during the day and write in the evenings. I temped for various companies, earning just enough to maintain my independence, but when I was offered a permanent salary working in Clerkenwell for a company just down the road from where I was lodging in Angel, I accepted with enthusiasm. I would have been far less enthusiastic had I met the woman I was hired to assist. Politeness she reserved only for those who could help her ascend the career ladder. She was rude to me from the beginning, persistently calling me Lauren despite repeated attempts to correct her. When I arranged meetings, she quibbled over the choice of room, rolled her eyes to clients in exasperation at me and ordered cups of coffee as if that were a suitable punishment for existing. I hated her. And in my expectation that I'd do something wrong, I began to make mistakes. I sent her daughter's X-rays off to the wrong hospital, arranged meetings in the office when she was working from home and once booked a taxi to take her to Heathrow instead of City Airport. By the time she looked up and realised she was heading west, it was too late to catch her flight. She phoned me at my desk in a rage that was murderous, spitting her threat to report me to HR. Had she been in the office, I don't doubt she'd have thrown a punch.

I accept that I wasn't a good assistant and should have resigned, but the room I'd rented in Angel was expensive and I just couldn't return to Surbiton. Working for a hateful Head of Marketing was better than returning home a failure. So I stayed. And on the afternoon of the airport debacle I put my head down on the desk and cried. Not at my mistake, but at the trap I found myself in. Andrea took her headset off and looked over. I could feel the stares of my colleagues, unnerved by the show of emotion in an atmosphere punctuated only by the sound of keyboards and laser printing. She put her arm across my shoulders and whispered to come outside with her. I slid from my chair and kept my eyes down, conspicuous with running mascara. When we got downstairs she offered me a cigarette and, though I hadn't smoked since Cambridge, I accepted it with reckless gratitude: I'd fucked up properly and there wasn't much more that could go wrong. I was shivering in the January afternoon, my tears cold on my face. The price of the cigarette was an explanation: Andrea nodded at my account and raised an eyebrow sceptically when I mentioned the HR threat.

'We all make mistakes,' she pointed out defiantly.

'Not as big as this one. I'm going to have to find a new job.'

'Listen. Find a new job if that's what you want, but not

because of this. You won't get the sack. Just say you made a mistake, or, you know, someone's just died or something.'

The suggestion shocked me. 'What if I forget, or then someone does actually ...?' I looked around for some wood to touch, frightened by the thought. Andrea grabbed my hand and put it to her own head.

'I do it all the time. I once told my boss I was pregnant when I messed up on some purchase orders. It's fine.'

'Didn't he have anything to say when you didn't have a baby?'

'Oh God, he didn't even notice. Couldn't give a shit. What I'm saying is, just don't worry about it.'

'Right. Thanks.' We were coming to the end of the cigarette, and my recklessness had given way to gloom. My mouth was full of nicotine tang, my boss was motoring back to Clerkenwell full of righteous anger and my new friend was advising appalling deceit.

She was right, of course. I didn't get fired that afternoon, and managed to stick it out for another two years. The woman I worked for moved to the Paris office in 2004 and her replacement, a middle-aged man called Patrick, was far more pleasant. I became comfortable and Andrea and I grew close. She was always willing to go for a glass of wine in Hatton Garden after work ('we might meet a rich diamond merchant') or to The Betsey for lunch.

One summer lunchtime in 2005, as we walked arm in arm away from the office, I explained that Betsey Trotwood was a character from *David Copperfield*. She held her cigarette away from her and stared at me. 'How do you even know that?'

'Because there she is, chasing the donkeys away,' I said, pointing to the sign hanging from the side of the building.

'She's David's great-aunt, and one of the few strong female characters in the novel. Dickens describes her as *inflexible*. As though bending is bad. I've always remembered that, for some reason.'

Andrea had been smoking as we walked. She looked at me steadily as she exhaled. 'You're wasted here, Laura.'

I laughed at her sudden earnest tone. 'I did an English degree. You have to know a bit of Dickens. I'm no F. R. Leavis.'

'Who?'

'Never mind.'

'Why don't you teach?'

I thought of my mother's friend Helen, teaching history to the unwilling of Hounslow, and demurred, saying I didn't have the conviction to teach.

'But you don't have the conviction to be someone's PA, either. Maybe you should be a bit more, you know, inflexible.'

I resigned from my job in Clerkenwell at the end of 2006 to write full-time. The small company I had joined almost three years before had been bought by a large corporate telecommunications firm and had begun to change considerably. It was the right time to move on. I handed all responsibility for my leave-taking to Andrea, who wrote 'Laura Leaving' on her list of things to do. She was swift and efficient at all things – including my leaving do. She reserved an area in a bar on Clerkenwell Road and presented me with the fruits of an office whip-round: a Montblanc pen and Moleskine notebook.

I got horribly drunk at my leaving do, encouraged towards potent cocktails by colleagues who volunteered their own frustrations, almost all of them about someone in the office. They wished me well and told me not to forget them.

I promised enduring friendship, became emotional when it was time to say goodbye and swallowed vomit in the taxi home. Andrea helped me up the stairs to my bedroom, took my shoes and jacket off and positioned me on my side with the wastepaper basket under my open mouth. She got into bed beside me and stayed there all night, explaining in the morning as she got ready for work, 'I didn't want you to choke in your sleep and die on the first day of your new life.' Her friendship was always no-nonsense and steadfast. The same impulse that motivated her to look after me on the night of my leaving do had brought her to my front door, that Friday evening in April, unwilling to leave me alone on my birthday.

She came upstairs and walked straight into my small kitchen. The work surface was busy with plates, cutlery and last night's wine glass. She put her bags down on the floor near my overflowing bin and took her coat off.

'What are you doing?' I asked.

'Cleaning up in here.' She picked up my nearly empty glass and rinsed it under the tap with her fingers. Then she extracted a bottle of cold white wine from her shopping bag, opened it and poured me a large serving. 'Go and sit down. I'll get things going in here and then we can talk.'

I did as I was told. I checked my emails to see if Andy had replied, closed the lid when I saw he hadn't and walked over to the bay window of my living room. As I looked down at the road below, at the unkempt hedges and uneven paving, I felt unblocked. It might have been the wine or the sound of Andrea banging around in the kitchen, but I felt pleased with myself; writing the articles, meeting a deadline, even having Andrea over made me feel as though normal was still a possibility for me.

I returned to the kitchen, drawn by the smell of chicken fajitas and the sound of order restored. Andrea had found an apron to cover her dress from the splashes and had poured herself a glass of wine. She looked up and lifted it to me. I moved over to her, full of sheepish love, clinked my glass to hers and pulled her in for a hug. I was so grateful, I couldn't speak.

'I'm here now,' she said. And then she turned back to the pan, wiping her own tears away. I laughed and backed away to lean against the fridge. 'I know how hard it must have been.'

'But you don't, Andrea. Your mum isn't dead.'

'OK, but—'

'No, listen. I'm not trying to get at you, but this is exactly what people say. And Christ, I've probably even said it myself before. But the truth is that the loss of . . . of her. It's just the most painful thing. I'm not the same person I was before I found her like that. On her own.' I fought the tears, not because I was afraid to cry in front of Andrea but because I wanted to explain. And the tears always shifted and trans-muted the explanation – they made my voice croak and the listener tut in sympathy. I didn't want an arm around my shoulder. I simply wanted her to understand. It was the same instinct that made me bash at the keyboard through the blur.

She nodded to me but continued looking down at the strips of chicken breast cooking in the seasoning she'd just tipped from a packet.

'OK. But listen, you still need to eat a proper meal.'

I picked up the fajita kit box, torn open on the recently wiped surface, and raised an eyebrow.

'I'm a working woman, Laura. What do you expect? Fuck-ing lasagne?'

But fingering the box reminded me of a task I had yet to complete. 'I still have to empty my mother's kitchen.'

Andrea looked up quizzically. 'Haven't you done that yet? The food will have gone off by now.'

'There wasn't much in the way of perishable stuff anyway. It was mostly packets, tins, that sort of thing. But I need to have a good sort-out anyway, and the kitchen's as good a place as any to start. What do you think?'

'I think you need to get your own kitchen in order first. The milk in your fridge scares me.'

'OK, but what room first? That's what I'm asking you.'

'Yes, Laura.'

'Yes what?'

'Yes, I'll come with you,' she looked around for a clean tea towel and decided to wipe her hands on the front of my apron instead. 'You've done enough on your own. And look at this place. It's obvious you need a bit of help. Now stop standing around and grate some cheese, please.'

Andrea emerged from Surbiton station exultant. She'd had the presence of mind to buy a roll of bin bags, marigolds and detergent, foreseeing 'we'll need to wipe down the cupboard shelves after we empty them'. I hugged her for too long, so much so she became efficient in her sympathy. 'Come on. Let's get this over with.'

It was a thankfully short journey up the hill to the house. I drove heavy with memory, slow to respond to Andrea's platitudes as I thought of that morning in February when I'd parked on the driveway, just a front door away from an event that altered everything.

I pulled up the handbrake and hung my head. Suddenly overwhelmed by the arrangements I'd made, the things I'd done to get us there. Andrea turned to face me in her seat, releasing her seat belt to get closer. 'Do you want me to go in first?' I nodded my head and began searching for the keys in my bag, but then I remembered the alarm.

'No, I'd better come with you.' The act of finding the right key, releasing the deadlock and deactivating the alarm – these were all physical requirements that kept my mind calm and pragmatic. I kicked at the heaped mail, takeaway menus and charity collection bags that pushed against our entry and stared down at the spot where she'd fallen.

I thought of all the times I'd stood at the bottom of the stairs, including that night in my pyjamas, looking for my mother in the wake of that terrible assault, and I felt suddenly territorial and possessive. I walked quickly into the kitchen and stared down at the work surface. It was the very spot she'd lifted me onto as she cried tears of frustration at her own mother. That brief expression of deep love for me, for what was hers – holding my small body to her own – took place beneath my adult fingers, splayed open in an attempt to retrieve and repossess. My pain felt almost physical; I wanted to pull at the past and make sense of it. I looked up to see Andrea watching me from the kitchen doorway.

'Are you OK?'

'Let's get to work,' I said, and began opening the cupboards.

We cleaned for several hours; I emptied and Andrea wiped. Our determined labour was interrupted, sporadically, by the kettle boiling for tea. At midday Andrea suggested ordering a pizza for lunch and, much like the cigarette she'd offered me that first afternoon we got to know each other, I deferred to her uncanny ability to propose something dirty at just the right time. She took her marigolds off and went to inspect the pile of menus I had kicked aside earlier. And returned holding a letter. It had been delivered by hand and was addressed to *the son or daughter of Katharine Lambton*. I stared for a long time at my mother's maiden name, long-neglected and joined to me by the cursive confidence of unfamiliar handwriting. I opened the envelope and read.

I hope you'll forgive the unsolicited nature of this letter. I have no address other than this one, but wanted to send you my deepest sympathies on the loss of your mother. We worked together before she was married but sadly lost touch in the intervening years. I'd be more than happy to meet, should you find that agreeable. I still live in Surbiton.
Yours,
Nicola

On a separate piece of paper she'd included her address and telephone number.

Part Two

Internal Examination

The stomach contained porridge-like material. There was a scar to the lower abdomen consistent with caesarean section. The lower urinary tract and genital organs were otherwise unremarkable.

One Monday morning, at the beginning of June, I phoned Helen at home. It had been several months since we'd spoken. When I discovered my mother's body, Helen was the first person I called. Tragedy bound us together – close and complicit – as we concurred on the choice of coffin and what she should wear within it. That her body was still present and dependent on our decisions drew us together, but deep and colourless grief awaited us both, like a long-overdue task, and so we withdrew from one another.

After a few rings she picked up. In the background was the sound of frantic barking.

'Laura. Hello. How are you? Sandy – get down!'

'I'm fine, thanks. How are you?'

'I'm sick to the back teeth of this yappy little shit.'

'You've got a dog?'

'Yes. I ought to be bloody sectioned. She'll be good company, people said. Well, I need good company now because nobody'll come near me. Laura, she does not stop shitting.'

'I don't know what to say. Would you like me to come and see you?'

'I would. Except it's probably easier if we meet in an open space, somewhere I can take her for a walk.'

'OK. How about this afternoon?'

She had not expected me to be so spontaneous. 'This afternoon? I can't see why not. We could do that. Can you get to Richmond Park?'

'Yes, definitely. 2 p.m.?'

I drove in through the Richmond gate of the park just before two. It is quite something to be met with such wide and expansive green after the narrow urban streets of Richmond's one-way system. But I couldn't indulge myself with a long drive through it; I turned right at the first roundabout and parked outside Pembroke Lodge, where we'd agreed to meet.

I saw Helen waiting by the toilets, bending down to admonish a small and unrepentant dog. She saw my boots before she saw me and straightened up at my sudden proximity. She looked smaller and older.

'Laura,' she said, pulling me to her with one arm. The other maintained a firm hold on Sandy's lead. I went to straighten up after a few seconds, but she wouldn't let go and held me harder. As though I were her other errant dog. And as our embrace continued, I allowed myself to slump into her. I felt her chest heave with her own sorrow and I joined her, crying suddenly and copiously into her scarf.

I pulled back to wipe my eyes and right myself. 'I'm sorry. It just hit me then. Seeing you.'

'Don't say sorry, Laura. You cry as much as you like. I've cried many tears.' She looked up and into my face with genuine sympathy. The kind of sympathy that's prepared to wait. 'Come on – let's get this one a walk and then we can talk.'

We crossed the road, pausing in our conversation to hold

hands gingerly as the cars slowed to let us pass.

'I cry every day,' she said. 'I still haven't come to terms with it. Don't know that I ever will.'

'Is that why you got Sandy? To keep you busy?'

'In a way, yes. I can't be bothered with other people at the moment. She makes more sense to me,' she said as she bent down to let her off the lead, 'and all she does is shit and sniff. There's a simplicity about that that appeals to me. When I'm not pulling my hair out. Does that make any sense?' As she spoke, she unclipped Sandy's collar.

'It does. Distraction is important—' I began to say, but Sandy had spotted a couple of ducks sitting on the grass near a pond and began tearing off after them.

'Oh, fuck. Hang on, Laura,' and with that, she began running, ineffectually, in Sandy's general direction. I broke into a run myself, seeing Helen had no chance of catching up with her. We spent ten minutes chasing Sandy in wide and concentric circles until another dog owner grabbed her by the collar and waited, with a sympathetic smile, for us to claim her. We were both breathless and grateful.

Helen put Sandy back on the lead. 'What the hell have I done? I've tethered myself to a furry devil. You naughty girl!' she shouted at Sandy, who accepted the compliment with great equanimity. 'Sorry, Laura, what were you saying? Something about distraction . . . it's good to be distracted?'

'Yes – well remembered. Just that I've been keeping myself busy. I've agreed to write a big piece on the Olympics, and that's been good for me, I think.'

'Well done! That's fantastic. Your mum would have been so proud.' She looked down at the ground then, still too out of breath to cry.

'I've been thinking about her a lot too. And about the past.'

She didn't say anything. Just looked up at me and waited as we walked. So I continued.

'About her and my dad. Trying to work out when things went wrong between them.'

'Have you spoken to your father about any of this?'

'No. Not yet. I mean, I can. And I will, but I want to try and get a few things clear in my head first. You know, things like . . .'

'Go on.'

'Well, why was she so keen to have Jenny around? She must have begun to suspect something was going on. I know my granny warned her.' I looked over at Helen. She was still staring down at the grass and Sandy's quick legs, listening intently and nodding her head. 'I mean, you knew her best of all. What do you think? Did she know?'

'About your dad and Jenny?' She looked up and to the right. As though the answer might be over by the duck pond. 'It's difficult to say. I believe so.'

'So why put up with it? And not just put up with it, *sanction* it. I remember her saying to him once, the night after Sue attacked her, "Never in the house". I mean . . . that's pretty odd, don't you think?'

'Odd isn't the word.'

'But why? Why did she let it happen?'

Helen stopped walking and allowed her right arm to be pulled up by Sandy's impatience at the end of the lead. She looked like a one-armed scarecrow trying to decide how frightening she could be.

'Because things had come to a head with them. I don't know how much of this I should be telling you.'

'What had come to a head?'

'It was complicated. I'm not sure of everything myself. But

I know that by the time Christopher was born, your mum had decided to stop sharing a bed with your father. Physically it was over between them.'

'When you came to stay?'

'You remember that? Yes, when I came to stay.'

'But my dad stuck around for another five years!'

'They agreed to keep things together. As normal as possible for you and Christopher. And your mum was happy for your dad to have a *life* outside the house. As long as it didn't interfere with your lives inside it.'

'But it obviously did interfere. I mean, eventually. He moved in with Jenny.'

'I tried explaining the same thing to your mum once. Laura, you have to understand that Kath,' she took a deep breath, 'your mum was complicated and stubborn. God, she was stubborn.' She smiled to herself and shook her head. 'And she couldn't be made to do anything.'

'What did you want her to do?'

'I wanted her to separate from your father.' She looked up at me and then back to the grass. 'I thought, in the long run, it would be better for all of you if they regained their independence. From one another.'

'Why did you come to stay after Christopher was born?'

'She needed me.'

'Why?'

'Because she almost died giving birth. And Christopher very nearly went the same way. It was a terrible experience, and she blamed your father for it.'

My mother went into labour on a Saturday afternoon. I was sent to go and knock on Sue's door and summon Jenny. When I returned, with Jenny holding my hand, my mother was sitting on the bottom step in the hallway. My father was on his knees in front of her, tying her shoelaces. She looked up and beckoned to me, silently. I walked over slowly, aware of being watched by three adults. She cupped my face and inhaled my features with a primal intensity. Our mouths met for a last kiss and I felt suddenly embarrassed by the depth of her emotion. She was crying at her own act of betrayal.

My mother had decided she was going to have another girl – she simply couldn't conceive of a birthing experience different to my own. But Christopher's passage into the bright light of the hospital was not to be straightforward. My mother was fully dilated upon arrival, but after fifty-five minutes of purple pushing she knew her baby was stuck.

A young and inexperienced midwife tried to encourage her. She mouthed platitudes, told her to keep pushing, that she was 'doing brilliant' and held her knee in maternal cama-raderie, but my mother just shook her head. In desperation she put her own hand down between her legs, hoping to feel the slippery globe of her baby's head, but there was nothing there. She turned to my father who was sitting beside her and spoke quietly, almost intimately: 'Where is she?'

'Your baby's coming, Mrs Rowan. You just have to keep pushing,' interrupted the midwife. My mother lay back against the bed, reprimanded by her insistence. She wanted to tell my father that she felt their baby's lack of strength deep down in her pelvis, but every time she opened her mouth to explain, he held her hand and spoke over her in an attempt to reassure: 'It's going to be OK, Kath. You're doing fine.'

She swallowed into her dry mouth, whispering to keep the contractions and the midwife at bay, and said, 'I know something's wrong. Please get me a doctor.'

My father, aware of the midwife watching them and

embarrassed by this overt attempt to undermine her authority, tried to mollify her again. 'Give it time, Kath. These things take time.' He looked to the midwife, seeking approval.

My mother felt his disloyalty like a sharp wound in her womb. Its immediacy quickly spread across her back and into the lumber region of her spine.

'Get me a doctor.' And then, because she saw the pained inaction in his eyes, she shouted louder: 'Now! Get me a doctor,' her voice rising to a scream as another contraction rolled in. The midwife approached my mother, leaning over my father's back as she tried to get closer to the bed.

'Mrs Rowan, please. Your baby is coming,' she said as my mother tried to move onto her side, away from the terrible pain of lying flat on the bed, but instead of helping her move, she leant over so that my father was forced from his chair. With her face hovering above my mother's, she pushed her rising shoulder back and said: 'You need to concentrate on pushing. Lie back and we'll get this baby out.'

'Get your fucking hands off me!' The midwife jumped back, her fingers burning from my mother's sweaty invective.

'Jesus Christ, Kath!' My father stood between the two women, powerless.

'Help me over,' my mother said to my father.

'Kath, I think we should do as we're told. You need to start pushing.'

But the new pain, like a barbed and twisted ball within her womb, was impervious to the contractions that came and went. It wanted nothing to do with pushing. She couldn't have known that her placenta had begun separating from the wall of her uterus, or that she'd soon start haemorrhaging, but she knew something was very wrong. So she held herself as still as she could and, looking above my father's head at the sky through the large window, said, in a suddenly calm and measured voice, 'This baby is going to die if you don't get me a doctor,' and, lowering her eyes to his face, said, even more quietly, 'and I will never forgive you if she does.'

The sudden transformation was enough to startle my father. My mother, in her terrible pain, had withdrawn enough to return with authority. He stood up and walked past the midwife and into the hallway, where he began shouting, his voice rising on the first note of panic, for a doctor.

The consultant who entered the room a few minutes later was a woman in her late forties, white and petite. Her name was Dr Lynn, and she fixed my mother with her small, fast eyes. 'Mrs Rowan. I understand you've requested a doctor. I'm the consultant obstetrician. Would you like me to examine you?'

My mother swallowed to lubricate her throat and nodded with an emphatic yearning that might have embarrassed them in any other context. But as Dr Lynn lifted my mother's thigh to peer between her legs, she saw the blood that had pooled beneath her. What had started as a trickle quickly revealed itself as the determined flood of placental abruption. Dr Lynn raised the alarm and worked quickly to stem the flow. The room was suddenly full of doctors, but Dr Lynn kept her eyes on my mother and spoke directly to her. 'Your baby is in distress. We need to perform an emergency C-section. Please don't worry. I'm going to take good care of you and your baby.'

The pathologist, in examining my mother's corpse, rightly deduced that the scarring on her abdomen was caused by a caesarean section. He couldn't have known that it was the result of an emergency procedure to safely deliver my baby brother and save her life. Or that Christopher's birth was the beginning of the end of my parents' marriage.

There was no shouting or panic as the birth loomed. Only my father's ashen face and sweaty hands as he realised things were about to go wrong. That his wife might bleed to death and take his second child with her because he hadn't wanted to contradict a midwife he'd never meet again, crushed him. He looked over at my mother who, in spite of the blood loss and considerable pain, had drawn her knees up and was breathing deeply. She was trying to give her baby space, the only thing remaining in her power, as the doctors desperately tried to staunch the bleeding.

My father did not know then, as he looked at his wife, that he would never reach her again. That she had failed to push their baby out but succeeded in pushing him away for good was a fact that would become apparent in the coming weeks. This was no time for painful recriminations or lacerating statements sharp with finality. She was too busy wrapping her maternal flesh around the distressed baby and preparing for the operation that would save their lives and scar her abdomen, ready for the pathologist's report some twenty-six years later.

On 13 September 1986, Dr Lynn made an incision in my mother's abdomen, parting the tissue and muscle so she could better reach her uterus. At 3.14 in the afternoon, she pulled my baby brother, Christopher Michael Rowan, from her punctured womb, grimacing and blue. His throat constricted by an umbilical cord reluctant to let go, he'd been just moments from death.

And that's exactly what she told my mother when she visited her on the recovery ward several hours later. My mother, who'd been given a general anaesthetic, was groggy and sore from the operation. She was confused by Dr Lynn's use of the word *death* in relation to the baby in the cot beside her. The baby that was not me. Or not even a girl like me. For days she felt as though her baby had died, had given up while inside her. Her nightmares were a variation on the theme of screaming – from the anguished shouts to my father, to the raw sobbing on being handed a lifeless baby.

Helen visited her on the Sunday afternoon following Christopher's birth. My father had already been and gone. My mother was staring into the middle distance as a nurse tried to position Christopher, forcing contact between his hungry mouth and her sore nipple.

'Kath?'

My mother's eyes didn't move. They simply filled with tears at Helen's voice.

Helen grabbed at the curtain and pulled it around my mother and her screaming baby. As she approached the bending nurse, she paused and looked down at her. 'And what exactly are we doing here?'

The nurse looked up at my mother and then, realising the question was for her, turned to Helen and said, 'Breastfeeding. We're trying to get mum to feed baby.'

'Mum looks like she could do with a feed herself. And an arm around her. Can we try again later?'

'This baby is very hungry.'

'So go get a bottle. I'll feed the little feller.'

'It's not a good idea. We need to keep mum's breasts stimulated.'

'Forget her breasts and do your job. Get me a bottle.'

My mother sucked in her breath and closed her eyes as she heard Helen sit down and take Christopher in her arms.

His anguished cry changed the moment he was against her. It became a raspy staccato full of expectation, and when she finally gave him the bottle of formula brought to her by the nurse, he was quiet.

'It's a boy,' my mother said, her eyes still closed.

'So I gather. And he has a fine pair of lungs on him.'

My mother's smile was too sharp and sudden to be anything other than a harbinger of pain. It forced the soft flesh of her cheeks upward until her eyes understood to cry.

'What happened?'

'I thought I was going to die.'

'But you didn't. And here he is. And you're both—'

'You don't understand. Even with him inside me and people around me, I felt so alone.'

Helen, made immobile by my brother's body and urgent sucks, tried to lean towards my mother. 'You'll get through this, Kathy. It's bound to be difficult for a little while, but I'll come and help.'

'Will you stay?' My mother turned and looked in her direction for the first time. And seeing her baby quiet and content in the arms of her best friend was like a balm to her aching wounds. Both the literal wound that throbbed in her abdomen and the sharper, more tormenting one in her head that kept closing and reopening.

'Of course I'll stay. I'll do whatever you want,' she said, smiling down at Christopher.

Helen. She was always there for my mother, holding her close when she felt as though she would surely fall.

My father came home on the afternoon of my mother's operation just as Jenny was preparing my dinner. His face was pale and fragile, as though he might cry at any moment. I jumped down from my chair and ran to him. He put his arms out in an automatic gesture of embrace, but I stopped short by a few inches to ask an urgent question. 'Is it a boy or a girl?'

'A boy,' he smiled sadly.

'A boy? That means I have a baby brother.'

'You sure do.' Then he stood up to face Jenny, who was standing behind me. 'Hi.'

'Hi,' she mumbled in return. They were quiet with each other. Comfortable.

'How's she been?'

'Oh, fine. We've been out to the playground, watched a bit of TV and I'm just making an omelette now. Would you like one?'

'No,' he said, grimacing at the thought. 'I could do with a lie-down, though. Are you sure you're OK down here?'

'Yes, definitely. Did it all go OK?'

He looked down at me and attempted to smile. Then looked back at her, mouthed *I'll tell you later* and went to walk out of the kitchen, his back suddenly strong and out of my reach. I followed him into the hall and pulled on his jumper.

'Is Mummy OK?'

He turned back, but his first look was to Jenny and then down to me. 'She's fine, sweetheart,' and then the more alarming, 'there's nothing to worry about.'

I stood still and listened to the heavy thump of his step on the stairs. Jenny and I remained in the kitchen. Suddenly strangers. She slid my overcooked omelette from the frying pan onto a plate as I sidled up to the chair I'd just vacated. 'Do you want some ketchup?'

'Yes, please.'

She cut my food up and slid the plate towards me.

'Will you be all right down here?'

I looked up at her, unsure what she was asking. 'Can I have a drink please?'

'Oh yeah. Sorry.' She quickly pulled a cup from the cupboard above the sink and filled it with water. I took a sip and winced at how warm it was – she hadn't let the tap run for long enough. But before I could say anything she had walked out of the kitchen and up the stairs. I ate a small, dry mouthful of omelette, got down from my chair and followed her, very quietly.

At the top of the stairs was standing room for one person – two, at a push – and a long and wide landing to the left. Our bathroom was the first door on the right, then my bedroom and, at the front of the house, a small box room – complete with cot, waiting empty for the baby – and my parents' large bedroom. On the second floor was another large bedroom, usually reserved for guests, and a small bathroom. I walked slowly past my bedroom, drawn by their whispering voices and the need to get closer. The first words I heard clearly were my father's. He was calling something a 'fucking disaster'. Jenny's voice was soft and soothing in return. 'It's all right, Rich. They're OK now.'

'But it nearly wasn't. I should have spoken up sooner.'

'What happened?'

'She asked me to fetch a doctor. And I didn't, and then . . . the blood. There was so much blood.' His voice drowned in the phlegm at the back of his throat. As he coughed to clear it, Jenny put her hand between his shoulder blades.

'It's not your fault.'

'Tell that to Kath,' he whispered to the carpet.

'You didn't know it was going to happen.'

'She can't even bring herself to look at me,' he said, turning to face Jenny. Their faces uncomfortably close.

'She's lucky to have you.'

He stood quickly, as though he'd suddenly understood something, and then saw me standing there. 'Laura.'

Jenny turned at the sound and got to her feet. I could see she was irritated by the interruption and, walking over quickly, tried to turn me out of the room and into the hallway. I became obstreperous and unmanageable – so much so that my father was forced to compose himself and join us by the door. 'Laura. What's the matter?'

'Why are you crying?'

'Because I'm being silly,' he said, trying to smile.

'What's wrong with Mummy?'

'Nothing. I'm just crying because I'm so,' he was casting about for a word, 'happy.'

I felt suddenly hot and angry as Jenny tried to steer me from the room. I was enraged that she was trying to keep me from my father and my father was trying to keep me from the truth. I shouted at her to *get off!* and pushed her hard in the hip. It caught her off guard and she stumbled sideways into my mother's bedside table, knocking the lampshade crooked. She was clearly shocked, as was my father, but the hot feeling made me charge on in the silence: 'I want to see Mummy.'

He looked at Jenny and then back to me. I stood still, ostensibly awaiting his next move but, in truth, it was his loyalty I wanted. He knelt down before me and put his hands on my shoulders. I felt my feet sink further into the carpet. 'We will go to see Mummy and your baby brother soon. I promise.'

'When?'

'In a few days. She needs time to get better.'

'Why does she need to get better?' I asked.

'Having a baby is very difficult, and sometimes it can make you feel poorly. So she needs to get some rest, and hospital is the best place for that. OK? Does that make sense?'

I nodded the assent of a powerless child.

'Why don't you go downstairs with Jenny now,' he said, looking up hopefully in that direction, 'and eat your dinner? I'll be down in a little while, OK?' I walked out of the room before Jenny could put her hands on me again. We walked downstairs in silence, to where my inedible omelette awaited me.

My father returned to the hospital that evening to drop off some clothes and toiletries. Jenny put me to bed, reading me several more stories than usual, perhaps in atonement for her behaviour earlier. I accepted her offering and the later bed-time because I wanted to be awake when my father returned. I thought he might have more to say and, if he thought I was asleep, his words might be more truthful. But I must have fallen asleep because when I woke, with a start, the house was dark and silent. I got out of bed and went into my parents' bedroom, expecting to find my father asleep, but he wasn't there. Instead I saw Jenny, lying on her side on my father's side of the bed. Her hair was splayed out on his pillow and in her arms was one of his jumpers, held close to her sleeping face.

It was the following week before my father took me, as promised, to visit my mother in hospital. He came to collect me from school, stopping to talk to the other mothers in the playground, many of whom demanded the headlines of my brother's birth with practised expectation. My father gave them what they wanted – weight, gender – and promised to confirm the name soon. He behaved as though nothing was wrong, that my baby brother didn't have a name because he and my mother couldn't agree and not because they hadn't spoken since the birth. I clung onto his hand, happily skipping towards the car, and made the facade plausible because I was so relieved to be finally on my way back to my mother.

We navigated the reception, a lift and several long corridors made bright and hygienic by shiny linoleum. It seemed incredible to me, as I walked beside my father, that we might find my mother in such a cold and efficient place. Our search eventually brought us to a garish curtain and, like a conjuror, my father pulled it back to reveal her. She was sitting up in bed and took a deep, joyful breath when she saw me. She didn't look at my father, was oblivious to him as he walked towards the cot on the right of her bed to peer at the baby. I took a few steps in her direction and noticed she was trying to stop her face from contorting as she inclined her torso towards me. I felt frightened by all that had happened to her since she last kissed me at the bottom of the stairs. All that had brought her to this place. She held out her arms and extended her fingers, impatiently.

I reached up with my hands, careful to avoid her sore bits. My hands ended up in her armpits, where the soft white cotton of her nightdress gave way to the moist, saggy skin. I looked up at her face and noticed her hair was flat and greasy.

'Come up here,' she said, patting the bedcovers beside her. I tried to get up, but the bed was too high. I gripped the bedcovers and tried lifting my foot to get some kind of purchase, but it was too difficult. My mother looked over to my father, who had lifted the baby out of his cot and put him to his shoulder. They still hadn't said a word to one another.

He walked round the bed in obedience to my mother's

silent request, but decided I should have the option of at least meeting my brother first. He knelt down to show me Christopher. I looked at his pursed lips and tiny palms – at the boy who had tried to break my mother – and continued scrambling up to my mother's side as though my life depended on it.

'So tell me all about it,' she said. 'What have you been up to?'

'Miss Jeffrey told the class you have a new baby and everybody clapped. And Michael told me you had to push him out of your moo-moo.'

She smiled and, looking over at my father, said, 'The baby didn't come out of my moo-moo. He got stuck. So they had to make a hole in my belly and pull him out that way.'

She looked down at her soft, deflated stomach and pulled the covers away. I could see the bandages beneath the thin white cotton.

'Is that where they had to cut you?' I asked, probing the edge of the bandage gently. She nodded. My father watched us both; he looked like he was holding his breath. 'Tell Mummy what happened in the playground today.' My mother looked at me expectantly.

'I fell over!' I said, revealing my scraped knee.

'How did you do that?'

'I was playing hopscotch with Isobel and she wanted me to let her win but I wouldn't.'

'And how did you hurt your knee?'

'I was jumping from five and six to seven.'

'And she pushed you?'

'No, I slipped. But she didn't help me up.'

'Oh dear. My poor little one.' Though it was my knee that was sore, her fingers were immediately busy about my face:

she was lifting the hair around my hairline and allowing it to fall as she ran her fingertips down the contour of my face. When she got to my chin she pulled my face forward slightly and kissed me, gently. 'I've missed you so much,' she said, terminating my chronicle of the playground.

The baby began to cry, bobbing his head on my father's shoulder. 'Kath,' he said, 'I think he's hungry.' My mother kept her eyes on me but reached out for the baby. My father leant in close and placed Christopher gently in her arms. He put his hand on her shoulder as she unbuttoned her nightdress.

'What are you doing?' I asked.

'I'm feeding the baby,' she said, suddenly exposing a huge red nipple. Her face twisted in pain as Christopher made contact. It lasted a few seconds, all of them silent and suspended, before she opened her eyes and looked for me again.

My father remained close, leaning over her shoulder. 'Is it getting any easier?'

'Not really,' she said quietly. Coldly.

'Can I do anything?'

'You could leave me alone with Laura.' He straightened up and reluctantly withdrew his unwelcome hand. He'd received the answer he was expecting. The fictitious joy exhibited earlier in the playground was gone, and in its place a growing – and more realistic – misery.

'I'll go and get a coffee. See you in a bit.'

My mother and I chatted as Christopher fed, and together we assumed some kind of flawed normality. I ignored the sucking demands of a new baby brother and she ignored the crisis in her relations with my father. The incision in her abdomen was not the reason their marriage failed, but I can see now that she simply didn't love him enough to get past it.

Breasts were unremarkable.

By the time my mother and brother came home a week later, Helen had already moved in.

Helen and my mother met in primary school, and remained close their whole lives. Helen taught History to a sprawling mass of recalcitrant youngsters in Hounslow, west London. An arts graduate, she trained to become a teacher in the early 1980s. Arming herself with lesson plans and noble intentions, she was determined to take her knowledge to the kids who needed it most. But after half a term in the classroom, she quickly dispensed with metaphorical armour and employed more tangible ones: sarcasm and detention. I admired her no-nonsense approach to life. She used honesty to cut through layers of bullshit in a way that made her strong and formidable. And after Christopher was born, my mother needed strength.

Her arrival, with a small suitcase the Saturday after his birth, was signalled by Jenny's abrupt jump from the sofa – where we had been sitting together – at the sound of the doorbell. My father was upstairs. Jenny walked to the other side of the room and craned her neck at the side of the bay window to see who was at the front door. But she wasn't fast enough, because within the space of a minute Helen had used a set of keys to enter, boldly and without hesitation.

Jenny stood where she was and waited for the incursion.

I was surprised and excited to see her. Having Helen in the house presaged my mother's imminent return. She put her suitcase down in the hallway, resting it against the bottom step, and walked into the living room where I was still sitting.

'Hello, monkey!' she said with borrowed enthusiasm. I could tell she was wary – that she didn't know exactly what she was entering. And then she saw Jenny standing in the bay, almost behind one of the curtains. 'Jenny. Hello.'

'Hello.'

'Is Richard about?'

'He's upstairs. Having a nap.' Helen nodded slowly. She returned her look to me, as though she didn't know where to begin, and sat down heavily on the sofa. Jenny didn't move but looked towards the hallway and at the staircase, willing my father to come down. When the silence became unbeara- ble she said, 'I'll just go and wake him up,' and left the room quickly. As she stepped over Helen's suitcase to go up the stairs, Helen said quietly to no one in particular, 'You do that.'

'Are you going to sleep over?' I asked, thrilled by the sight of her suitcase.

'Yes. Is that good news?' I poked my arm through the crook of hers and squeezed myself against her.

'How many?'

'How many what?'

'How many sleeps?'

'Oh – I'm not sure. You'll have to ask your mum that. As many as she needs me here for.'

'Can you sleep in my bedroom?'

'I don't think so.'

'Why not?'

'Well, correct me if I'm wrong, but don't you have a tiny little bed?'

'It's a big girl's bed.'

'Not big enough for this big girl,' she laughed, patting her chunky thighs. 'I'd bust your bed. And then where would you be?'

My father came down the stairs, stepping over and wide of Helen's suitcase. He picked it up quietly and put it against the wall. Jenny followed a few paces behind. 'Helen. Hello. Kath didn't mention you were coming.'

'Did she not?' Helen stood up. 'Well, she's asked me to come and help. With Laura and the baby. I hope that's OK.'

'Yes, of course. No problem at all. But what about work? Aren't you still teaching?'

'I am,' she smiled. 'But Kath seems to think I can drop Laura in at' – she looked behind my father for Jenny – 'Sue's in the morning and then drive to work. I should be able to do it.'

'Can I make you a cup of tea?'

'No thanks. I'm about to head off to the hospital and collect them.' The colour drained from my father's face. He looked as if he'd been slapped.

'You're doing what?'

'She asked me yesterday afternoon. When I went to visit. Look, it's no big deal – I'll go and get them and bring them back here.'

'I think I should be the one to bring them home,' he said firmly.

'No, Richard. I don't think you should.'

My father spoke over his shoulder to Jenny. 'Could you take Laura into the kitchen, please?'

They held their silence until I was in the kitchen and the door had been closed behind me. The exchange, whatever it consisted of, didn't last long. Within a few minutes, Helen joined us in the kitchen and asked if I'd like to go with her to the hospital. She pushed my shoulders gently towards the front door and, as she helped me into my coat, turned my body so I could put my other arm in. I had a direct view into the living room, where my father was sitting on the edge of the sofa, his head in his hands. He looked totally demoralised. Helen turned me back to her sharply so she could do my buttons up and then opened the door, ushering me out into the September sunshine.

My mother's bag was packed and she was busy stuffing some dead flowers into a small bin when Helen pulled back the garish curtain. She smiled and began walking towards us, dressed in a loose shirt and baggy trousers with slippers on her feet. Christopher was sleeping peacefully in his cot, oblivious to the arrangements taking place around him.

'Shall we wake him up?' Helen asked.

'I think we'll have to. Can you carry him?'

'Of course I can. Who's going to carry your bag?' Helen asked, eyeing the bandages over my mother's abdomen.

'They're sending a porter with a wheelchair for me. It can go on the back of that.'

'Right, OK. Laura, do you want to come with me down to the car, or wait here?'

'She'll wait here,' my mother said, and turned to pick up the small warm body that was Christopher. He pursed his lips at the interruption but didn't open his eyes. Helen took him gently from my mother and pressed him to her shoulder, holding him in place with her left arm as she slid her protective right hand up his back and onto the furry dark hair at the base of his head.

While we waited for the wheelchair, I asked my mother if Helen could sleep in my bedroom.

'No, sweetie. She's going to sleep in my room.'

'But what about Daddy?'

'He's going to sleep upstairs for a while.'

'Why?'

She looked at me, long and steadily, before answering. 'Because your brother is going to be waking in the night. He'll need feeding at all kinds of funny times. So it'll be better for Daddy if he isn't woken up.'

'But what about Helen? She'll be woken up.'

'Helen doesn't mind. And it's only for a little while, until I'm feeling a bit stronger.' My immediate concern was that I'd been overlooked to share a room with Helen, but I was also dimly aware that my father's banishment upstairs was unusual. And unsettling.

My father's car was on the gravel in front of the house, which meant Helen had to park on the road a few doors down. We emerged from the car slowly – a feeble procession – and shuffled along the road with Helen at the front holding Christopher. I walked behind her and ahead of my mother, who took small, considered steps. She kept her head down, sometimes holding onto the wall to steady herself. I kept looking back every few seconds, making sure she followed.

My father was waiting for us at the end of the path, the front door wide open. There was no sign of Jenny. He blocked Helen's entry to the house with his body and bent his knees to take Christopher from her. Helen looked behind for my mother and stepped to the side to wait for her. My father's face broke into a smile when he saw me and moved so I could go inside.

'I'll go and grab the bag from the car,' she said to my back as she returned to the road.

My father knelt down with Christopher and presented him to me again. 'What do you think? He's a cracker, isn't he?'

'Yes, Daddy, you've already shown him to me.' He pulled me close to him and kissed my ear. 'I'm just so pleased to have my best girl and my best boy home.' He stood up and smiled as my mother finally walked up the path with Helen behind her. He put his hand out to help her up the step but she held the wall instead and paused to catch her breath. She looked at how he was holding Christopher and said nothing.

'How are you feeling?' he asked, putting his hand on her back surreptitiously as she stepped past him.

'OK. Better.'

'I'd have come to get you, Kathy,' he said as he waited for Helen to come in before closing the front door. 'You didn't need to trouble Helen.'

'It's no trouble,' Helen said quickly.

'I'll make tea and you can get into bed. Helen, I've put your bag upstairs.'

My mother was leaning against the bottom post of the banister. She looked exhausted. The C-section had left her particularly weak, but the blood transfusion had also triggered an allergic reaction; her ankles and thighs were red and itchy and covered in hives.

'Please,' she was breathless, 'can one of you help me upstairs?' Helen made a move but my father was quicker. 'I'll help you,' he said, handing Christopher to Helen and taking my mother's hand. She put her weight on it immediately, pausing at every step to plan her next move. My father stood beside her, happy to support his wife in some way. Helen, Christopher and I went into the kitchen where she proceeded to make tea. My mother must have waited until she was in bed before delivering her instructions on the new sleeping arrangements, because just as Helen and I sat down at the kitchen table, we heard the dull thud of drawers shutting and doors slamming with barely repressed violence. Helen closed her eyes and said nothing. I sipped my milky tea and waited; just as thunder must follow lightning, we waited for shouting. But there were no raised voices. Just the sound of my father walking quickly up and down the stairs to the second floor. He had been ordered up to the top of the house. His acquiescence was angry – we heard his quick step down to the hallway and the unstoppable bang of the front door as he got into his car and drove away. Helen stood up as though my father's departure had been planned from the beginning.

'Where are you going?' I asked.

She put her hand out to me. 'Come on, monkey. Let's go upstairs and see Mummy.'

Helen put Christopher down in a Moses basket positioned on my mother's side of the bed and made sure she was propped up comfortably before going back downstairs to locate the painkillers and antihistamines she'd been prescribed. I sat at her feet and rubbed cream onto the red patches. She twisted her ankles under my touch, as though she were purring inside, willing my nails to dig deeper into her angry skin.

Helen moved her things into my mother's bedroom and slept beside her that night and for many nights thereafter. She helped her to sit up in bed for feeds, lifting Christopher from his cot into my mother's practised arms. She sat beside my mother, with her arm across her shoulders, as the ducts in her engorged breasts carried milk to the many openings at the tips of her nipples. Nipples that were red and cracked from Christopher's hungry mouth. Helen enabled her to love, and go on loving, her baby. And she reminded my mother how to love and take care of herself again. Every morning, as I trudged sleepily into the bathroom to wee, Helen – all dressed for a day of teaching – would crouch beside the shallow bath my mother was sitting in, and, as my mother stared into the middle distance, squeeze a sponge over her warm, soapy shoulders. To shield me from my mother's morning sorrow, she used to greet me cheerfully.

'Morning, monkey.' I sat with my eyes closed and let the water flow out of me. 'I'll make you some porridge in about ten minutes, OK?'

'I'm not hungry.'

'Go and get dressed now.' Helen ignored anything inconvenient or beside the point. I could have been one of her pupils declaring I hadn't done my homework, or her best friend in the depths of depression – if she didn't want to acknowledge something, she just pushed on regardless. But I enjoyed having Helen to stay. She was exactly what we needed at the time. And she loved porridge.

'Laura? Porridge?' As if it were a question.

'No, thank you.'

'With honey?'

'I don't want porridge.'

'Then you need your bloody head checked. What do you want instead?' We were in the kitchen, preparing for another day at school. Helen poured the oats into a pan of milk.

'Cornflakes.'

She pulled the cutlery drawer open and angrily extracted a wooden spoon to stir the warm, oaty mixture. 'Let me tell you something. If you love yourself you'll start the day with a bowl of porridge.' And then, because she saw I was unmoved, 'Do you know what cornflakes will do?' I said nothing. It was obvious I couldn't win. 'They'll do a silly little dance in the milk, flutter against the insides of your stomach and scratch your bum on the way out. They're absolutely bloody pointless.' Placed before me, five minutes later, would be a large, steaming bowl of inevitable porridge.

After breakfast, Helen walked me over to Sue's house where Jenny would be waiting to take me and Sam to school. One drizzly morning in October, as she took my hand to cross the road, she said, simply and quietly: 'She's getting there, Laura.' It was a curiously vague phrase for a five-year-old, but I knew what she meant.

'I know.'

'It's a tough business.' Then, because I didn't say anything, she clarified, 'Having a baby.'

'Is that why you haven't had one?'

'Not every woman wants to have babies, Laura. Remember that.'

'Helen?'

'Yes?'

'Why is she so sad?' The silence was unexpected and prolonged. We'd long since crossed the road, but still she held my hand. I looked from our hands up to her face, where I saw it folding in on itself. She shook the sorrow that had swarmed her face and regained control. 'I wish I knew.'

The months after Christopher's birth marked a uniquely unsettled period in my life. The very fact of Jenny and Helen's heavy involvement in our family life pointed clearly to the breakdown of my parents' marriage. They were dysfunctional in the most obvious sense. My father accepted his failure as a husband and my mother withdrew into the distance that opened up between them. And yet he did not move out.

My mother's strength and willingness to parent two children emerged from the darkness of a difficult labour and a troubled marriage. Around the beginning of November, my mother – finally able to wash and dress herself in the morning – told Helen she could go home.

'And what about Richard? When can he come home?' It was early one morning. Their voices were quiet and measured from behind the door of my mother's bedroom.

'He is home.'

'You know what I mean. Come back down here.'

'I don't know.'

'I think you need to make a decision.'

'That's easy for you to say.'

'Kath, I'm not saying it's easy or that you have to stay with him, even. But this can't go on. And Laura will understand. If not now, then one day.' I heard the bed creak as Helen got out and opened the door. She wasn't particularly surprised to see me there.

My father did not move back into their bedroom after Helen left. Instead the house was plunged into a tense silence that made me long for her return. But things did settle down into a kind of normality: my mother began getting up early to supervise my breakfast and feed Christopher in time to walk me to school for the bell at nine. I used to watch her retreating back from across the playground, slightly hunched because the handles of the pushchair were too low for her height, and wonder what she and Christopher would do until the gates reopened to admit parents at three. When she would be there again, relieved and smiling. As if she'd just walked round the corner and waited for six hours.

One winter afternoon, just before we broke up for Christmas, Jenny came to collect Sam and me from school. My mother had taken Christopher for a check-up at the doctor's. As we walked home I listed all the things I'd asked Father Christmas for. But the thing I wanted most of all was a My Little Pony. A girl in my class, Stacey Hesler, already had one and derived great pleasure from publicly combing her rainbow mane. My jealousy was unbearable and bordered on obsession.

'I'm sure Father Christmas will bring you one,' Jenny said with a knowing smile that irked me.

'How do you know?'

'Grown-ups know these things.'

'What have you asked him for?'

'To lose her virginity!' Sam chirruped loudly, and started galloping sideways in celebration.

'Pack it in!' she shouted, leaning over me to try to land a thump on his retreating back.

'What's virginity?'

'It means doing sex on someone!' supplied Sam.

'Shut your filthy little mouth or I'll tell Mum!'

'You want Richard to do sex on you! I heard you tell Kelly in your bedroom.'

Jenny's face coloured upward like a glass of Summer Fruits squash. Reluctantly she looked down at me, awaiting my question, but I was too distracted by the spiky little word that Sam had used to connect the name Richard with my father. That came later. When it was too late to ask any more questions.

Helen remained a fixture in our lives, coming to see us at least two or three evenings a week but staying away at weekends.

She came with a bottle of wine, a packet of cigarettes and a humorous tale from the classroom. My mother would drink, listen and laugh, lifted by the camaraderie after spending the day alone with my brother and his inarticulate demands.

I used to look forward to Helen's visits too. Excited by the prospect of her becoming a part of our household again. Always in my pyjamas by the time she arrived, I would hang off her arm in a crude attempt to make her stay. If my mother was in a good mood I would be allowed to stay up beyond my usual bedtime and watch television in the adjoining living room. I was sitting there, with the volume turned down low, the night Helen and my mother argued.

One of Helen's colleagues had a baby at about the same time my mother had Christopher. She'd left a small hole in the teaching schedule of the English department, a crack that became a crater when Colin Ball, a sallow and malnourished bachelor of fifty-five, finally threw in the towel on his teaching career, walked out of a fifth-year lesson on *Romeo and Juliet* and straight into The Royal Oak at the end of the road. There had been no moment of rebellion, no lurid pun on his surname, just Friar Laurence's quietly convincing view that 'powerful grace … lies in herbs'. He thought of the hops that must go into every pint of beer and decided to take himself – both wise and slow – to the nearest boozer.

Helen had been asked to fill in while the school found a suitable replacement. 'There's no one else, apparently! I'm supposed to lend *historical context*, for God's sake.' She laughed to herself and said, 'And do you know what one of the little shits asked me?'

'What?'

'Did Juliet ever suck on her own mother's tits?'

My mother giggled quietly.

'I said to him, I said, "I don't know about Juliet, but you'll be sucking on this piece of chalk if you ever use that language in my classroom again." Little fucker.' *Spink-spink*. The sound of a cigarette being lit followed by a loud and eye-watering inhalation.

'You'd miss it, though.'

'I would not.'

'But you have something to *do* every day. Every day feels like the last one for me.'

Helen smoked into the silence.

'I just wish I had something to focus on. Some direction.'

'You'll find direction the moment you start living again.'

'What's that supposed to mean?'

'Richard.'

'Not that again.'

'Listen to me: it was a mistake. You should never have married. I get it. So why won't you leave him?'

'Why *would* I leave him? Because he goes out to work every day and puts a roof over our heads and food on the table? Because he loves his children?'

'Because you don't love him! Because you've every reason,' Helen lowered her voice to a wet, urgent whisper, 'to believe his head's been turned by your little babysitter. There are two reasons for you. Let's start with those.'

'So what?'

'So that's OK, is it? And what exactly do you get out of this?'

'A home, a father to my kids, a——'

'A cover for the truth!'

'Call it that if you want.'

'I don't want! I don't want any of this.'

'I'm keeping it together for Laura and Christopher.'

'And I'm telling you Laura and Christopher deserve better.'

'Than what? A good home, a mum and dad who love them?'

'None of that has to stop. Just because you live apart doesn't mean they won't benefit from your love. And there's a good chance your happiness will make them happier.'

'I can't, Helen.'

'You can.'

'No, *you* can. You always can. But I need to put my children first. As soon as they're grown up and move out, I'll do it. I'll tell them the truth.'

'For fuck's sake.'

'For fuck's sake yourself!'

'And Jenny?'

'What about Jenny?'

'Don't pretend she isn't gunning for Richard. And when that happens, when he finally gives in, what happens to your little suburban dream then?'

'He won't.'

'Kath, he's human. He has needs like all of us. And when someone offers companionship, comfort, love—'

'Helen . . .'

'—the sensible thing to do is take it.'

'I can't.'

'There you go again.'

I heard the gritty grind of a spent cigarette in the glass ashtray. And then Helen's hurried and farewell exhalation. 'I should have known. Always the bloody same.'

My mother made no response. She just sat there as Helen pulled her coat from the back of the chair and put it on. The quiet, awkward shufflings of an unexpectedly frosty goodbye.

She walked past the open door of the living room, where I sat in suspended anxiety, towards the front door. Before she opened it – my ears alert to every sound – I heard the swift and rapid pad of my mother's bare feet running to her. And then the soft drop of sobbing caught by earnest shushing. I don't know who was crying or who was shushing. Perhaps they both were. But I know something was resolved by this discreet emotion.

Helen was right. Eventually Jenny was the one to pull my father away from his marriage. In 1991 he moved out, and I hated him for doing so. I was too young to understand that my mother's silence and inaction had permitted it. That it was no marriage. I simply saw her as the victim and it made me unhappy. And angry.

Christopher was also unhappy – at five years of age his unhappiness manifested itself in tears and tantrums – but he wanted my father enough to still see him. He was able to accept that contact had to be at the weekends and under another roof. I envied him his pure and direct love, because my own had become so contaminated by all that I was starting to understand and the many things I could not. Ultimately I just couldn't forgive him for leaving us. We didn't speak for many months, and I never stayed the night at his new place.

They moved to a small two-bedroom flat in New Malden. It was all they could afford, because my father insisted on keeping up the mortgage repayments on our house in Surbiton. Even after the mortgage had been paid off in 2001, he never suggested selling it or that he and my mother should get a divorce.

In 1994, just one month before my thirteenth birthday, Jenny gave birth to a little girl. My father telephoned my mother to ask if he could come to the house – without Jenny – and introduce us to his new daughter. It was a watershed moment for all of us, seeing him with his baby. His pride was boundless and he wanted us, his first family, to share this moment of achievement with him. I understood then, on the brink of adolescence, that my mother, in her rejection of him after Christopher's birth, had deprived him of a great chunk of joy. And in Ellie he regained what was rightfully his. It made me want to be his daughter again.

We started slowly; my secondary school was in Kingston, so on at least one afternoon a week I'd take the bus to New Malden and spend an hour with Jenny and Ellie before he came home from work. I didn't exactly help, and I certainly didn't wash up or cook like she did for my own mother, but I took an interest in Ellie and played with her, something that – I'm assured by friends who are now mothers – is help enough to any new parent.

By the time I was offered a place at Cambridge, in January 1999, my father and I had rebuilt some semblance of a relationship. When I got my results the following August, I drove with some friends to the bank he worked in to show him the slips of paper. He was so thrilled, he asked if he could hug me. And I remember crying on his shoulder, not because of my results, but because he'd felt the need to ask.

I wasn't the only one to soften towards him after he moved out. My mother wasn't friendly, but she was perfectly happy to see him when he came to collect Christopher for the weekend or drop him off on a Sunday evening. The quietude of a broken home; when the walls first crack, all is panic and upset, but once the damage has been assessed and accepted, it's possible to live calmly under its roof again. I'm not saying my mother wasn't right to be worried about the impact of a break-up on Christopher and me, but she underestimated the great benefit of peace and harmony.

My meeting with Helen in the park had helped me to see that Christopher's birth was the catalyst for a process that was already well under way. Helen was right – my mother did freeze him out, I remember it myself – but I still wanted to know when, and if, they were ever happy. And I knew my father was the only one who could answer that question with any certainty. I've covered many stories in my professional life, interviewed people in the aftermath of great trauma, and yet I felt myself cringe at the thought of asking my father how he really felt about my mother. Before things went wrong.

The Friday that followed my meeting with Helen was a gloriously sunny day. The kind of June morning that makes you feel sudden panic that plans are not in place to enjoy it fully. I put on shorts and a T-shirt, found my trainers at the bottom of my wardrobe and, tying my hair up, went out for a run. I realised as I made my way towards Clapham Common that I hadn't even brushed my teeth. With every stride I got further away from my flat, her report and the sorrow that had engulfed me for so long. I did a lap of the common and then ran back to my flat, against the flow of commuters, at around nine and showered. I made breakfast to *Desert Island Discs* and sat down with a cup of coffee around ten. I continued working on my fourth article; it was about the rush to buy property near the Olympic Village. I was playing around with the title: 'Are We the Village Idiots?' and the decidedly weak, 'The Only Doorway in the Village', when my father phoned.

'Hi Dad.'

'Hi, Laura. What are you up to?'

'Just doing a bit of work. I'm writing some articles on the Olympics.'

'Very good. Got a tough deadline?'

'Not especially tough, no,' I said, rolling my eyes. My father liked to believe I worked in a smoke-filled, cut-throat Fleet Street office full of hard thinkers and straight-talkers.

'Well, let me know when it will be published.'

'*Printed*, Dad. I'm not writing a book.'

'Well you should. And you could.'

'What can I do for you?' I asked, looking out at the sunshine.

'I haven't seen you in a while. Jenny and I have got you a little birthday present here. Ellie would love to see you.'

'I'd like to see you guys too. I've been meaning to phone you, actually.'

'OK, well, can you do this weekend?'

'Yeah. Tomorrow afternoon – say around four?'

'Great. I'll let the girls know. Ellie will be pleased. See you tomorrow.'

With the mortgage on my mother's house almost paid off, in 1998 my father and Jenny moved to a small three-bedroom house. It was still in New Malden, but in the catchment area for a much better primary school. On the edge of a big housing estate, their road is swamped by cars and impossible to park on. I underestimated how long it would take to find a space and ended up knocking on the door late and ever so slightly out of breath.

Ellie opened the door, standing tall in heels with self-consciously long hair. Her face, so heavy with new beauty, looked almost perilous on her neck. As though it might tip over into womanhood at any moment.

Their hallway was narrow and cluttered. My father's bike was leaning up against the wall, and Jenny and Ellie's shoes filled most of the space in between. Ellie had to open the door and press herself against the wall for me to enter before we could hug. 'They're in the kitchen,' she directed.

'Happy birthday!' my father said as soon as he saw me. Jenny was vigorously stirring a small pot on the stove. She turned her body to wave briefly.

'It's not really my birthday any more. But thank you,' I said, accepting the small package he'd picked up from the table.

'It's only a little thing. Ellie chose it.'

'Can I open it?' I asked her.

She nodded, grinning excitedly at the wrapping paper. Inside the wrapping paper was more tissue paper, and within that was a gold sequinned evening top. The kind that is either sexy or desperate.

'I've got one. It looks really nice with jeans.'

'Thank you. I love it,' I said, knowing I would never wear it.

'I've still got the receipt if you don't like it.'

'No, I really like it. Thanks Ellie,' I said, giving her a kiss. My father walked over to take one too. I lifted my hand to Jenny, as though she'd just allowed me to cross in front of her car, and said, 'Thanks, Jenny.'

'You're welcome.'

'Do you think it would suit me?' my father asked us, holding the top up against his chest. Ellie rolled her eyes.

'It's a bit understated for you, isn't it?' I said.

'I could pair it with some jeans and go out on the town with you two.'

'Nobody goes *out on the town*, Dad!' Ellie turned to me in mock horror.

'He's never going to get less embarrassing. You know that, don't you? This situation,' I said, pointing to my father, standing there eager like a little dog, 'is never going to get any better. Next time just buy him a top too. You'll save yourself a lot of hassle.'

'Come on, Laura. Have a drink with me. What would you like? I've got some Pinot Grigio in the fridge, or you can have a beer. Jen?' He looked over at her cautiously. I could tell from his deliberate change in tone that they'd had some sort of argument before my arrival. She turned from the stove to face us. 'Glass of wine with Laura?'

'No thanks. But you go ahead, Laura,' she said, attempting to smile.

'Actually I won't, thanks. I'm driving, so I'll stick to the soft stuff. Can I have a cup of tea?'

'Why did you drive?' my father asked, outraged. 'Did you manage to park?'

'Yes, down on Dennon Road.'

'You want to get yourself a bike. Like your old dad. Best thing I ever did, getting rid of the car. Cycle to work every day.'

'That's great. Good for you.'

'We got rid of the car because we couldn't afford one,' Jenny corrected him, 'not because you couldn't find a place to park it.'

He smiled uncomfortably. 'Let's go and sit down in the living room, shall we?' And he herded me and Ellie out of the kitchen while he made the drinks. Even at the height of summer their living room was dark. Ellie turned the light on and we sat down together.

'My mum wants to move,' Ellie said by way of explanation.

'Why's that?'

'She thinks that now your mum has gone they should sell the house in Surbiton.'

'I see. And what do you want?'

She shrugged her shoulders. 'I like it round here, but I can understand why my mum wants something nicer.'

'How's school?'

'School's finished. I had my final exam last Thursday.'

'Oh, wow. Sorry – I should have known that. How did they go?'

'OK, I think. I messed up on a couple of questions for the Media Studies paper, but I'm hoping my coursework will carry me through.'

'What do you need?'

'Kingston want three Cs.'

'Kingston University?'

'Yeah. You sound surprised.'

'I am. Don't you want to get further away than that?'

'If I go to Kingston I can live at home. And save money.'

'Ellie, it's not only about the money. Don't you want to just'– I thought about the weed and shagging of my first year at Cambridge – 'go somewhere completely new and find out a bit more about yourself?'

'I can still socialise with people. And if I change my mind about living at home, I can apply for accommodation in my second or third year.'

I felt sad for my little half-sister, so unambitious and practical. She stood up as my father came in. 'I'm just going to go and get ready.'

'Get ready? You look gorgeous!' I exclaimed.

'I need to straighten my hair. I'm going *out* out.'

'Bloody hell,' I said, taking my cup of tea from my father, 'I feel so tame in comparison.'

My father smiled at her and then down at me on the sofa. I could see that having both daughters under one roof made him happy. He sat down in an armchair and visibly relaxed as he sipped at his pint of lager.

'So what's going on, Laura? You say you're working at the Olympics?'

'Not at the Olympics, no. I'm working on a series of articles *on* the Olympics.'

'Right, right,' he said, nodding his head and taking another sip. 'What are you saying about them?'

'Just examining the overall effect on places like Stratford and Docklands. Are they going to benefit in the long term? That kind of thing.'

'If you bought a flat in Stratford five years ago, you're going to benefit. I can tell you that for nothing.'

'It's not just about house prices, Dad. I'm interested in those who have no hope of buying property. The ones that haven't been invited to the Olympic party.'

He was smiling at me, no longer listening to what I was saying. Just pleased I was there and talking to him.

'But I've been thinking a lot about Mum too.'

He put his pint down on the floor beside him and shifted forward to the edge of the armchair. Like he wanted to be ready to take my hand at any moment.

'Me too.'

'I've been thinking about both of you, actually. Perhaps this isn't the best place to talk about this stuff,' I said, looking at the hallway and the open kitchen door on the other side of it.

'No, it's OK. Go on.'

'I've been replaying things in my head. When you and Mum—'

'When we separated?'

'Before that, actually.' I squirmed. 'I have no memories of you and Mum ever being, well, happy.'

He reached down to collect his pint from the floor. 'We were happy, Laura. But things got in the way.'

'What things?'

It was my father's turn to glance up at the doorway. 'Just things – or events, I should say. You were one of them,' he said, smiling at me.

'Is that why you got married? Because she was pregnant with me?'

'Well, yes and no. We didn't *have* to. But Granny, Mum's mum, wanted us to do the right thing. I don't want you to get the wrong idea – I wanted to get married too.'

'So what happened?'

'What do you mean, what happened? We got married.'

'Why did it go wrong?'

'I don't know. I suppose I just wasn't right for her.'

'In what way were you not right?' My shyness had gone. I just wanted answers.

'Do you know how we met?'

'In a library. Mum worked there, and you kept borrowing books as an excuse to see her.'

'Well, sort of, yes. Mum worked there, but I wasn't reading or studying or doing anything particularly productive. I had no direction, no job, nothing going for me, really. And she sort of . . . took pity on me.'

'Took pity on you how?'

'She let me take her out a few times.'

'And you had sex?'

'Christ, Laura!'

'Sorry. I'm just trying to work it out. I was born in April

1981, so you must have conceived me in the summer of 1980. Is that when you started sleeping together?'

'Yes. But it wasn't . . . we weren't . . . you know.'

'You weren't what?'

'*Doing it* all the time. We just weren't very careful when we did. That's all.'

'Did she blame you for getting her pregnant?'

'Something like that.'

'But presumably it took two to tango?'

'It was a long time ago, Laura.'

We continued talking quietly until Jenny called us into the kitchen where she'd served up a meal of pasta and tomato sauce. Ellie ate just enough to fill her stomach and then disappeared out with her friends. My father and I kept up a companionable conversation in which we took it in turns to invite Jenny to say something. It was hard work. She stood to clear the dishes as soon as I put my fork down, even though my father was still eating. Their argument hung unfinished in the air. I decided to pretend to have something to do. I grabbed my things and said goodbye. Jenny waved from across the table.

My father walked me to my car. 'I'm sorry about that, Laura. It's just hard for Jenny sometimes. You know, with Ellie growing up and me out at work all day. She gets pretty lonely.'

'It's OK. Don't worry. I'll see you soon, Dad,' I said, putting my arms out for a hug.

He pulled me close to him and hugged me hard and then, his breath wet with the tang of beer, spoke into my ear. 'I love you, Laura. I really do.' I swallowed the sudden lump in my throat. 'And I'm your only parent now,' he said, pulling away so I could see his face. 'I'm sorry I haven't always done the right things. But I have always loved you. You know that, don't you?'

I nodded.

'OK, drive safely. Do you want me to help you back out? That's a very tight space.'

'No, it's OK. I've got parking sensors.'

He shook his head at the unstoppable march of automotive technology and kissed my cheek. I got in and drove away, watching him walk, sad and slow, back to the house from my rear-view mirror.

The heart weighed 670g. The cardiac valves were healthy.

My mother taught me to read. Not the mechanics of reading – no memorising of tricky words or how to sound out letters – she left all that to my teachers. The lesson she taught me was a more enduring one. She showed me that it was possible to withdraw into literature: to find your place in a dream-rapt landscape. Her shelves at home were heavy with Victorian and twentieth-century novels, and Hardy was the weightiest of all; *Tess of the d'Urbervilles* was almost always splayed open by her bedside, where she nightly dipped in and out of Tess's story. The tragedy of a young girl wronged by parent and man became a sort of talisman for her own life.

She loved the second-hand book tables under Waterloo Bridge. The journey to the kaleidoscope of spines laid out amid the grey concrete of the South Bank was a pilgrimage worth making, as far as she was concerned. Whenever we arranged to meet up in London, my mother was always quick to suggest the South Bank.

I remember one Saturday afternoon in May 2005. It must have been a warm day because neither of us wore a coat. She was there early, her brown wavy hair falling forward as she pored over the titles, each one presenting an opportunity to recognise or scrutinise. She was voracious in her handling of books, greedy for title and edition, reluctant to release.

I went up to her and tapped her shoulder. She looked up, momentarily annoyed at the intrusion, but smiled when she saw it was me.

'Laura,' she said, pulling my face towards hers for a kiss. 'How are you?' But before I could answer, she held up a paperback, exultant. 'Look at this!'

'What is it?' I asked, bending my head to read the title.

'*The Sea, the Sea* by Iris Murdoch. I read it when I was just eighteen. Before I had you,' she added, already busy reading the back.

'Is it any good?'

She looked up, almost annoyed again. 'Oh yes. It's wonderful. It's about a theatre director who just gives up on his London life and goes to live by the sea. And he eats all sorts of crazy things. I loved it.' She had begun leafing through the first few pages.

'Why don't you buy it?'

'Yes. I think I will. Do you mind?'

'No. Go for it.'

We walked to the Festival Hall, where we sat down and had a coffee on the terrace overlooking the river and the people. She watched me tear open a sugar sachet and pour the granules onto the soft foam of my cappuccino. I waited for them to sink through the milk before I began stirring. She knew I wanted to talk but didn't know how to begin.

'What's the matter, Laura?'

'I'm just a bit stuck, I think. I don't know what I'm doing with my life.'

'Does anyone?'

'Well, I'd like to know a bit more. I'm twenty-four years old and I hate my job.'

'And what is it you want to do?'

'I don't know. Not be someone's PA would be a start.' I was still stirring. Still scowling.

'But I bet you're very good at it.'

'I'm really not.'

'OK, so if not a personal assistant, then what?'

'Write. I want to be a writer.'

'So write. What's stopping you?'

'This job. I'm so bloody knackered at the end of every day that I can't think what to write about.'

She smiled and looked straight ahead at the river. 'Sometimes life happens to us. And there's not much you can do about it. But if you want something, you have to make room in your life. For whatever it is you want.'

I didn't say anything. I was resisting the urge to rail against the generic clichés. *Life happens to us. Make room for what you want.* I drank my coffee and watched the people wandering comfortably along the South Bank, their faith in the Thames and the London Eye strong enough to justify the afternoon.

'Have you ever thought about writing?'

'Me? God, no.' She seemed surprised by the question.

'Why not? You love literature, stories – why not write something?'

'I like retreating into a book, you know – into what's already there. I remember the first time I read *Tess*, I felt like I was sitting on a warm, green hillside looking down at Angel paying attention to Tess more than the others. I can't explain it, but it made me feel as though I could take my eyes off the characters for a little while and look around. But that's Hardy for you. I wouldn't have a clue how to create that world myself.'

I followed the buildings east to St Paul's Cathedral and thought about what she'd said. 'Look at that.'

'What?' she said, following my gaze.

'The dome of St Paul's. I can see that from my bedroom window in Angel.'

'Can you? That's quite a view.'

'Well, when I say *see*, I have to lean out the window and crane my neck.'

She laughed and sipped her coffee. And as she put her cup back down to meet her saucer, said, 'So why don't you write about that? Think of the life it's seen.'

'You want me to write about St Paul's?'

'I just want you to do the thing that will make you happy. And I worry sometimes that you're too like me. Scared to make a change.'

'And what changes are you scared to make?'

'Oh, I don't know.'

'Have you ever thought about moving? You could come and live closer to me.'

'I'm too old for London.'

'I hate to think of you in that big house on your own.'

'Don't worry about me,' she said, looking down into her lap. 'I'll find my own way.'

'But are you happy?'

'Yes, I'm happy,' she said, grabbing my hand and pressing my fingers together too tightly. 'I'm happy because I'm with my lovely daughter.' I remember feeling embarrassed when she said this. As though it was too much. And now the only thing that is too much is the memory of it. I marvel at how wealthy I was that day – surrounded by my mother, her honesty, her touch – and I didn't appreciate it. I wish I'd returned the compliment and told her how precious she was to me. But the terrible truth is that I didn't know I felt that way until she was gone.

We walked around the Tate Modern for an hour or so, and then I accompanied her to Waterloo and said goodbye on the platform. I felt her take a deep breath, smelling my skin, as she hugged me to her. She boarded the train, found a seat beside the window and immediately presented Hokusai's great wave – the front cover of *The Sea, the Sea* – to the glass. She didn't look up again to wave goodbye.

I decided to walk back to Angel that afternoon and, in doing so, passed the statue of Sir Hugh Myddelton on Islington Green. I'd lived in Angel for a year and a half, had walked past it many times, and yet I'd never looked closely at the inscription. I thought of what my mother had said about St Paul's, and made myself cross the road and have a closer look. I went back to my room and began researching the New River Company of 1613. I printed a map of the forty-mile route, designed to bring drinking water to Londoners from natural springs in Hertford. I highlighted the sections that ran under my house on St John Street, and began thinking about how I might approach my first piece of writing. I wrote of how simultaneously elusive and plentiful water was to the occupant of a shared house – that despite Sir Hugh Myddelton's best efforts, I found it very difficult to get into my bathroom in the morning because of the rampant overcrowding of dwellings in EC1. I described how the stuff flowed freely in the kitchen, hydrating the house's hungover occupants, but was rarely used to clean the furry scum generated by several disconnected human beings living together. I concluded my piece by noting how much of my small salary was spent on this essential utility, and yet the waiting staff in neighbouring restaurants still looked askance at my decision to decline *still* or *sparkling* and opt instead for *tap*, the perfectly adequate stuff I had already paid for. It was the first post of *Lost Angel*. And I had my mother to thank for nudging me towards it.

Five years later, on 13 March 2009, with a lot of saving, a large mortgage and some money from the sale of my grandparents' house, I moved into my flat in Balham. I remember walking from room to room, smiling at the unopened boxes and thinking of how much space there was for even more of me and mine. I kept looking at my front door and wondering at the luxury of being able to open and close it to whomever I wanted. It was a uniquely enjoyable feeling, and one I wanted to share with my mother. I phoned her as soon as I'd worked out how to turn the oven on and put a pizza in. She answered quickly, as though she'd been waiting for me to ring.

'Laura? Are you in?'

'Yes. I'm in and I've got my dinner on.'

'Oh, well done, darling. I'm so pleased. What's it like?'

'It's perfect. And it's all mine,' I said, opening the oven door to check it was getting hot.

'When can I come and see it?'

'As soon as you like. Tomorrow?'

'Tomorrow? Hang on, let me just check . . . yes, I can do tomorrow. What time?'

'Any time. I'm just going to be here unpacking boxes.'

She rang the bell at ten the following morning. In her arms were a bunch of yellow roses and a tall, cut-glass vase still wrapped in tissue paper. 'I stopped off in Kingston on the way. Bought you this. And these,' she said, offering me the flowers.

'Thank you,' I said, opening the door wide. 'I'm up on the first floor. Come on in.'

She stepped into the carpeted hallway gingerly, glancing up at the stairs ahead of her. 'How many flats are there?'

'Three. One here,' I said, pointing to the door on her left, 'mine's on the next floor up, and then one at the top.'

'Oh, I see. And how do you get your mail?'

'It all comes through the same letter box,' I said, closing the door behind her and pointing, unnecessarily, to the slot. She nodded her head. 'Come on up. I'll put the kettle on.'

She took each step with careful precision as she ascended into the darkness.

'The light bulb needs replacing up here – it's pretty dark,' I said, opening my front door so that the light from my flat would illuminate the last few steps.

When she stepped into my little hallway, her face suddenly opened into a smile. 'Oh, Laura.'

'Do you like it?'

'I love it. And it's all yours.'

'I know, I know. I keep thinking that too. I can't believe it.'

'I can.'

'Shall I show you round?'

'Yes. Here, take this,' she said, handing me the vase. 'It's for the flowers. Where's your loo?'

'Just in here,' I said, attempting to push open the bath-room door. I'd left a half-emptied box of toiletries behind it. 'Hang on,' I said, putting the vase down so I could push with both hands. 'There's some toilet roll on the side of the bath.'

I went into the kitchen and boiled the kettle. She came in a few minutes later, wiping her hands on her trousers.

'Sorry, I need to find the towels.'

'Don't worry about any of that. I think it's absolutely brilliant. I'm so proud of you.'

'The area's really cool. At first I was a bit worried about leaving Angel, but actually everything's on the doorstep. And it's very handy for the Northern Line.'

'Yes, so I see.'

'And it's not that expensive. Compared to Surbiton, I mean.'

'You never looked at Surbiton, did you?'

'No, but I'm thinking about you.'

The kettle had boiled and the room was quiet again. 'Where are your cups?' she asked, suddenly businesslike.

'Oh . . . I need to wash these ones up.'

'I'll do that for you. Do you have any milk?'

We made tea and sat down in the living room. I didn't have a sofa yet, but I had managed to buy two chairs and a small dining room table on eBay the previous week. We sat opposite one another.

'So, how about it?'

'How about what?'

'Moving. I hate to think of you alone in that house. Especially now Christopher's gone.'

'Balham is great for a young girl like you, but what am I going to do here?'

'It doesn't have to be Balham. You could look at other areas that might suit you better. But at least you'd be closer to me. And you don't need so many bedrooms.'

She leant forward on her elbows and looked down into her cup of tea. 'I have thought about moving, actually.'

'You have? That's great.'

'But not here. I was thinking of Twickenham, or somewhere like that.'

'Twickenham? Isn't that where Helen lives?'

'Yes. That's right.'

'It's pretty expensive. And isn't even on a tube line.'

'I know, but it's near the river. And Richmond Park. You know how Helen and I like to go walking together.'

'But wouldn't it be nice to be near me too? Clapham Common is just down the road.'

'Laura, come on. It was just a suggestion.'

'I don't understand why you'd choose living near Helen over me.'

'This is silly. I'm not choosing anyone or anywhere.' She got up from her chair and stood beside mine. I remained, petulant and unmoving, in my seat. She put her hand under my chin and lifted it gently. As I looked up at her she bent down to kiss my forehead. Then she patted my cheek and said, 'Come on. Let's unpack your kitchen.'

The business of the boxes absorbed both of us for a few hours. Just after two, she went to find her coat in the living room. I stood beside her as she buttoned it up, waiting for the right moment to speak. 'I'm sorry about earlier. Of course you should do what you want. I just want to see more of you, that's all.'

'And you will. You're closer now, anyway. Why don't we try and get together on a Sunday for lunch? Either here or at home? It doesn't have to be every week, just when we can.'

'That sounds nice. I could drive over to you. I think it's about forty minutes.'

'There we go. There's always a solution,' she said, kissing my cheek.

After I'd waved her off and come back upstairs, I saw she'd trimmed the stems of the roses and arranged them in the new vase on my mantelpiece. And for some reason, I started to cry. At the time I put it down to tiredness, but perhaps, deep down, I knew my mother had tried to give me something infinitely more precious that day. She'd tried to offer me the truth.

Driving back from New Malden to Balham took a long time. The traffic was awful, and after trying several alternative routes, I found myself in Tooting, very near Andrea's flat. I decided to pull over and phone her. I wasn't ready to go home just yet. Her phone rang and then went to voicemail. I tried her again in case she hadn't managed to get to the phone in time.

'Laura. What is it? I'm on a date.'

'Oh shit. Sorry.'

'Well, almost on a date. Just waiting for him to turn up. Can I phone you back?'

'Can't you bin it and come out with me instead? I need to drink wine and feel like the rest of the human race.'

'No, I can't. He's got a really good sense of humour.'

'He hasn't arrived yet! No one's banter is that good.'

'No, silly. It said so on his profile.'

'Jesus.'

'You need a bloke, Laura. I love that you've phoned me, but what you really need is to have sex again. And then that person is obliged to listen to you. Do you know what I mean?'

'Not really.'

'I'm serious. You need to start dating. Look, I'll come over one night in the week and we'll get you registered with a dating site, OK?'

'Don't worry. Have a nice date with Mr Charisma. I'll speak to you soon.'

'Oh, come on. Why won't you even try it?'

'Because I don't want to meet anyone new. Sometimes I don't even want to talk to you, Andrea.'

'OK, but what if you end up meeting the one?'

'And what if that's total bullshit? Have you met *the one*?'

'No, but I've met some really nice guys. You remember Rob with the carrots? Come on, Laura, you need to get back out there. How long has it been?'

'I can't think about that right now. I'm happy the way I am, where I am.'

'You're not happy, Laura. You're busy. There's a difference. Oh, fuck, I think that's him. He's fat. I'll phone you later.'

I hated the thought of marketing myself to others. I was having enough trouble maintaining the few friendships I had, let alone admitting someone new into my life. Someone who would ask me questions and wait for me to show an interest in them. The idea exhausted me. But out of respect for Andrea – who averaged two or three dates a week – I permitted her to come over one night and create my dating profile. We ate dinner, and as soon as I'd opened another bottle of wine, she began casting about for my laptop. She opened it up, the backlight illuminating her face like an eager witch.

'Where can I find a nice photo of you?' she asked.

'Can't you just take one of me now?'

'No. You look like shit.'

'Yes, Andrea! Because this is what I look like.'

'Hang on. I'll find one.' And, with renewed vigour, she logged into Facebook, determined to find a suitably misleading image.

'Here you go,' she said, turning the laptop screen to me in triumph.

She'd found one of us on a night out in Angel, before my move to Balham. We'd ordered cosmopolitans in self-conscious mimicry of *Sex and the City*. As we lifted our glasses, Andrea had leant over to the barman and asked him to take a photo of us. We looked like young, fictionalised versions of ourselves.

'Andrea, that was taken over three years ago.'

'Yes, and you look fit. I'll crop me out.'

I left her to it. To her credit, she did a very good job of making me appear an attractive prospect. Her descriptions pointed to someone motivated, driven to succeed and eager to engage with life. This, coupled with my photo, prompted several messages from men keen to meet. I went on a few dates, all calamitous in their own way. One confident twenty-five-year-old asked me – within five minutes of meeting – for my favourite sexual position. I sat there stunned, not just by the nature of his question but at his sense of entitlement, probing quickly for something not readily on display. I told him to go fuck himself.

Andrea's attempts to push me back into the world had relied upon airbrushing out what was new about me. The deep loss I'd experienced, the slow uncovering of an uncomfortable past – they had changed my outlook. And my face. I was thinner than I was at the beginning of the year; dark circles from late nights and uncontrollable weeping underlined my eyes. I no longer wore make-up. So I did what I should have done in the first place: I took a photo of myself with my laptop camera and edited my profile to include the fact that I am a writer prone to spending long periods of time alone. And it all went quiet.

By mid-July, just as I was finishing my final article ('The Olympic Flame: London Lets the Light In'), written to coincide with the opening ceremony the following week, I received a message through the dating website from someone called Tom. I hadn't exactly forgotten about my profile, but the radio silence that followed my edits had, more or less, convinced me I'd be left alone. His enquiry was simple and willing: *What are you working on? Tom.* Without thinking, I typed, quickly and casually, *Just something on the Olympics. Laura.*

He responded almost immediately: *Sounds interesting. Fancy meeting for a drink?*

I looked around my empty flat and then at my profile picture. And realised I did want to meet. That I felt ready to tell someone about myself again.

We agreed to meet in a bar in Clapham the following Thursday. It was almost 8 p.m. by the time I got there. He was standing up against the bar, his jacket in his hand, watching the door for my arrival. He was very short. My heart sank as I took in his five feet four inches. I tried to rescue my reaction and look at his face. It had a feminine quality I found disarming – he was almost pretty. And he beamed the moment he saw me. As though there were no one he'd rather meet. I blushed at his obvious pleasure, conscious that I couldn't muster the same enthusiasm. He insisted on buying me a drink and ordered a bottle of beer for himself. I sat on the only available bar stool and, raising myself up even further, took off my jacket. There was nowhere to put it, so I folded it up on my lap and looked around for something to say. He stood below me, short and expectant, like a loyal subject.

'So, tell me about the Olympics,' he said with open invitation. I felt myself recoil in embarrassment.

'What do you want to know?'

'Just what you're writing about. Are you a journalist?'

'Yes. I write a mix of things, really, but I was looking specifically at how parts of east London have remained untouched by monumental changes like the Olympics and the LDDC.'

'What's the LDDC?'

'The London Docklands Development Corporation.'

'And that's a bad thing?' he smiled.

I smiled back apologetically. 'Look, I'm sorry. I shouldn't have come out tonight. I'm tired and I don't really want to talk about my work.' I turned back to my glass of wine and waited for his reaction in my peripheral vision. A woman on the other side of him got up and gave him her stool. He took it gratefully and pulled it over to mine. He climbed up comically, as though he were scaling a mountain, huffing and puffing at the effort, and then feigned vertigo as he looked down. I chuckled despite myself and looked back at him. His pretty face was full of humour.

We began to talk more easily then. He worked as an IT project manager for a healthcare company and owned a flat in Wimbledon. He'd had one serious relationship that had ended the year before and little success with women ever since, telling me how he had come to recognise the dark shadow that passed over their faces as they took in his height. Dates were rarely salvaged after that, he said, quickly ordering a second round of drinks. I became more relaxed and open – telling him about the guy who'd asked for my favourite sexual position. He laughed, and matched my anecdote with one of his own: a Polish woman who had asked him for his exact height measurement as though she were conducting a medical.

'What was her conclusion?'

'She closed her eyes in compassionate understanding and

asked me whether I had bought my own property. I mean, it's the obvious follow-up question.'

'She was probably just thinking of you – you know, whether you'd be able to reach the lock, turn the lights on, stuff like that. God, how awful. Did you tell her where to go?'

'Absolutely I did. The following morning.'

'You mean, you slept with her?'

'That's a very personal question. Shame on you.'

We drank into the early hours, moving on to shots and then into a cab. I sobered up enough to direct the driver to my house. When I invited him up, he had the presence of mind to decline, saying he'd watch me go in and call me in the morning.

My phone sounded its alarm at six the following morning and I reached for it in despair. I had been asleep for about four hours. And had neglected to take a glass of water to bed with me the night before. The result was a mouth that was dry and unyielding. I got up to have a wee and then trudged into the kitchen for water. I gulped it too quickly and retched into the sink, disgusted with myself. Then I re-membered Tom's refusal to come upstairs, and groaned with remorse.

I went back to bed, too hungover to cry, and was woken at nine-thirty by my phone ringing. I didn't recognise the number but, thinking it might be Andy, coughed my voice back to normality and answered.

'Hello?'

'Well, good morning! And how are you feeling?' It was him. I must have given him my number.

'Tom. Hi.'

'Hello. I was just phoning to see how you are. And to say how much I enjoyed last night.'

'Me too. I don't remember much after the shots. I blame you for my complete loss of memory.'

'That'll be the Rohypnol. I know it's not the done thing to drug someone on a first date, but when you're under five and a half feet you've got to use every tool in the box.'

'Did you just call me a tool?' I could hear him laughing at the other end.

'I'd really like to take you out to dinner. And give you the opportunity to finally seduce me. Are you free Saturday night?'

'As in tomorrow? Erm, I don't know.'

'You don't know? Well, you do now. You're coming out with me.'

'You're bossy.'

'I just know what I want.'

'And what's that?'

'Someone who's really pretty, funny and intelligent. With massive tits. I'll pick you up at seven.'

'OK, see you then.'

'Laura?'

'Yes?'

'I can't wait to see you again.'

I got out of bed, motivated by the thought of a cup of tea and a chance to replay our conversation in my head. I went into the kitchen to boil the kettle and, as I went to open the fridge, saw Nicola's note pinned to the door. I'd brought it home and put it somewhere prominent. So prominent that I'd forgotten all about it. I had the whole day to myself – the Olympics stuff all done and dusted – so I decided to phone

Nicola and take her up on her offer. It would take my mind off agonising over what to wear for my date with Tom.

A young female voice answered. 'Hello?'

'Oh, hello. Is that Nicola?'

'No, she's not in, I'm afraid.'

'Can you tell me when she'll be back?'

'This afternoon, sometime. She's gone into town to get a few things. Who shall I say is calling?'

'Laura Rowan. I'm Katharine Lambton's daughter.'

Nicola phoned me back a couple of hours later, just as I was unloading some shopping from the car onto the pavement. She suggested meeting at one o'clock, outside Surbiton Library. I looked at my watch – it was eleven forty-five.

'That's a bit tight for me. I don't live in Surbiton any more. I'm in Balham.'

'Oh, I see, I'm sorry. Well, I can do four, if that's any better?'

I hadn't planned to spend my afternoon driving back and forth across south London, but Nicola sounded keen and she'd gone out of her way to post that note in the first place. We arranged to meet at four.

The day contracted before me and I tried to do too much. I unpacked the shopping, washed my bed sheets, tidied the flat and then filled the car up. By the time I hit traffic on the A3, it was three fifteen and the only number I had for Nicola was a landline. I decided to phone her before she set off for the library and tell her I might be late, but nobody answered. I sat in the traffic, sweating and angry with myself. It was twenty past four by the time I sped up the hill to Surbiton. I parked at the back of the library and sprinted to the front of the building, searching urgently for the woman who wanted to meet my mother's daughter.

There was no one there. I pulled out my phone in futile remonstrance at myself. I was standing at the top of the ramp that led to the large, open doors of the library, facing the road, looking for a retreating figure that might be her. I was clammy and breathing hard. From behind me I heard a quiet voice, cautiously warm: 'Laura?' I turned and saw a small woman with a neat grey bob staring up at me. She searched my face and inhaled sharply before smiling. Then she put her arms out to hug me, buoyed by having found my mother's face, after so many years, in my own. I bent down to meet her embrace, envious she had found something I was still looking for.

'Let's sit down over there,' she said, indicating the benches in front of the war memorial adjacent to the library.

'Did you want to go for a walk first, or grab a coffee?'

'No. There's something I need to show you first.'

'OK. Sure.'

We walked over to the war memorial and I stared, suitably sombre, at the names etched on the stone. I thought she was going to tell me something of the local history, indicate the name of a fallen relative, but she walked past it without so much as a glance and sat down.

'Your mother and I worked together in there,' she said, indicating the library on our right. 'Before you were born.'

'Yes, I know.'

'She was a very gifted librarian. A custodian of quiet,' she said, and smiled sadly to herself.

'And she left to have me?'

'No.' She screwed up her eyes, momentarily hesitant, and then looked straight ahead at the cars motoring past on the Ewell Road. 'She left because she met your father. And what happened to her on that stretch of road over there.'

My mother hated school, not because she wasn't intelligent or academic enough to succeed. She hated school because she had no friends. Her reticence and inability to communicate with others had become so marked and acute by the fifth year that all she could do was wait for her sixteenth birthday and the opportunity to walk away from the girls that had angled their chairs away from her for years.

My grandmother was devastated: she believed that her failure to provide a sibling was the source of her daughter's crippling loneliness. She cajoled, engineered and finally pleaded, but my mother's desire to withdraw from the world had a momentum of its own.

In January 1977, on the morning of her sixteenth birthday, my mother decided to stay in bed. She buried herself beneath the blankets and waited for my grandmother's peremptory knock; it wasn't to seek permission, just to alert her to the fact that an intrusion was imminent.

'Happy birthday, darling,' and then, without waiting for a response, 'you're going to be late. Get up, please.' She spoke to the unmoving mound beneath the covers. 'Katharine! I'm *talking* to you.' She marched into the room and opened the curtains. 'Time to get up. You'll be late for school.'

My mother still didn't make a sound. She defied through silence, and it drove my grandmother berserk – she began shaking my mother's body under the blankets, rolling her to and fro and into action.

'I said get up. Get up!' Her voice was high-pitched now, and starting to fray at the edges. In despair she pulled the covers from my mother's warm, pale body and watched as she drew her legs up into a foetal position, protecting herself from the woman who had only ever wanted her. Who had desired her being with an intensity that had begun to turn in on itself. My grandmother looked at her body, soft and diffident, and felt a sudden urge to bite. To consume this flesh that had failed. In her anguish she looked around the room and saw my mother's bra, hanging from the bedpost like a flaccid flag.

My grandfather appeared at the door then, drawn by his wife's raised voice. 'What's going on? Why are you shouting?' His wife's frustrations with their first and only child were nothing new to him. He remembered how her desperation to conceive my mother had nearly driven her mad. Literally. He had come home one afternoon from work and found her still sitting on the toilet, knickers kicked away, crying at the menstrual blood dripping, irrefutably, into the toilet bowl. Her extreme sorrow, every twenty-seven days, was cataclysmic. It closed them off from other people and made him fear for their life together.

'It's seven thirty, and look at her!' My grandfather looked at his daughter's nearly naked body, vulnerable and exposed, her breasts held behind the insufficient cover of knees hugged up in defence. He was deeply embarrassed. And then angry.

'Cover her up!'

'Paul, it's seven—'

'I said, cover her up!' he roared. And then, because my grandmother was too shocked to move, he pulled the blankets over my mother himself, careful not to touch her skin and complicate his feelings further.

'Jean. I'd like to talk to you downstairs.'

From her bedroom, my mother heard them argue, my grandfather adamant that my mother be left alone to make her silent protest on the morning of her sixteenth birthday.

He knew exactly what she was doing, and in his own way he supported it.

They left her at home alone that morning in January. When she heard the front door close as they went off to work, she got out of bed and dressed herself. She went downstairs, breathed in the musty freedom of an empty house and made herself a cup of tea and some thickly buttered toast in the kitchen. It was the most liberating experience of her life – to be at home alone, while the world outside continued to turn. She thought of the other girls in her class, settling down to their lessons, answering questions, raising an eyebrow to her empty seat, and she felt happy enough to laugh. After breakfast she searched the bookshelves for something to read and went upstairs to run herself a deep bath.

My mother avoided baths – they made her feel too vulnerable. She grew up in a home where locks were not allowed. My grandmother would not allow it. And so, lying in water, naked, waiting to be looked upon, was something she couldn't bring herself to do. My grandmother said it was a safety measure, but as my mother grew into adolescence, she knew it was a way of keeping an eye on her.

On my mother's sixteenth birthday she treated herself to a deep bath. She immersed herself in the hot, soapy water and luxuriated in the sensation of quiet and privacy. And used her fingers to smooth, clean and connect with her body – and in this moment of perfect pleasure, resolved never to return to school again.

The happiness of that morning became a working prototype for many others. The next day my grandmother made an abortive attempt to get her up. When it didn't work, she left her to sleep, slamming the front door with empty vengeance.

As with all uncompromising decisions, on the third

morning my mother was forced to admit she'd inadvertently denied herself access to something she needed: the school library. The small, overcrowded room at the top of the tower had been my mother's sanctuary during anxious lunchtimes. The exacting silence was the perfect social leveller for someone like her. Instead of running a bath, she put her shoes and coat on and walked down the hill to Surbiton Library. A grade-two listed building, built in 1896, its imposing arched entrance at the summit of a long ramp belied the timid courtesy of its interior, where the few quietly and unobtrusively sought something to read. My mother found shelves of nineteenth-century novels and crouched down on her haunches to have a better look. They were all there before her, authors long dead who beckoned to her from beyond the spine to a private landscape she could make her own. She picked up *Middlemarch* and took it over to a chair near the window, where she was immediately captivated by Dorothea Brooke. She had been in her seat for over two hours when the librarian came over to return some books to a nearby shelf. She saw my mother's absorption and looked for the title of her novel.

'It's a wonderful book, isn't it?' she whispered.

My mother looked up, her brow creased in irritation.

'Sorry. I didn't mean to interrupt you.'

My mother shook her head, as if to say she hadn't. And smiled.

'Have you read *The Mill on the Floss*?' the librarian asked kindly.

My mother shook her head again.

'Well, you must. It's Eliot at her very best, in my opinion. I'm Nicola, by the way. The librarian here.' She extended her hand down to my mother.

My mother looked at the hand and then up at the smiling face, and decided to take this social opportunity. She shook Nicola's hand and said, simply, 'I'm Katharine.'

My mother began visiting the library every day. She arrived at the same time, sat in the same seat and worked her way through *Middlemarch*, before moving on to *The Mill on the Floss*. At the end of February, Nicola approached her again, but this time with a direct question: 'We're looking to hire a junior librarian with responsibilities three mornings a week. Is that something you might be interested in?'

My mother tried to speak but her voice was dry and raspy. She managed to nod, whereupon Nicola went to get her an application form.

My mother closed her book and began completing the form. At the end of the afternoon, she handed it in to Nicola behind the desk and walked down the ramp and out into the chill air with a renewed sense of purpose.

My mother was invited to have an interview with Nicola, but as she was the only applicant, what was billed as an interview was in fact an induction session. Her first responsibility was to reclaim and reorder the library's property: she was shown how to categorise returned books and position them correctly on the trolleys for redistribution.

She didn't tell my grandparents about the job. They had been coexisting in an uncomfortable stand-off until one of my grandmother's friends told her they'd seen Katharine pushing a trolley full of books around in the library and then asked the obvious – and to my grandmother, galling – question, 'Is Katharine no longer in school?'

My mother didn't try to explain herself. She heard my grandfather counsel patience to his wife from her bedroom upstairs. And over time, people grew to accept my mother's new job. She went about her duties with a discreet and methodical professionalism that recommended her to Nicola and readers alike. In May 1977, just three months after she'd started, Nicola asked her to do three full days instead of just mornings. My mother accepted, and grew in confidence as she mastered subcategories and reference books. She was quick to spot and replace books that had been mindlessly returned to the wrong shelf. It was a job that required her to blend, unobtrusively, into the background. It was the perfect job for her. And she did it happily for almost four years.

At the beginning of the 1980s, the local authority wanted to reinvigorate reading areas for children, and Nicola thought my mother should take responsibility for that. My mother disliked small children – she used to shrink at their confident clamour – and would have been happier if she'd been asked to lead a project on keeping them out of the library. But she recognised a vote of confidence when she saw one, and began looking into brightening up a suitable corner.

As the weather turned warm and bright outside, she began to notice a young man who arrived at a quarter to nine every morning. Just fifteen minutes after Nicola had opened the doors. He was tall – just under six foot – but stooped and uncertain in his gait. He arrived at the library every morning in order to do very little. My mother was intrigued by him; he couldn't have been more than twenty-one or twenty-two, and yet he was dedicated to a routine of nothing. He entered the library and went to his usual table in the natural history section. My mother watched him nose around the shelves, take several books, or sometimes just one, over to his desk and then, instead of reading them, he rummaged in his jacket pocket for a packet of tobacco and a lighter. He smoked just outside the doorway, his right foot resting against the building and his neck stooped so he could watch the ground. My mother used his first cigarette break of the day as an opportunity to peer at the titles he'd pulled down from the shelf. *Birds and How They Live* was a favourite, as was *The Observer's Book of Trees.*

My mother watched him return to the books he'd carefully selected and then disregard them entirely for the rest of the day. She suspected they were mere placeholders: a means by which he could secure space. He broke the day up by smoking cigarettes, buying cups of coffee, reading newspapers or completing a crossword. He was killing time in the most obvious sense, unable to concentrate on any one activity for longer than twenty minutes. At around four thirty in the afternoon, he began gathering his things up and, striding quickly past the issuing desk with his head down, left the library for the day.

My mother grew curious and, as the weeks passed, her curiosity got the better of her. One morning, in June 1980, she went outside ten minutes after opening the doors in order to witness the prompt arrival of a man tasked with doing nothing. Sure enough, at the appointed time a red Austin Maxi pulled up outside the building and the young man emerged, leant in to speak to the driver and then closed the door with a bang. He turned to trudge up the ramp, his every step observed by the middle-aged woman behind the wheel. As he passed my mother, standing under the arched entranceway, he smiled, surprised by her presence there, and said, by way of explanation, 'She watches me until I'm inside.' My mother looked back at the car and saw the woman return to a driving position, signal left and rejoin the flow of traffic.

My mother got on with her work: ordering books, making posters, painting boxes in bright primary colours, but try as she might, she couldn't ignore the disconsolate young man who wandered around. Her interest was not purely observational; she detected in him the same writhing obedience to a controlling matriarch. He was aimless precisely because he was so used to being directed.

By the end of June, the children's book corner was almost complete. With no chairs for the children to sit on and no more money to furnish the area, my mother had begun reading up on how to make her own beanbags – the material and filling could be obtained at little expense. The task she had accepted with quiet disdain had absorbed her so much that she now pushed at the boundary of expectation.

She was flicking through a pile of textile books in the reading room one Monday lunchtime when he approached her desk and waited for her to look up. When she didn't, he coughed quietly.

'I'm just going down the road to buy a sandwich. Can I get you anything?'

'No, thank you. I brought my own sandwiches.'

'OK. Just thought I'd ask.' He turned to walk away.

'Wait. I could do with a walk, though. I'll come with you.'

They walked down the hill to a café, where he bought a sandwich and a cup of tea. He suggested they sit on the bench behind the war memorial and eat their lunch.

'I'm Richard,' he said, extending his right hand across his body to shake my mother's limp fingers.

'Katharine. Nice to meet you.'

'And you.'

My mother opened her carefully prepared cheese and ham roll while Richard foraged in his paper bag for his egg sandwich. He kept looking cautiously sideways as though to check she was still there. My mother stared straight ahead at the names etched on the yellow stone.

'Is that your mum who drops you off every morning?'

He'd just taken a huge bite of his lunch and had to nod in answer, his mouth full of bread. He chewed quickly, gulping down the silence that was suddenly everywhere.

'I'm supposed to be applying for jobs. I finished university two years ago and still haven't worked out what I want to do.'

'What did you study?'

'Mathematics.'

My mother raised her eyebrows in surprise. 'I thought you were going to say natural history, or something.'

'Why? Do I look like I should be a zookeeper or something?'

My mother laughed. 'No. Just, you always have that bird book on your desk.'

'Oh yeah,' he said, grinning. 'I do actually like birds. My dad used to take me birdwatching when I was younger. But no, I keep my papers in there.'

'Your papers?'

'Rizla papers. You know, for making rollies.'

My mother looked blank, so he reached into the inside pocket of his jacket and pulled out one of his cigarettes. 'Do you want one?'

My mother shook her head emphatically.

'Do you mind if I smoke?'

'No.'

'So what about you?' he asked, putting the cigarette between his lips and lighting the end. 'Why are you here?' He leant against the back of the bench and lifted his right ankle to rest on his left knee.

'I work here.'

'Permanently? Is this what you want to do?'

'I like it. I like the quiet,' she said, looking down at her lap, 'and Nicola's really nice.'

'Is that the other one? The one with the short hair?'

'Yes. She's the senior librarian.'

'Have you left school, then?'

My mother nodded her head. 'Over three years ago now.'

'Don't miss it?'

'No.'

'Me neither. But my mum is threatening to enrol me in the army if I don't get my act together.'

My mother looked at her watch and stood up. 'I'd better get back. Nicola will be wondering what's happened to me.'

'OK,' he said, standing up to join her. 'I'll be in in a bit,' he said, putting the cigarette to his lips again.

'Bye.'

'See you later.'

On Saturday morning I woke feeling well and refreshed. I went for a run and managed a few hours of writing after lunch. With nothing left to do but anticipate the evening ahead, I put on the red and blue tunic dress I'd selected the day before. I wore it over leggings with black boots. I blow-dried my hair straight and noticed, as I tried to hide the split ends behind my ear, that it was in urgent need of a cut. I pulled my make-up bag from the bathroom cabinet and began applying foundation, eyeshadow, liner and mascara. I stared at the face that slowly emerged and remembered it from the morning of her funeral. The last time I'd applied make-up.

Tom rang when he arrived downstairs. I went to the window of my living room, holding the phone to my ear and looking down. I couldn't see him on the footpath, but then

I looked at the road and saw a car with its engine idling, waiting for me.

'Do you want to come up?' I said.

'No thanks. There's nowhere to park, anyway. Our table's reserved for quarter to eight so we'd better get going.'

We drove out to Kew, where he'd booked a Michelin-starred restaurant near the station. I felt underdressed as we walked from the car to the restaurant. A feeling that deepened when I saw the thick white tablecloths and self-consciously friendly waiting staff.

He ordered two glasses of champagne and folded his arms, leaning on them to force his shoulders towards me, conspiratorially. He was wearing a light blue shirt under a grey jumper. He looked very smart and I realised, with a thrill, that I fancied him.

'What's the matter?'

'It's a bit posh, isn't it? I'm not really dressed for this.'

'You look gorgeous. And the food is amazing. Just wait till you try it.'

Our champagne arrived. He lifted his flute to mine and said, 'To you.'

I looked around, embarrassed, and then back to him. 'To me?'

'Yes, to you, Laura. Thank you for coming out with me tonight.'

He was uncompromisingly straight with me from the beginning. His height had made him grab (literally, sometimes) at what he wanted in life. And he wanted me. I found his honesty both mortifying and refreshing – his enthusiasm made me blush and his sincerity made me want to be the Laura he liked more fully.

We drank water with dinner; he was driving, and I felt too

self-conscious to drink alone. We spoke easily and openly about previous relationships, jobs and university. He told me he'd proposed to his last girlfriend and together they'd bought the flat in Wimbledon, but the reality of planning a wedding and waking up next to the same person for the rest of her life had been too real. She had sent him an email from work, telling him she was too conflicted to marry him and asked him to stay away that evening while she packed her things up.

'What did you do?'

'I did what any sane person would do under the circumstances: got completely shit-faced and went home to beg her to stay.'

'And what happened?'

'She was there with her mum and dad. Moving stuff out. Every time they put something in the car, I took it out again. It took a long time for her to go, and her dad almost punched me.'

'Shit,' I said, laughing despite myself. 'That's terrible.'

'Yep. But I got myself together, bought her half of the flat and slowly replaced things. We're still quite friendly, actually.' He searched my face for a reaction. 'How about you?'

'What about me?' I said, smiling, looking down at the tablecloth.

'Any significant others I should know about? Former lovers, ex-husbands, disgraced footballers? That sort of thing?'

'Let's see. I slept with my ex a few months ago.'

'A significant ex?'

'He's certainly significant to someone else.' Tom looked steadily at me. 'He's married, living happily in Buckinghamshire somewhere – that sort of thing.' I ran my hand through my hair and wished my glass of water was wine.

'And is it over?' he asked.

'It's *very* over. He was a mistake I won't be making again.'

He lifted his glass to me, relieved. 'Here's to fucking exes. I mean, not literally – that's not an instruction. Please don't fuck him any more. You know what I mean.'

The waiter appeared, on my right, to offer us a variety of breads, and in doing so broke the gentle momentum we'd established. We ordered our food and tried to talk again. To find the banter that had united us over a week ago. The restaurant was too stuffy and we were too sober. We scraped for conversation: favourite films, TV box sets, where we'd grown up. I thought of Andrea's instruction – that I needed to have sex – but couldn't quite fathom how that might come to pass.

Tom insisted on paying for dinner and invited me back to his flat for coffee. I leant against the work surface of his small, square kitchen and waited for the move that would take us beyond talk of cafetières and milk and sugar. He reached behind me for something inconsequential and our faces came close enough to finally stir. He kissed me gently at first and then with more certainty, holding my face, my hair, and pulling me to him. It had been a long time since I'd slept with someone sober. We went into his bedroom and took our clothes off with perfunctory requirement. His hands were powerful, holding me to him and to his life as long as I wanted to be there. When he got on top of me, I felt my body act alone as if it had an undeniable physical need for his love. But I had to switch my brain off to access it.

I woke early the next morning to the light that flooded his bedroom. I looked around at the bare walls, the bulb hanging from the ceiling and over to the large, uncurtained window.

Tom slept with his back to me, the sheets pulled up under his chin in happy composure. I lay there, warm and naked under the sheets, until just after six, thinking about my mother and her job at the library.

Tom woke when I got up to use his bathroom. He was smiling and stretching when I returned to the room, naked. I jumped back into bed in an effort to cover myself with the sheets. He pulled himself up on his elbow and looked down at me as I tried to cover my nipples, and grinned.

'What is it? Why are you smiling like that?'

'Because you're beautiful. And I've already seen them.'

'I'm not a good naked person.'

'No, me neither,' he agreed solemnly. 'I did suggest Naked Friday at work, but they were all, oh that's gross misconduct. Any more suggestions like that and we'll have you fired.'

'Some people are so narrow-minded. What did you do?'

'I insisted on my right to work with my bollocks out. What else could I do?'

'Exactly. I mean, what's wrong with testicles in the workplace?'

'We speak the same language, Laura. Now let me have a look at those puppies again,' he said, pulling the covers down.

I grabbed hold of the sheet. 'Two things: one, they are not puppies and two, where the fuck are your curtains?'

His ex-girlfriend had piled the curtains and many of the other soft furnishings into the back of her parents' car the day she decided Tom was not the one for her. As we made love again that morning, in the bright Sunday-morning sunshine, my rational mind returned to my aroused body in joyful gratitude that this girl I'd never met, who'd taken so much that afternoon, had left me her Tom.

The brain weighed 1230g and showed no abnormality externally. The vessels at the base of the brain were unremarkable.

My mother felt sorry for my father. He was like a troubled stray, hiding out in the sanctuary of the library, and after years of feeling isolated and unhappy herself, she was able to recognise his need for companionship. It didn't matter that she wasn't a suitable companion; she befriended him simply because he needed her.

One afternoon, after my father had gone home for the day, while tidying the books away my mother noticed an envelope sticking out of his bird book. He had returned all the others to the shelf. It was addressed to her, though he'd written her name incorrectly, spelling it *Catherine*. I have the note here before me – she kept it safe and secure in her notebook from 1980: *I enjoyed talking to you on Monday. Perhaps we could go for a drink sometime? We don't have to. Richard.*

My mother put the note back inside its envelope, folded it in half and put it in her pocket. She didn't know how to go for a drink. Because she'd had so few friends at school, she'd never been invited to the pub or to the park with a bottle of cider. Having missed out on this seminal lesson of adolescence, she felt the want of learning as she read my father's self-effacing note. So she did what she did best: she hid.

My father looked for her the following morning, but she stayed in the back room, telling Nicola she wanted to recategorise the children's books ahead of the opening of the new reading corner in July. At midday, he asked Nicola where she was, but my mother had cycled home to eat her lunch there.

He went outside to sit on the bench and wait for her return. When he finally saw her cycle up the Ewell Road and round to the back of the library, he got up and went to meet her. She was locking her bike up as he approached. 'I've been looking for you all morning.'

She continued fiddling with the lock. 'Sorry. I've been busy.'

'Did you get my note?'

She stood up. 'Yes,' and then quietly, 'thank you.'

'And?'

'And what?'

'Do you want to come out with me one night?'

'Where do you want to go?'

'Just down to the pub. I thought we could have a chat and get to know each other.'

'I don't drink.'

'OK. That's OK. What would you like to do?'

My mother shrugged her shoulders. 'We could go for a walk.'

'A walk? Yeah, we can do that.'

They arranged to meet at Alexandra Recreation Ground at six o'clock the following Saturday. My mother wore a simple white cotton dress and her hair down. As she cycled down the hill towards Tolworth, she felt the wind push the soft fibres against her legs, exposing them to the cars that were too close and fast. At the first opportunity she peeled off the main road and pedalled harder, feeling nimble and free as her dress rose up above her thighs. The warm evening air was light and playful about her face. As she coasted towards the meeting point, she couldn't help smiling and the movement of her facial muscles triggered sharp, almost painful goose-bumps to her arms. For a brief moment she forgot about meeting my father, about my grandmother's disapproving silence as she left the house. The hair follicles tightening in exquisite physical pleasure forced her to forget everything. And remember herself.

My father was waiting at the gate to the park, too smart for a walk on a field. He saw my mother in the distance, a vision in white, coasting down the hill towards him, and felt a jolt of joy. She was beautiful. And a secret. And he'd had the good sense to ask her out. He was beaming at her as she slowed down and came to a stop. She locked her bike up and allowed my father to open the gate as they stepped onto the path that skirted the recreation ground.

'Do you come here a lot?' It was a terrible chat-up line but my father sensed, rightly, that my mother was unaware of the cliché.

'Not really. I don't go out much.'

'Why not?'

My mother looked puzzled. 'I don't have any friends.' It was such a simple declaration. He didn't know what to do with it.

'How come?'

She shrugged her shoulders. 'None of the girls at my school wanted to talk to me.'

My mother's lack of embarrassment surprised him. 'None of them?'

'My best friend moved away at the end of our second year.

To a new school. So I was on my own after that.'

'That's why you left as soon as you could?'

'On my sixteenth birthday,' my mother confirmed.

Her candour and his interest were enough to propel them round the field several times. As the sun began its descent my father reached for her fingers. My mother allowed her hand to be held and, as she unlocked her bike for the ride home, she let him kiss her cheek. My father's courtship was not something she sought, but when it was upon her, she capitulated.

The following Monday my father did not turn up at the library as usual. Nicola noticed his absence but my mother, it seemed, did not. Even after the warmth he'd shown her on Saturday, she felt no proprietary interest in him.

He returned the following day, at eight forty-five, looking for my mother. He found her in the children's corner with Nicola, discussing the new shelving arrangements.

'Richard,' Nicola said as she turned to him. 'We missed you yesterday.'

'I had a job interview,' my father said, looking at my mother, 'in a bank.'

'Good for you.' Nicola also watched my mother and attended to the conversation as a translator would an interview: 'And? How did it go?'

'OK. I think. They said they'd let me know next week.'

'That's great news. Well done.' Nicola looked at my mother, who had kept her eyes trained on the carpet, and decided to leave her and my father alone.

My father asked her if she'd like to go for a walk after the library closed on Friday. She nodded her head in quiet agreement, but as 5 p.m. on the appointed Friday rolled around, so too did the dark clouds that presaged rain. He took her hand as they walked down the ramp and round to the back of the library. The first big drops of rain began to fall from the bruised sky.

'What about that drink instead?'

'I don't drink.'

'I know. But they sell soft drinks in the pub. And we're about to get soaked.'

My mother allowed him to pull her down into Surbiton town centre to a pub just outside the station. She found a small table in the middle of the main saloon bar while my father went to order the drinks. She put her hands in her lap and her head down, avoiding eye contact. He returned to their table with a pint of lager for himself and an orange juice for her. As he sipped his drink, she watched a gradual change come upon him. He leant in further, ostensibly so he could hear her better, but before long he reached for her hand with confidence. His conversation loosened as he drank; he spoke more fluently about how he'd loved his father and how his sudden death when he was just nine had changed his mother and therefore him. She never let up. Was always on at him to do something constructive. 'The interview was her doing. And I thought I'd go because, well, I thought it might impress you.'

She'd been watching the effect of alcohol on him so closely she hadn't actually heard what he'd said.

'Did it work?' he prompted.

'Did what work?'

'Are you pleased I went for an interview?'

'I don't know. Yes. Good for you,' she said, borrowing Nicola's response from earlier in the week.

My father smiled. 'I'm going to get another. Orange juice?' My mother looked at her glass and then at the other people sitting at nearby tables. 'What's that?' she asked, pointing to a tall glass on the table nearest to them.

My father followed her gaze. 'A gin and tonic, I think. The one with the lemon in it?'

My mother nodded.

'Probably a gin and tonic. Would you like one?'

My mother wanted to go where my father had gone. He was happy, chatting openly and looked excited about the next one. 'Yes. I'll have one of those.'

She sipped at her drink and noticed my father's smile of approval. She was surprised by how easy it was to join others after years of feeling so left out. The slice of lemon sitting on top of the ice forced her to slurp the gin, sharp and uncompromising, until the alcohol prompted the production of dopamine in her brain. She began to feel good, so much so that when my father jumped up to get another round of drinks, she assented readily to the apparently innocuous, 'Same again?'

The second gin and tonic tasted stronger. It was so fizzy she began to burp. After two of them her stomach felt full and uncomfortable. She got up to go to the toilet, but when she returned another one was on the table. They were appearing with bewildering frequency so that as she finished one, more of the same quickly appeared. She became confused and eventually dizzy, her instincts blurred and, as she felt herself drowning in drunkenness, reached out for my father's hand. 'Please. Take me home.'

'Are you OK?'

'Take me home.'

He put his cigarette out, downed his pint and escorted her outside to the cool, reviving night air. The pavements were dirty with aftermath; as she watched people stumble in a clumsy search for more, she pulled her cardigan more firmly round her and felt grateful for my father's arm steadying her. When they approached the top of St Mark's Hill, my mother had to stop to vomit. She bent over and belched the effluvium onto the pavement and her shoes.

'I'm sorry. I shouldn't have let you drink so much.'

'My mother's going to kill me,' she slurred, staring at her wet shoes and tights.

'Why don't you come back with me? My mum will be in bed by now. We can get you cleaned up and then I'll walk you home.'

She agreed to his suggestion not simply because her neurotransmitters were soggy and slow or the alcohol had dampened her ability to respond. She agreed because she couldn't face my grandmother's disapproval. She nodded her head and he guided her back to his quiet, dark home. But instead of going to the kitchen, my father led her, creeping, upstairs. My mother – the consummate librarian – observed the rule of silence.

He was excited to have her in his room with him. The successful stealth of the operation made him jubilant. He didn't pause to consider how drunk she was, that what felt like freedom to him – closing the door – could be viewed as a kind of constraint for her. He sat down on his bed and reached under it for the small tin that contained his stock of rolling papers, tobacco and a block of cannabis resin.

My mother watched him, no longer curious, just distracted by the dexterity of his fingers. He rolled a joint with the serious concentration of a professional and invited my mother to sit beside him. The bed looked steady in a room full of flux. She wanted to get near those fingers that smoothed and rolled, skilful in their ability to create even after so much alcohol. That my father did not appear drunk impressed my mother. She felt like an amateur. He lit the joint and sucked the situation into being, inhaling to a beat in his own head and tapping the seconds that passed with his right foot. It prompted him to stand up and walk towards the record player, a trail of smoke hanging to indicate the path he'd taken. My mother narrowed her eyes in an effort to focus and out of the grey, amorphous smoke returned my father, who held the joint in his right hand so that his left was free to settle on her thigh. She looked down at his fingers, the ones she'd been admiring just a few seconds ago, and wondered what they could do to her. And just as he'd reached across his body on the bench to shake her hand a couple of weeks before, he now proffered the joint and encouraged her to join him.

'Do you want some?'

She shook her head. 'I don't know how to.'

'Just suck and then pull it back, into your lungs.'

Passing the joint with a subdued benevolence, he watched as my mother met his fingers with her own and put it to her lips. She did as my father instructed and felt her lungs roar in angry rebellion. And began coughing.

'Don't take so much in. Take a smaller puff next time.'

My mother banged her sternum with an upturned fist. 'Puff? As in blow?'

'Sorry, no. It's just a phrase. Do what you just did but, you know, less.'

My mother pulled a small amount of the psychoactive stimulant into her lungs and this time they accepted it. With a few more inhalations her tired neurons began firing in unexpectedly euphoric rhythms. Her usually strained face relaxed into a smile as she lay back on her elbows and blew the smoke up to the ceiling. And laughed. The sound surprised my father – he'd never seen my mother look amused, let alone laugh – it had come out of nowhere, piercing the silence, and commanded his attention.

He took the joint back and exhaled, sending the smoke over her breasts and pursed mouth – both pushed up in an attitude of complete surrender. She felt freed by the loosening in her face and throat and, without looking at him, held her fingers out for the joint.

'Is this what you want?'

She didn't move but smiled in answer. And my father, mistaking her private joy for mutual arousal, put the joint into an ashtray on his bedside table and lifted the palm of her hand to his lips. The hand that had told him she wanted more. She pulled it back, surprised by the wetness he'd left there, but by then he had knelt down in front of her, his hands busy lifting her skirt and pulling at her knickers. She became inert. Unmoving, as he put his finger inside her in crude imitation of what she liked to do to herself. Alone. And as her brain replayed those moments – in the bath, in her bed at night – she felt her body relax. My father felt the tension leave her and, pulling her hips towards him, noticed how heavily her limbs had sunk into the bed. He stood up and began unzipping his jeans. My mother still stared up at the ceiling.

'Is this OK?' he whispered, pulling her into position. He took her silence for consent, her physical arousal for permission and, without waiting for an answer, entered her body for the first time. In doing so he sent forth sperm that surprised and ambushed her waiting egg, forcing it to divide until a life had been created.

*

At the beginning of August, Tom went on holiday to Tenerife with three of his friends from university. It had been booked long before I was on the scene and, while I was perfectly happy for him to go, he was at pains to reassure me that I had nothing to worry about.

'Why would I worry?' He'd driven over to Balham to cook me dinner. It was the evening before his flight.

'That I might be unfaithful.'

I laughed out loud, thinking he was joking.

'Don't laugh. I'm serious.' He was stirring something aromatic and pointlessly complicated.

'I'm not laughing at the idea. Just your choice of words. *Unfaithful.*'

'I consider us to be ... going out, that's all. You know, exclusive.'

'Exclusive!'

'Fucking Jesus, Laura. What's the matter with you? I'm trying to tell you I really like you. And I'm not planning to have sex with anyone else. Is that blunt enough for you?'

He was suddenly red in the face. I'd never seen him angry before. Our shared banter operated like a shock absorber – it generally carried us smoothly over bumps and potholes – but my levity had finally offended him.

'I'm sorry.' He turned back to stirring. I walked over to him at the stove and put my hand on his arm. 'I'm sorry. I know what you're saying, and I feel the same way.'

'Is it what you want, though? Because you don't sound particularly pleased,' he said, petulantly.

'Of course it is. Tom, I'm shit at this.' He nodded in agreement. 'I don't know how to have these conversations without taking the piss. Come on,' I said, prising the wooden spoon from his hand. 'Kiss me. Let's kiss and make up.'

He agreed to the kiss. It was a brief, dry one. 'That's all you deserve.'

'You're right. I'm a very naughty girl.'

'Please leave the kitchen immediately.'

Dinner was lamb tagine. The rich smell of cumin and garlic lingered in my kitchen for days afterwards. We sat at my small dining table and drank red wine. He moved two church candles from the hearth to the table and lit them as the light began to wane. It was an effortless evening, full of conversation and subtle plans, lingering looks and mingled fingers. We refilled our glasses and, taking them through to the bedroom, left the dirty dishes in lazy offering to the morning. We had sex quickly and without preamble – our movements had become more practised and familiar.

Tom woke very early the next morning – his flight was at seven thirty from Gatwick. He kissed me briefly before letting himself out and I slept on for several hours, waking at around nine thirty. I got up and walked into the living room, preparing myself for the sight of last night's dishes, but he'd already washed up. A small domestic gesture but, as I stood and stared at the plates and cutlery draining casually beside the sink, I knew the generosity of it meant more to me than his fumbling attempt the night before to tell me I was his girlfriend.

I decided to get dressed and go for a run. By the time I returned to my flat, the postman had been. One of my neighbours had already sorted the mail into discrete piles on a shelf above the radiator. I had one letter, and it was from the Coroner's office. They were writing to inform me that the inquest into my mother's death was to be opened the following week – on Wednesday 8 August in Woking. And then, like that first day in Cambridge when I realised I'd waved my parents off when I still needed them, I felt suddenly frantic that Tom had gone and caught a flight when, unbeknown to both of us, I would have to face Her Majesty's Coroner's Court on my own. I was absurdly, deeply upset, and before I could get upstairs to my front door the tears were upon me, hot and wet on my red cheeks. I felt completely abandoned: by Tom, but most of all by my mother, whose life was still the subject of official correspondence but whose being was permanently nowhere. Hers was an absence that still had the power to surprise me.

In searching for my mother, I sought out Helen. I thought she would want to attend the inquest, but she didn't return any of my phone calls or texts. Assuming she was away somewhere, I sent her an email with the date and time of the hearing and the address of the Coroner's Court. My father had also been contacted – he was still officially her husband, after all – and we arranged to meet outside the Coroner's Court at ten.

I was called as a witness and asked to give my account of how I found my mother's body. The proceedings were clinical and efficient; it took just over half a day to record a verdict of accidental death. And then it was over, her death certificate finally available; my mother's life had passed through the administrative spectrum of colours.

'Can I give you a lift?' I asked my father as we walked down the steps.

'I think I'll get the train.'

'Don't you have to change, though?'

'Only once. At Surbiton.'

'You need to decide what to do about that.'

'About changing train? I think that's a matter for South West Trains.'

'No, sorry – I'm jumping ahead. About the house. It's probably yours now. Technically.'

'There's nothing technical about it. But yes, I take your point.' He stopped and looked at me. He reached into his inside pocket for something, eventually pulling out a packet of cigarettes and a lighter. 'Do you mind if I smoke?'

'No, I don't mind. You do what you need to do,' I said, eyeing the cigarette.

'I've been trying to cut down. The girls have been on at me to stop, but what with all this—'

'With all what?'

'With your mother, and Jenny. It's hard.' He blew out some smoke and looked behind him at the steps.

I held out my fingers for his cigarette. He looked at me, surprised but not displeased. 'May I?'

He nodded. And then, in an effort to demonstrate his nonchalance, offered me my own one.

'No thanks. I just want a few puffs.' I took a deep drag. 'Why are you here, Dad?'

'What kind of question is that?'

'I'm not trying to get at you, but you're here as her husband. Or rather her widower.' He dipped his head as though I'd just knighted him. 'And the house. Why didn't you divorce and sell it?'

He looked at his shoes and shrugged his shoulders. 'Guilt, I suppose.'

'For having an affair?' I exhaled and passed the cigarette back to him.

'Well, yes. And other things.'

'Like what?'

'She was never mine to marry.'

'What do you mean?'

'It's complicated, Laura.'

'You keep saying that. And so does Helen. But I can deal with complexity. It's the constant evasion that frustrates me.'

'She was in love with someone else. How's that?'

'Before you?'

'Yes.'

'Who was it?'

'I don't know, exactly. Just someone she met at school.'

'Would Helen know?'

'I'm sure she would.'

'And you feel guilty because she married you? That doesn't make any sense. How is that your fault?'

'She married me because she had to. She was pregnant, and your grandmother pressured her into doing the right thing.'

'OK, so you got married in 1981. And what then?'

'And then we tried to make a go of it. We had you and then Christopher, but after his birth, things just sort of fell apart.'

'And you got into bed with Jenny. When was that, exactly?'

'Listen, your mum wasn't entirely blameless, you know.'

'So you say. She went and got herself knocked up – not once but twice – and then, when she decided to stop having sex with you, you decided to do it with someone else. Is that an accurate summary?'

'No, it bloody well isn't!'

'Then tell me the truth.'

'The thing with Jenny. It wasn't a decision. It was a . . .' He looked at me for the right word, his eyes circling above my head. 'An impulse. A feeling. I didn't want to feel alone any more. Can you understand that?'

I nodded my head. Sex. That little word Sam had taunted

Jenny with on our way home from school. And, unbidden, I pictured Christopher's terriers – Buster and Ruby, fucking and howling – and remembered his words of caution. That I was overthinking things.

'What does Jenny think?'

He looked at me again.

'About Mum and the house and all this,' I said, turning around to indicate the building behind us. 'Presumably she wants you to sell the house?'

'She's pretty fed up of New Malden.'

'I can understand that,' I said, thinking of her stirring at the stove in their dim and cramped kitchen.

My father nodded and took another deep inhalation. I sat down on the step behind us. 'And what do you want?'

He crouched down and joined me. 'I want to sell it. And give you and Christopher and Ellie some money. You know, a bit of a leg-up in life. God knows it hasn't always been easy for you three.'

'And what about you and Jenny?'

'The way I see it, I've still got another four or five years left at the bank before I can retire. With money from the sale of the house, and if we continue to save, we'll be able to move wherever we want.'

'Well, let me know if you need any help. I could phone round some estate agents for you.'

'Don't worry. I need to square things with Jenny first. Anyway, this is my problem. You've got enough on your plate at the moment.'

'I really haven't, Dad. All the Olympics stuff is finished. But I should probably let you know that Andrea and I cleared the kitchen a few months ago. Just the perishable stuff – what was in the fridge, that kind of thing.'

'I didn't know you'd done that.' He put his head in his hands. 'God, Laura, I'm sorry you've had to take on so much.'

'Honestly, Dad, don't worry. I'm fine.'

'I know you are.' He turned his body to look at me properly. 'You're still my best girl. But for the record, I am sorry. For all of it.'

I kissed his cheek and stood up. 'Let me know what you plan to do with the house,' I said in farewell. He nodded and lifted his hand to wave.

I checked my phone. Still no word from Helen. Or Tom, for that matter. We had spoken the night before: he made a point of calling to wish me luck. With the taste of my dad's cigarette in my mouth, I started the car and thought about where I might go. And then, on a whim, I did something stupid. And completely unforgivable. I phoned David. It rang and rang, the sound of him not picking up echoed by the idling engine. As though my car were also in a suspended state, wondering when we could move on. I didn't leave a voicemail and put my phone back in my handbag, open on the passenger seat. I reversed out of the space, and just as I was about to put the car into gear my phone rang. I didn't need to see his name to know it was him. He still wanted me. I pulled up the handbrake and answered it.

'David.'

'Hi. This is a bit of a surprise. What's going on?'

'Oh, nothing really. I just wondered if you're free. Well, not free, but around. For a drink or something.'

'Yeah, yeah, I could do that. When were you thinking?'

'I'm in Woking, of all places, but I can drive to meet you somewhere.'

'Like, now?'

'Yeah. Sorry, that's what you asked. Now, or later, if you prefer?'

'I'm working from home today but I could meet you somewhere nearby. Can you get to Amersham?'

'I'm sure I can. I'll stick it in the satnav.'

We met in The Kings Arms Hotel on Amersham High Street. David was sitting at a table by the window with a half-empty pint, his laptop open, watching the entrance to the bar. He stood up as I approached, unsure what contact he could make with my body. I kissed him lightly on the cheek, a move that emboldened him to hold my arms and go for a kiss on the other cheek. 'Such a nice surprise. To hear from you.'

'Yes, sorry. Not much notice.'

'No, I was pleased to see your missed call. Can I get you a drink?'

'Yes, please. I'll have a glass of dry white wine. Large.'

He went to the bar and returned with my drink and another pint for himself.

'I wasn't expecting to hear from you after, you know ... last time.'

I took a big swallow of wine. 'I know, I'm sorry.'

'It's fine. Totally fine.'

'The thing is, that morning you left—'

'Listen, we don't have to dredge all of that up. I was just saying it's a surprise, that's all. But really nice to see you. I'm not complaining.' He smiled.

'I was going to say, after you left I went home, or to my mother's house, I should say ... and she'd died. I found her body.'

His jaw fell open. He sat back in his chair, his face so full of surprise it was almost theatrical. 'Fuck.' He rubbed his working-from-home stubble. 'Oh, God. Laura, I had no idea.'

'I know.' My eyes filled with tears. It was an involuntary response to any conversation that included details of how my mother died. And his sympathy was very convincing.

'I'm so sorry.'

'I've just come from the inquest. Accidental death. That's where I was when I phoned you.'

'Right. I see.' He nodded his head as though only Her Majesty's Coroner's Court could account for such an unusual booty call.

'It makes no sense. I'm sorry – I just didn't want to be on my own. And I thought of you.'

'S'OK,' he said, looking around him, and then reached out to touch my hand.

'Do you know people around here?'

'Not exactly, but the village we live in isn't far from here.'

'OK.'

'Sorry – I don't mean to sound paranoid. I'm not suggesting you have plans to jump on me or anything.' He was blushing.

I felt emboldened by having survived the efficient administration of death I'd witnessed earlier. As he danced around the big question that hung in the air between us, I thought of the cold, precise examination I'd just undergone and then the clean and considered judgement. I wanted to rip it up. To lift my skirt and shit all over their pointless paperwork.

'I really want to fuck you.'

He put his pint down and stared at me.

'Is that a yes or no?'

'Christ.' He ran his hand through his thinning hair and smiled. 'Well, you know I'd love to. But is it a good idea, what with all you've been through?'

'I don't want to think about it. I just want to do it. Do you want to have sex with me or not?'

He put both hands on the table and, with deliberate care, pushed his chair back. He stood up and walked over to the bar. I sipped my wine and looked out of the window at the cars going past, mothers holding their children's hands as they crossed the road, and waited for David to return. I wanted to be taken beyond this pedestrian life: to grab and bite and moan and cry.

David ordered a bottle of Prosecco at the bar and had it sent up to the room but we didn't have time for it. I kicked off my heels as soon as we were inside and took my jacket off. As I pulled my blouse from my skirt, he walked towards me, conscious perhaps that undressing me was his job. But his fingers were too slow; I didn't want to watch them grapple with every button on my blouse. I did it myself, and stood before him in my bra and skirt, my tights still on. He didn't know where to start or how to go about opening me. I unclasped my bra and threw it on the bed, half-expecting his eyes to follow it, but he kept them trained on me. A curious blend of desire and caution – he sensed my unpredictability.

I cried when it was over. The tears rolled down my cheeks and into my ears as I stared at the ceiling. I thought of my mother and the first time she ever had sex with my father. How that mistake was the beginning of my life and this mistake.

'I knew this was a bad idea,' he said.

'These tears aren't for you. Or about us. It's more complicated than that.'

'Tell me what's wrong. Is it about your mum?'

I blinked and turned to face him. The water ran out of my

ear. He stroked my face with his hand and said, 'I love you, Laura.'

'What?'

'I should never have married Sarah.'

'That's a big statement.'

'I know. But it's true.'

'But you *did*. And you have a daughter.'

'I've gone over it all a thousand times in my head. Since February.'

'Don't go over it any more.' I pulled his hand from my face. 'You should stay with Sarah. It was probably a blessing you were too *lily-livered* to ditch her.'

'Post-coital Goneril. Nice.'

'Just be grateful it's not post-coital gonorrhoea.'

'You see. I fucking miss this. I miss you. I've never had this with anyone else.'

'Had what?'

'This connection.'

'Dave. I can't help you. You didn't want me enough when it mattered.'

'I did, Laura. I always wanted you. I'm just a fucking dick. They were your words at the time, not mine. Remember?'

'I remember. And I stand by them.'

'Why did you phone me if I'm such a fucking dick?'

'Because it would appear I am one too.' He put his hand on my hip and tried to pull me towards him. 'I'm seeing someone.'

'Who?' he said, withdrawing his hand.

'His name is Tom. He's pretty short.'

He laughed nervously. 'Is it serious?'

'I think so. Or at least it was before I did this. Now I'm not so sure. So don't worry, you're off the hook. Go back to Sarah. I don't want anything from you.'

'Come on, Laura. Don't do that. With Sarah, it's difficult. After Bea, we found out we couldn't have any more children and I—'

'I don't want to hear it.'

'I'm just trying to explain why—'

'There was a time when I cared. When I really tried to understand why you chose her over me. But that time has gone. I'm sorry I phoned you earlier – I shouldn't have,' I said, sitting up and swinging my legs round to hang off the bed.

'So that's it? You're just going to say goodbye until you find yourself at a loose end again?'

'No,' I said, reaching down to pull my knickers on. 'No more loose ends. This is already a bad memory.'

I went downstairs and out to my car. It was around six o'clock, and the car park had begun to fill up. I thought of David up in the room I'd encouraged him to book with the bottle of Prosecco still unopened in the ice bucket. I went back into the bar and decided to pay the tab. I tried Helen again but she didn't answer, so I started the engine and began the journey back to Balham.

There was a diaphyseal fracture to the right ulna. Dynamic compression plate used to correct this. Hardware still present.

My mother woke several hours later. Her skirt and knickers were in a heap on the carpet. She got up – soundlessly – dressed and tiptoed out of the house and into a Saturday morning transformed by what had happened to her. Once home, she employed her own version of the previous evening's stealth entry and made her way up the carpeted stairs to the sanctuary of her bedroom. She dared not shower, even though the moisture at the top of her legs felt cloying and alien. Running water at such an hour would invite questions from my grandmother. And she had no explanation for what she'd experienced. So she got into bed and pulled her knees up to her chest and tried to make sense of all her body had undergone. But the chain of events was too puzzling in its unreality and so, despite the dawning of a new day, my mother decided to bury her body beneath the blankets and sleep on until late morning. She couldn't have known her reproductive system was alive to its first major task. As it set about hosting the event of a lifetime, my mother slept.

She returned to work the following Monday, still stupefied by Friday and the actions of the young man who had put himself inside her. It was the day her new children's corner was to be unveiled, the date designed to coincide with the beginning of the school holidays. A small gathering of regular visitors to the library and a representative from the local authority listened as Nicola congratulated my mother on her successful execution of the initiative. She pointed to the bright beanbags – disarmingly low upon the carpet – and told of my mother's determination to encourage children to stay and read. My mother stood to one side and burned with shame. Not because of modesty but because my father had just tiptoed into the room and joined the small crowd at the back. He smiled at her and put his right thumb up, full of praise and pride at his secret knowledge.

The children's corner proved popular that first summer of 1980. My mother was busy enough to ignore the sporadic ache on the right side of her abdomen and the rising nausea whenever it was time to eat. Ignoring my father proved more difficult – he asked her out again and again. When his persistence went unrewarded he began following her around the library and then home one evening, desperate to know what he'd done wrong. Nicola saw it all: my father's slumped shoulders and dejected expression, and then the look of determined cruelty on my mother's face. She was freezing him out – for the first time. She tried asking my mother if anything had happened, but my mother's silence on the matter appeared absolute. In an effort to resolve matters, she sat down at my father's table. He looked up hopefully, his face visibly disappointed when it wasn't my mother.

'How are you?' Nicola's voice was a concerned whisper.

He shrugged but didn't reply. The pain of hoping for the junior librarian and getting the senior one was still too sharp.

'What's happened between you and Katharine? You were getting on so well.'

'Ask her,' he whispered. 'One minute we're going out, the next she won't even look at me.'

'Did anything happen?'

'No. We just went out for a drink. Like *normal* people.' He felt spiteful towards Nicola, my mother and even his own mother – women who wanted something inscrutable. And his inability to understand led to a persistent failure to deliver.

'Did you hear back from the bank? About the job you went for?'

'Yes. They don't want me either.'

By October my mother's morning vomit had become routine. Nicola, a quiet observer, was able to piece things together. Sensing my mother's growing unhappiness and inability to make a decision, she asked her to stay behind one evening after work. She locked the main door and told my mother to take a seat in the reading room.

'Katharine, I'm very worried about you. I know, I know,' she said, putting a hand up to my mother's immediate open-mouthed objection, 'you're going to tell me nothing's wrong. Or perhaps that it's none of my business. But something is definitely wrong. You can tell me.'

'There's nothing to tell.' She spoke quietly but with determination.

'I think you're vomiting because you're pregnant. And I have a fairly good idea who is responsible for your condition.'

My mother began to cry into her hand. Nicola knelt down at my mother's side and tried to hug her. The angle was all wrong; she stretched her arms across her chest and shoulders, trying to link her fingers on the other side of my mother's sobbing torso.

'There, there. Don't cry. We'll work it all out.' She gave

up trying to hug her and sat back on her haunches. 'Do you want to tell me what happened?'

My mother shrugged her shoulders and looked down into her lap. She delivered fragments of the story: the alcohol, going back to his room, the following morning.

'When was this?'

'In July. Just before we opened the reading corner.'

Nicola calculated the weeks in her head. 'About ten weeks then. OK, we still have options. If you don't want to have this baby, we can arrange for you to see someone. And then you won't be pregnant any more. Do you understand what I'm saying?'

My mother nodded her head. Nicola wrote the details of a clinic on a piece of paper and told my mother to think about it.

'I'll drive you there and wait with you. You don't have to do this alone.' My mother took the slip of paper and held it in her lap. She thought of the rock, paper, scissors game she used to play with Helen. It was hard to believe that a piece of paper could destroy the small unstoppable thing inside her.

But a week later my mother, who had promised to think about an abortion, continued to avoid any discussion of her condition. Nicola tried to get her to make a decision but my mother withdrew into silence and clothing that was too big for her. Weeks passed, so that by November the pregnancy was becoming more obvious. Her window of opportunity was closing, but still I grew within her.

On 24 November she woke without the hollow feeling that preceded her daily vomit. She had a shower and went downstairs, where she made herself some toast, chewing slowly as she stared at the lawn levelled by mist. The day was waiting for her, ready to pull her down the hill and into work, but she wouldn't go. Not yet. For a few moments she stood still and steadfast, with her hand on her stomach, encouraging the life that had established itself. My first foetal reflex came to assure her, in that moment of private communion, that she was not alone.

She picked up her bag and keys and went outside and unchained her bike. She began cycling down the Ewell Road full of me and the knowledge that she would be my mother. It was still very early in the morning, the mist effacing the hard white of the give-way lines. As she approached the library, with her eyes primed for a view of the war memorial, my mother neglected to see the car pulling out of the road on her left, blocking her lane in its patience to turn right. She hit the side of it and was flung over the roof and onto the road a car's length away. As she flew through the air she pulled her legs up to cover her stomach and landed heavily on her right arm, like a badly formed question mark, causing the ulna to snap in two. The pain was extreme and unrelenting in its sudden force. The bone that had been intact and silent seconds before the impact screamed in outrage. She lay on the road absolutely still and unmoving – it was the only offering she could make to the exacting agony. The effort of perfect stasis in perfect pain threatened consciousness. She began counting to herself – anything to keep the dark edges from encroaching into her field of vision.

The motorist, a man in his mid-thirties who had been on his way to work, sat shaken in his car. His hands still on the steering wheel, he couldn't bring himself to look at my mother's body. The driver's door had been dented by her front wheel so that when he did finally emerge, it was out of the passenger door, having climbed, without dignity, over the gearstick.

The man knelt by her side and began shouting for help. In desperation he left her and ran to the fire station twenty yards down the road and raised the alarm. My mother placed her left hand on her stomach, willing her secret occupant to take courage and stay with her. By the time the ambulance arrived, screaming its legitimacy to the other cars on the road, a crowd of curious bystanders had appeared. One of the paramedics, a woman in her late thirties, jumped down from the vehicle efficiently, inured to the sight of cyclists lying broken at junctions. Her concern was professional and capable: *What's your name? Where does it hurt? How old are you?* My mother tried to answer, but the pain in her arm was getting impatient. It had become warm and wet. She couldn't even move her head to nod. The paramedic read the position of her right arm, pinned down beneath her body, and tried to reassure my mother. She asked her if she had any pain in her back and neck. My mother wanted to mention her baby but articulating the pregnancy she'd kept secret for so long was a strain too far. She decided to close her eyes and rest in the darkness for a little while.

Twenty minutes later, she resurfaced again briefly and discovered she was no longer outside. She'd somehow found her way into a noisy cave, held there by people who were shouting to the enraged sirens outside. *Katharine. Nineteen. Suspected fracture to the right arm.* She sank back under and decided to stay down for as long as she could.

When she woke again, it was in the Accident and Emergency department of Kingston Hospital. My grandmother was standing in the corridor, talking to someone, her voice floating to my mother through the half-open curtain. My mother remembered her arm and tried to look for it but her neck wouldn't oblige. As she attempted to move her head, she felt her chin strain against the unyielding collar.

My grandmother pulled the curtain aside and walked back into the room. 'Katharine,' her voice was breathless and urgent, 'darling. You're awake. Thank God.'

'My arm. Where is it?'

My grandmother smiled and stroked her left hand. 'It's still where it should be. But it's a bad break. I've just spoken to the senior registrar and he thinks you might need a metal plate.' My mother wanted to ask about her baby but any conversation with the doctor was impossible with my grandmother hard by. Surrounding her with close, suffocating concern.

'Nicola.'

'It's OK. Everything's OK. She's outside. With a young man who says he knows you from the library?'

'Where's Dad?'

'He's on his way.'

The only other person unaccounted for was me. She closed her eyes, hoping I'd held on.

'What shall I say to Nicola and the chap she's with? I didn't ask his name.'

'Richard.'

'Richard. What shall I say to them?'

'Tell them to go home.'

My grandmother walked alongside my mother as she was wheeled to a waiting room in the Radiology department where an X-ray had been scheduled. The radiologist knocked quietly on the door and entered. My grandmother greeted her with a wide and predatory smile.

'Katharine Lambton, is it?' she asked, as she opened her folder.

'It is,' confirmed my grandmother.

'Before we proceed to X-ray, I need to ask you if there is any reason to believe you might be pregnant?'

'I should think not,' my grandmother chortled, full of middle-class certainty.

'I take it you're her mother?'

'Yes. I most certainly am.'

'Mrs Lambton. Can I ask you to step outside, please? I need to speak to Katharine alone.'

'Anything you need to say to my daughter you can say to me.'

My mother saw her opportunity. 'Mum. Please. Can you wait outside?'

'Kathy, I'm here to look after you.'

'Please. Let me speak to her alone.'

My mother confirmed her pregnancy to the radiologist, who arranged for her to be transferred to the maternity ward, where she was examined by an obstetrician. He went about his task with sprightly efficiency, bending down to my mother's small bump with a Pinard stethoscope. He smiled when he heard my heartbeat.

'Is she OK?'

'She?'

'Is my baby OK?' she almost shouted.

'Yes. Nice strong heartbeat. She's been shaken but not stirred.' And in response to a crappy James Bond joke, my mother began to cry. The obstetrician thought they were tears of happiness, natural to a mother who has just learnt that her foetus is still alive. But the truth was something she could never hope to articulate. She cried because there was no longer any alternative to the fate that awaited her. She was going to mother the baby that had survived within her and, as soon as her own mother discovered how that baby had come to be, she'd be compelled to share a life with my father. Her accident, her flight through the air, was really the end of any other possible life. The obstetrician had confirmed more than just a heartbeat: he'd told her of my strength and determined grip on her body, and that my existence would require her to concede a significant chunk of her own.

My grandmother absorbed the news of her daughter's pregnancy with a disbelief that quickly gave way to anger. She surmised immediately that the young man waiting downstairs in Accident and Emergency was the father. Nicola had returned to the library, but my father remained in the waiting room; he was midway through a crossword. My grandmother sat beside him and asked him what he planned to do.

'What can I do?'

'About *the baby*,' she mouthed, keeping her voice low to maintain the *entre nous*.

'What baby?'

'Don't play the fool with me, young man. My daughter is pregnant. And I suspect you had a hand in it.'

My father stood up and looked down on my grandmother in bewilderment. 'How do you know?'

'She's being examined in the Maternity unit,' my grandmother whispered with venom. 'I know what maternity means!'

'So she hasn't told you?'

'What does that have to do with anything?'

'I'm just trying to understand,' he said, sitting down again. 'Katharine hasn't actually said that she's pregnant?'

'I haven't had a chance to speak to her yet,' my grandmother conceded, 'but I will. And when I do, I expect you to be available. You've caused this problem, and I'm going to make sure you're part of the solution.'

The following morning my mother's arm was operated on. The surgeon repositioned the shattered bone fragments and then screwed a metal plate to the outer surface of the ulna. As my mother recovered and her strength returned, my grandmother became efficient on her behalf. She contacted Nicola to explain that her daughter's injuries would prevent her from continuing to work at the library. It was a simple headline to a much more complex story – and Nicola knew it. But she accepted my grandmother's explanation and wished my mother well, full of sorrow for her broken life.

My grandmother set about interviewing my father for a position my mother knew he'd jump at. She asked him about his relations with my mother, what his plans were, where his parents were. Jan Rowan, the woman who had diligently dropped her son at Surbiton Library every morning in the hope of his applying for a job or a course of study, received a phone call from my grandmother, who told her, very bluntly, that her son had made her daughter pregnant and would she please come up to Kingston Hospital where Katharine was recovering from a road accident. Their baby was still alive and due in April.

On Thursday, 15 January 1981, just two months after her accident and five days before her twentieth birthday, my mother and father were married at Kingston Registry Office. Nicola had read the notice of their upcoming marriage and went along, uninvited. She sat at the back of the room and noticed another young woman who stood with her head bowed for most of it, and who left just before the end.

My mother and father made their way to their first home together, a rented two-bedroom flat on Lovelace Road, Surbiton. The first three months' rent had been paid by Jan Rowan in apology for her son's actions. My father had until his child was born to find himself a job.

Tom returned from Tenerife the following Sunday evening. He emailed his flight details, but because he'd left his car at Gatwick we decided there wasn't much point in me driving out to meet him. His flight landed at half past four and he was at my front door just after six o'clock.

I had already decided to tell him about Dave. I spent the days before his return going over events, trying to downplay the seriousness of our relationship. I'd managed to order things around the absence of the *l*-word and reasoned that, because he'd held back from telling me he loved me the night before he went away, we were still at the beginning of something. I thought that my honesty would open up the possibility of forgiveness.

But seeing his face when I opened the front door hit me hard: it was both tanned and happy, eager and joyful. He dropped his bags and opened his arms. Of course he wanted me. I felt his chest meet my body as the first stone hurled at a ruined woman. The impact of his love felt like some kind of judgement on my stupidity. I'd really gone and fucked things up.

He took a deep breath of my hair and my neck and began kissing my chin and then my lips. 'I've missed you so much.'

'I know. Me too.' I wanted to go with him. As he pulled me towards the bedroom, I saw that it wasn't too late. That with a simple withholding of the truth I could join him again.

We made love quickly, urgently, afterwards remarking on his tanned bits and what we were going to order for dinner. I felt the heavy weight of duplicity – it was suddenly everywhere: the lone pubic hair shed on the sheets, the pillow Tom had folded in half to prop his head up. Our life together suddenly built on a lie.

'Will you order? I'm just going to have a shower.' I walked into the bathroom, sat down on the toilet and cried quietly to myself.

By the end of August, the deception had become part of me. Like an unsightly skin tag, my only option was to tie a rubber band around it and cut off the blood supply. I hoped that by pretending it had never happened, I could kill off the recollection entirely. In private apology to Tom, I became a much more enthusiastic girlfriend.

We spent every weekend together; he drove over to Balham after work on Friday night, where we'd order a take-away and drink wine on the sofa. On Saturdays we woke late and headed down to Borough Market on the tube. Tom loved to agonise over cuts of meat and vegetables, prompted to his purchases by an impossibly complicated recipe, while I sipped my coffee and rolled my eyes. And sometimes he'd buy me a bunch of flowers. If I hadn't been too sneering.

Afternoons were spent back at my flat: I'd sit at the table in my living room and write or edit, while he simmered dinner into submission. And we were happy. Or he was happy, and I was content to have made him so.

One Sunday morning at the beginning of September my father came to see me. His visit was unannounced, and his voice at the end of the intercom completely unexpected. Tom was in the shower, singing to himself.

'My dad's here,' I shouted as I opened the door.

'What?' He had been washing his hair but quickly put his hands over his soapy groin.

'My dad. He's coming up.' And then, looking at the position of his hands, 'I'm pretty sure he won't ask to see your knob.'

'Very funny. Let me rinse off.' I went to go and open the front door. 'Laura! Close the bloody door!'

'Sorry. Sorry.'

My father was apologetic and sheepish. 'I should have phoned first. I'm sorry.'

'It's OK. Don't worry. Come on in.'

'Thank you.' He stepped into the hallway and heard the shower. 'Do you have company?' He was wary.

'Yes.' It was my turn to be sheepish. 'Someone I'm seeing. A boyfriend, in fact. His name is Tom.'

'Oh, right,' he said, nodding. 'Laura, I'll leave you to it. I didn't mean to interrupt.' He began stepping back towards the door.

'No, Dad, don't be silly. I'd like you to meet him, and I should have said something. Come on in. He'll be out in a minute.'

We walked down the hallway, past the bathroom door and into the living room. I put the kettle on while my father sat down on the sofa. As I was pouring the hot water into three cups, I heard Tom open the bathroom door, pad across the hallway and go into my bedroom, closing the door firmly behind him.

'So what's up?' I said, sitting beside him on the sofa.

'What isn't? That would be a more accurate question. Oh, it's nothing. Just had a little disagreement with Jenny, that's all,' he said, looking sideways at the entrance to the living room. Waiting for the boyfriend he'd been told to anticipate.

'What's the matter with Jenny? Is this about the house?'

He nodded. 'I need to sell it, Laura. It's not just about some money for you and the other two. Jenny wants to move to Guildford, and if I don't sell the house she'll be moving there without me.'

'What's in Guildford?'

'Her mum and dad bought a bungalow there a few years ago. She wants to be near them.'

'And she's not taking no for an answer?'

He nodded again. 'I always knew we'd have to decide what to do with the house. One day. I just didn't expect your mother to go so—'

'Suddenly?'

'Exactly.'

'I don't know what to say, Dad. Are you sure you want to sell?'

'I think, on a purely practical level, it would benefit everyone.'

Tom walked into the room, wearing the shirt he'd worn on Friday when he came over after work. My father put his cup of tea down on the carpet and stood up. They shook hands. He sat down again quickly, perhaps embarrassed by the difference in height.

'I made you a cup of tea,' I said, to break the silence. 'It's in the kitchen.'

'Thanks.'

I got up and pulled one of the dining chairs over. He gave me a grateful look as he walked back into the room, sipping tea that was patently too hot.

'What do you two have planned for the weekend? Or what's left of it.'

Tom coughed his voice into action. 'We were going to walk up to the common and have lunch.'

'Is that Clapham Common?'

'Yeah, there are quite a few places round there. You're very welcome to join us.'

'No thanks. I won't stay long.' He turned to me. 'I just wondered if I could take you up on your offer to phone around estate agents.' He raised his eyebrows significantly. 'I just think it's probably better if you do it.'

'Of course. I'll make a note of some of the local ones and get them round for a valuation.'

'Thanks,' he said, picking up his cup of tea and slurping loudly. He asked Tom where he worked, what he did, but I could tell he wanted to get going. The questions were a filler for the uncomfortable conference we suddenly found ourselves in. He stood up as he gulped the last of his tea and held out his hand to Tom. 'It was nice to meet you. Take care of yourselves,' he said, turning to me.

'I'll walk you out.' Tom took the cups into the kitchen while we went downstairs to the entrance hall.

'He seems like a nice chap.'

'Yeah. He is.'

'Listen, about the estate agents. Phone me on my mobile, not the landline, OK?'

'OK. Bye, Dad.'

'Bye, darling.'

My mother's house had been standing empty since February. It was common knowledge among the local estate agents that the sole occupant had fallen down the stairs and died. In other words, they were waiting for my call. I arranged for three of them to come and value the house on the second

Saturday in September. As I followed the first one round, listening to the prosaic agent-speak, I began to see how the house of my childhood was to be marketed. I nodded my head to his view that it would need 'updating', but that its 'generous proportions' would attract young families. I suddenly saw my mother leaning against the work surface of the kitchen-diner with scope to extend, smoking away the trauma of that morning in the playground. The south-facing bedroom – with room for an en-suite shower – was the scene of her great depression and rejection of my father. And the entrance hall, with original coving, was where I'd stood as a little girl in pyjamas desperate to reach my mother and as a thirty-year-old woman who had failed to catch her.

I phoned my father later that evening with the three valuations. He was happy for me to choose the agent I wanted to go with. I opted for the first one, not because I thought he was better than the other two but because I didn't think there was enough of a difference between them to justify protracting the decision.

I called on Monday morning and officially put my mother's house on the market. There was to be an open house the following Saturday, and I had to drop off a set of keys to allow access to the property for viewings and marketing photographs.

On Wednesday lunchtime I received a call from the same estate agent. He'd been into the house to take some pictures but, as he was locking up, the woman next door had asked him what he was doing. 'I told her the family had made a decision to sell the house.'

'OK. She probably just wants to know what's going on.'

'I'm sure she does, but she said she'd also like to speak to you.'

'To me? What did you say to her?'

'I said I'd pass the message on.'

'OK, thanks. I'll try to remember to give her a knock when I'm next over there.'

He phoned again the following Saturday afternoon, around five thirty. The open house had been a big success in estate agent terms. They'd had seventeen viewings and four offers. All despite the fact that nobody was able to walk out of the kitchen and into the garden.

'I told you, the key's on a hook beside the French doors.'

'I looked there and couldn't find it. Do you have a spare set? We have another viewing on Monday at eleven.'

'Not for the French doors. I'll come and have a dig around in the house for it.'

'OK. Well, if you find it, would you mind dropping it off over the weekend sometime? You can just pop it through our letter box.'

'Will do. Thanks.'

I was working on an article on the increasing number of council flats being sublet across the capital's housing estates. I'd had a tip-off that there were a handful of unofficial tenants in Peckham who might be willing to speak to me, but – perhaps worried by the prospect of eviction – they had all become very difficult to track down. My big exposé was looking decidedly tenuous.

Tom volunteered to take my car and drive to Surbiton to look for the key. I carried on cutting and pasting until the copy became so fragmented it ceased to make sense. I was just about to phone Andy and concede defeat when Tom came home. He closed the door quietly. I waited for him to walk down the hallway but several seconds passed and still he didn't move.

'Hello?' I shouted and stood up.

He was standing by the door, his hand on the latch. He hadn't taken his jacket off.

'You were a long time. Did you manage to find it?'

'No sign of it. I had to call a locksmith to fit a new lock.' He delivered this information without looking at me once.

'OK. Thank you. What's the matter?'

He had a piece of paper in his left hand. It was hanging by his side.

'What's wrong with you?'

'What were you doing at The Kings Arms Hotel on the eighth of August?'

The receipt. He'd found the receipt for the room and Prosecco in my car. I'd stuffed it in the door pocket that day as I tried to phone Helen. I opened my mouth to say something but no sound came out.

'On the way home I tried to come up with all sorts of reasons why you might check into a room on your own. And order Prosecco! But then I remembered that ex-boyfriend of yours. The married one. He lives in Buckinghamshire, doesn't he?'

'I'm sorry.'

He hung his head and smiled. As if it all made sense. But then I saw his shoulders heave with a huge sob. I walked towards him but he put his hand up. The one still holding the receipt.

'Please, Tom. I'm so sorry.'

'So that's what you were doing. While I was away thinking about you, worrying about the inquest, you were busy fucking someone else.'

'It was a moment of insanity. Totally stupid. I wish I could take it back.' My gaping inability to speak had given way to clichés.

I watched his hand on the door latch and thought desperately of what I could say to bring him back to me. But I knew it was the absence of speech that had done for me. I should have told him. The truth would have given us a chance. He took his hand off the latch and fished in his pocket for my car key and the new keys to the French doors. He threw them on the floor, dropped the piece of paper and opened the door.

'Please don't go,' I whispered as he closed it hard behind him.

The mouth, tongue and thyroid gland were unre-
markable. The nose was intact and the nostrils were
unobstructed.

When faced with calamity, our first instinct is to find out
what happened. We probe the edges of something before
moving to the centre – an external examination before
the internal one. I was so angry with myself for leaving
the receipt in my car that, as I stood in my hallway staring at the closed front door, I began castigating myself for
my stupidity: if only I'd thrown it in the bin, shredded it,
left David to pay the tab. I wasn't ready to really consider
why I'd betrayed Tom in the first place. I kept going back
to the moment I got into my car after leaving the hotel. In
my absurdity I found myself blaming Helen: if she'd only
answered my fucking calls and emails, I wouldn't be in this
mess.

And as if to confirm my hypothesis, Helen phoned me
that afternoon. I was sitting on my sofa, half a bottle of wine
down and starting to feel hungry.

'It's about time. Where have you been?'

'I was on a school trip to Croatia and then ... well, then
September happened, and I've been trying to keep my head
above water since then.'

'I sent you an email about my mother's inquest. You never

even replied.' The wine and heartbreak had made me bolshy.

'I know. I know it all. I couldn't bring myself to attend, and I knew I couldn't explain it to you over email. Laura, I'm sorry. Did you go on your own?'

I thought of David on top of me – his mouth hot and hurried as he thrust inside me. I closed my eyes and felt them burn. Poor Tom.

'Laura, are you there?'

'Yes, I'm here. No, my dad came along as well.'

'Oh, he did. That's good. Listen, I'd love to see you again soon. Do you fancy another walk in Richmond Park?'

'I'm not sure. I mean, yes, but I need to let the dust settle here for a bit.'

'Is everything OK?'

'It's fine. I'll give you a ring next week.'

'OK. And listen, I'm sorry for going off the grid there.'

I wanted to tell her that my life was in pieces again; that I felt broken and unreachable. But she'd already gone.

I came into a light sleep at around six on Sunday morning. I could tell from the effort of opening them that my eyes were puffy from crying. I checked my phone, hoping for a message from Tom. Even an angry one would have been something, but his silence was like a substantial wall built suddenly over-night, ugly in design and uncompromising in its message. There was nothing to say. I knew I couldn't spend the day alone. I phoned Andrea.

'Hi love. How are you?'

'Tom and I have broken up.'

'Shit! You're joking. Why? When?'

'Because I slept with David. Yesterday.'

'You slept with David yesterday?'

'No, he broke up with me yesterday. I slept with David back in August.'

'Fuck. Oh, God. I'm so sorry.'

'Thanks.'

'Why did you do it?'

'Because I'm an absolute idiot. I don't know, Andrea.' I started to cry. 'I just felt like I needed to do something crazy, sort of destructive. It makes no sense. But anyway, it worked. I've ruined the one good thing in my life.'

'Oh, love. Maybe when he's had time to think about it he might come round. You've had a pretty rough time of it. You never know, do you?'

'I know he won't forgive this. And I don't blame him.'

'I'd say come over, but I'm up in Derbyshire for the weekend. My train gets in at quarter past five. Do you want to meet me at St Pancras for a drink and a chat?'

'Don't worry. I'll be OK.'

'I'll give you a ring when I get home, OK?'

'OK. Speak to you soon.'

'I love you, OK?'

'Yep.'

I had some breakfast and a second cup of tea and decided I'd drive over to see Helen. She had seemed quite keen to meet up when she phoned the day before. She was also the closest thing I had to a mother.

I had never been to her house before; Helen always came to see us when I was a child, but I had her postal address and had used it last February to send her some reading suggestions for the funeral. She lived in a small cottage behind Twickenham Green, in an impossibly narrow street. It took me a long time to park, announcing myself with frustrated revs of the engine and endless corrections as I finally forced my car into a tiny space. By the time I emerged from the driver's side, sweating and stressed, Helen was watching me from her window. She looked surprised. She opened the door just a crack, not willing to admit me. Then I heard the scrabbling paws of Sandy and understood.

'Hi Helen. Hello Sandy.'

'What are you doing here?'

'I'm sorry it's unannounced. I just wanted to come and see you. Can I come in?'

'Yes. Of course. Hang on a second – let me shut the dog away.' She closed the door for a couple of minutes and returned, opening it wide to admit me. She was wearing a dressing gown over jeans and a turtleneck jumper. When she hugged me, I felt how cold her face and hands were.

'Are you OK? You don't look well.'

'No, I'm not. Bloody cold – I can't shake it. Come on through.'

She led me into the small living room at the front of the house. She'd lit the fire and had evidently been reading when I arrived. Her book was splayed open on the table with her glasses folded across the pages.

'This room is so cosy – and warm. Do you spend most of your time in here?'

'Yes, and sometimes the nights too. It's like a bloody womb. The rest of the house is so cold. Sit down, Laura, I'll make you a cup of tea.'

'That's OK. I can make it. You're the patient here.'

'Don't be silly. Sit yourself down.'

I sat down and reached for her book. Her glasses fell from the pages, landing face down on the lenses, and as I righted them, I saw she was reading *Tess of the D'Urbervilles*. It was the same edition my mother had kept beside her bed: a Penguin English Library edition with Stonehenge on the front cover. It looked as though it hadn't been very well cared for; the front cover had been torn and repaired with sticky tape. I got up from the sofa and walked into the kitchen, where the kettle was boiling and Helen was carefully pulling a teapot from one of the cupboards.

'Is that my mother's copy of *Tess*?'

She put the teapot down quietly and closed the cupboard door. 'Yes, I found it the other day. Kath must have left it here.'

'Here? When?'

'Oh, I don't know. One afternoon.'

'How long ago?'

'I don't know. I've only just found it. You can see – I'm only a few chapters in.'

She fired two tea bags into the pot and laughed. 'I wasn't keeping it from you. Do you take sugar?'

'Yes. One, please.'

She reached up to a different cupboard and began rummaging inside. In her effort to locate the sugar, she pulled down a box of porridge oats and left it on the work surface.

'She lived here, didn't she?'

Helen stopped in her tracks. The steam from the kettle continued to climb in powerful spirals.

'She lived with you. That's why her book is here.'

She put the kettle down and turned to me. 'So, she left her bloody book here! So what? We were friends. She came to see me from time to time, and must have left it here.'

'You're lying to me.' My insides burned. 'I know you are.'

'How can you say that to me? Of course I'm not *lying* to you.'

'She had porridge the morning she died. It was in her stomach when the pathologist opened it with his scalpel. And there wasn't a single porridge oat in her kitchen.'

'Oh, Jesus.' She leant on the work surface for support and hung her head between her taut arms.

'That's why you've never invited me here. And didn't want to open the door to me a minute ago. It's because—'

'She didn't want you to know, Laura.'

'She didn't, or you didn't?'

'I've always wanted to tell you. But she wouldn't.'

'Why not?'

'Because she thought you'd already experienced too much. The mess with your father, the thing in the playground ... She was convinced, when he finally left, that you needed a simple life. And she wanted to give that to you.'

'When did she move in?'

'When Christopher moved to Australia. In 2007.'

I heard the numbers and tried to make sense of it. 2007. Two years after that day by the South Bank. When she'd told me to make room for the things I wanted.

Helen stood up straight and poured the boiling water into the pot. She was calm again. 'Five years. She was here with me for five years,' she said impassively. She put the teapot, some milk and two cups on a tray and lifted it to her chest, suddenly substantial: 'Let's go in and sit down. We need to talk.'

I turned on my heel and walked back into her living room. I made my way over to the corner where Helen had been reading and picked up my mother's book. I closed it shut in righteous defiance of her attempt to mark her place.

'You should have told me.'

'I couldn't, Laura. It was your mother's decision, and she didn't want you to know.'

'Didn't want me to know what? That she was gay?' The reality of what I'd uncovered was starting to dawn on me. 'It all makes sense now. You shared a bed with her after she had Christopher.'

'That wasn't what you think. That wasn't sexual. I was there to support her as a friend, at a very difficult time in her life.'

'But the reason she rejected my father was because—'

'No, Laura.' She was shaking her head emphatically. 'No.'

'It was because of you. You were the reason she didn't want to be with him any more.'

'That's not true. Your mother never wanted to be with him *full stop*. She got pregnant, and then your grandmother saw to it that she got drawn into a life she never wanted.'

'Bullshit! You were very keen to step into his shoes. And she let you.' My lungs were hot with pain: the injustice of my father's rejection and then, devastating in its connection, Tom's humiliation at my front door.

'Your father knew. Your mum had told him there'd been someone from her schooldays. And then, as time went on, he came to understand that it was me. But they decided to give things a go. Christopher was the child they set out to have together. He was planned in a way you weren't. He was her big effort at the heterosexual wife.'

'And what happened? She just gave up trying?'

'Christopher's birth, and her depression afterwards, it frightened her. She felt very alone. Like no one could help her. I tried to convince her to end the marriage.'

'So she could be with you?'

'Well, ultimately, yes. I'm not going to lie to you, Laura; I wanted your mum to be with me.'

'But she wouldn't.'

'She knew that if she left your father her options were to be alone or come out as gay. And she couldn't do the latter while you and Christopher were still young. So she tried to maintain the status quo until you left home.'

'The status quo? You mean she lied to me.' I broke down and wept. I looked at the book on the table and felt wave after wave of my own misery.

'Please listen to me. I loved your mother very much – no, listen, Laura. You may not want to hear this, but it's the truth. I loved her and she loved me. And it wasn't about being gay or lesbian or anything like that. It was just the two of us. And we always loved each other. From the very first day of school.

'You're looking for her, Laura. I know you are. But the trouble with your mother is she liked to lurk in the shadows. She was very reluctant to be herself. I wanted her to own the situation with your father, I implored her to end things because I could see what it was doing to you and Christopher. And I can still see its effects this afternoon. But she was stubborn. And she had to do things her way. I tried, Laura. I tried to encourage her out.'

'You mean you wanted her to *come* out?'

'I just wanted her to be herself. And if that was a gay woman in her fifties living with her lover, then so be it.'

'And she wouldn't?'

'No. She drifted into a strange middle ground where she was living with me but pretending she wasn't.'

'Were you supporting her?'

'How do you mean?'

'Financially. Who paid for her life here with you? I'm assuming my dad had stopped paying any maintenance for me and Christopher. The house was paid off.'

'You have to understand that your mother and I, we didn't spend much. We went for walks, cooked together – having your mother here was no great expense.'

'So you did, then? You kept her. Like a wife.'

Helen sighed. As though I was deliberately misunderstanding her. 'I took care of everything until 2009, when she sold your grandmother's house. She gave some of the money to you and Christopher and kept the rest for herself.'

'What did she do all day? While you were out at work?'

'She read, she walked a lot down by the river, prepared an evening meal. And when I got home she'd bleed me for details.' She smiled down at her knees. I knew that grieving smile – a reflex of the facial muscles before they fold in pain. 'I'd save up stories for her, Laura,' she said, her face smooth and appalled. 'Sometimes I'd embellish them and make up details I knew would make her laugh. Because I loved to hear her laugh. Oh God, I miss her. I miss her so much.'

'And the day I found her?'

'She got up early and took the bus to Surbiton.'

'To maintain the fiction.'

'I'm afraid so.'

'So tell me about her, then.'

My mother was extremely shy as a young girl. And Helen was the only girl she wanted to play with. On her first day at school she watched Helen playing with another girl on the carpet – they were building a house together – and decided she wanted to build a house. With Helen. Not the other girl. They were sitting cross-legged, happily constructing a building bright with primary colours and its own impermanence. My mother walked over to them and, without speaking, crossed her ankles and dropped down next to them. Helen reared up like a snake, suddenly attentive and full of venom: 'This is *our* house. Go and build your own!'

My mother was stung by how angrily her bid to join in had been inspected, spat upon and passed back to her. She did the only thing she knew to do in such circumstances. She sought out the nearest adult and cried to them. Her teacher, Ms Rogers, called Helen over and asked her what had happened. Helen bowed her head so that the greasy, unwashed strands could fall forward. She continued to stare through them at my mother, the interloper, who was now crying with fresh vigour.

'Katharine, what's the matter? Did you want to play with Helen?'

My mother nodded her head.

'Helen, Katharine here is very shy. Would you please let her join you and Christine in your game?'

'No,' she said, defiantly.

Ms Rogers sighed with mock sorrow and told my mother and Helen to join hands. 'Helen, you're going to look after Katharine. We all have to play together, so I want you *both* to go and sit in the reading corner and get to know one another.' It was a terrible outcome for Helen. She and Christine had been talking through plans for the roof when my mother came along and used emotion to bulldoze the project. My mother, on the other hand, was delighted with Helen's hand. She was full of admiration for Helen's strength and defiance. And now she was hers to play with. Ms Rogers had made that clear. Except as soon as they'd walked a few paces from their teacher's desk, Helen dropped the hand she had never wanted to hold. My mother tried to grab it up again, but, like a reluctant fish, Helen twisted it away from her. 'I don't want to play with you,' she said to my mother's confused face. And with this devastating statement set off in search of Christine and the housing project my mother had so mindlessly delayed.

But my mother didn't have time to indulge her sorrow. Helen was walking away. Quickly. She had to get her back. She sat down beside her. Too close.

'Go away.'

My mother picked up one of the blocks and offered it to Helen.

'We don't need your help!' Helen shouted with the callous cruelty of a young child.

'Helen Saunders! Come here right now, please.' Ms Rogers had heard, with her own ears, Helen's cruel rejection of my mother's advances. She was furious. Helen approached the desk with contempt. At just five years of age, she was already angry with the world and all that it wanted from her.

'I heard what you said to Katharine. I thought I told you to go and sit together. Katharine! Come here please.' My mother returned to the scene of their earlier peace agreement and began crying at the failure of it. Helen folded her arms across her chest and turned her back on the girl who wouldn't leave her alone. Ms Rogers pulled at one of the arms firmly and turned the recalcitrant body back to face my mother. 'You two are going to go and pick up all the blocks on the carpet and put them in the box. Come back and tell me when you're finished.'

My mother's optimism was renewed; she wiped away her tears and smiled happiness at Helen. Who would not look at her. Together they put the blocks away, my mother handing blocks to Helen who put them solemnly in the box. She would have happily used them to build a wall between herself and my mother, but for Ms Rogers glancing in their direction every few seconds.

Despite my mother's best efforts, they did not become friends that day. But they did enter into a relationship of sorts: my mother attached herself to Helen and sought strength from her hard and implacable exterior. She hoped that one day Helen would relent and let her in. In fact, Helen simply accepted my mother's need for her and eventually grew accustomed to her faithful company. Their unity was established and noted. It became a matter of interest for the adults, who realised that a class divide neither girl was aware of had been crossed. Their friendship troubled my grandmother for many reasons. It's true that she wanted nothing to do with this family from the local housing estate, but in her heart, more troubling than the social difference was the fact that my mother's reticence deepened as the friendship continued. Helen began speaking for my mother. She answered questions on her behalf, made decisions about where they'd play and who might join their game. She was my mother's mouthpiece, and my mother was very happy to withdraw into silence.

My grandmother tried to push at the soft, pliable infancy of their friendship, fancying she could change its course. She was cold and cutting to Helen. And yet every morning my mother reattached herself to Helen's side in the playground and stayed there until it was time to go to their different homes.

Helen's poverty stemmed from her mother's poor education and poor choices. She had two sons from a previous relationship and Helen, her youngest child, from a relationship that foundered days after Helen's birth. Her father was very young – just eighteen when she was born – and completely unprepared for the physical assault of a newborn baby on a home. He didn't care to bring up his girlfriend's two boys, and after being woken every three hours by hungry cries, didn't care to raise his own daughter either. So Helen was brought up by a woman who had been flattened by life; who had only a dim perception that her need to feel wanted by unworthy men had led her to this damp and disappointing existence.

When Helen was nine years old, Ms Rogers knocked on the door of their flat. It was a Tuesday morning and Helen was at school. Her mother answered the door and assumed, not recognising the face in front of her, that it was somebody from the council asking her to account for her son's absence from school. John was in the living room watching television. He hadn't been to school in over eight months. He said he was being bullied, but when she'd tried to raise this with the headmaster he informed her that John was the bully – that he made the lives of the younger boys a misery. She had no answer to his accusation, concluding only that she too was as weak as her son's victims. That she wanted to push him out and away but he was too strong for her.

But the woman at the door was not from the council. She was Helen's teacher from her year in Reception. 'Mrs Saunders? I taught Helen a few years ago. May I come in?' Helen's mother simply nodded in the face of authority, grateful for the opportunity to compose herself as they made their way, awkwardly, to the living room, where John's face was lit up by the glare of the television. She switched it off, emboldened by the presence of a stranger who had come to speak to her about Helen. John continued watching the now dark screen as though nothing had changed. Ms Rogers looked from him to Helen's mother, who was sitting down on the edge of the sofa expectantly, and decided she'd better get to the point.

'I'd like to talk to you about Helen.'

'What's she done?'

'Oh, nothing! Nothing at all. Mrs Saunders, I'm here because I think Helen is very bright.'

Ms Rogers had hoped the adjective, heavy with meaning, would convey her daughter's academic potential and serve as a springboard for her proposal. But Helen's mother remained impassive. She was waiting for something more substantial. Something she could understand.

'I think she should consider sitting the eleven-plus and trying for a place at the local grammar school.'

'Helen's not eleven yet.'

'No. The eleven-plus is the name of the test the children sit. It determines whether they're bright, er, clever enough to go to grammar school. To a selective school. Mrs Saunders, we have one of the finest grammar schools right here in Kingston. If Helen passes, you could send her to one of the best schools in the country.' Helen's mother finally understood that Ms Rogers was barking up the wrong tree.

'Miss . . . um . . .'

'Rogers. But please, call me Liz.'

'Miss Rogers. Look around you. I don't have that kind of money. I'm glad you think Helen's clever, but I can't afford to send her to private school.'

'No, no. Mrs Saunders, grammar school is still state education. There would be no fees to pay. She just has to pass the test, and I'm confident that, with some tutoring, she'd stand a very good chance.'

'Tutoring?'

'Yes,' Ms Rogers gulped and continued, 'one-to-one

tutoring. I'm here because I'd like to tutor Helen myself. For free,' she added quickly.

'Why would you do that?'

'Because she's clever. And because I'd hate to see a girl like Helen miss out on opportunities because of . . .' she looked over at Helen's older brother, still staring at the blank television screen '. . . circumstances beyond her control.'

Helen's mother agreed to the arrangement. Ms Rogers began tutoring Helen in her classroom after school every Monday. Helen's sharp, darting intellect quickly settled into the required framework. She was spiky in her selection, quick to digest the logic and move on. And as the months passed, she began to grow confident and optimistic. She knew that my mother – over in Surbiton – was being prepared by my grandmother for the same test. After five years of almost constant companionship, Helen needed my mother as much as my mother needed her. She worked hard for Ms Rogers, not because she saw an opportunity to improve her lot in life but simply because she couldn't foresee a life without my mother by her side.

For my grandmother, the eleven-plus was her longed-for means of separating my mother from Helen. A place at grammar school was the only way, short of moving to a new area, to ensure the two friends were finally pushed in divergent directions. It was an inadvertent slip by my mother that finally alerted her to Ms Rogers's tutoring intervention. My mother wanted to know how she would travel to and from her new school.

'By bus. The number 65 takes you straight there,' my grandmother answered, matter-of-factly.

'Will it go past the Cambridge Estate?'

'No.' My grandmother paused. 'Why would you ask that?'

'Because I want to go with Helen.'

'Darling, Helen won't be going to your school.'

'Yes, she will. She's very clever. Ms Rogers said so.'

'Ms Rogers? Your teacher from Reception? What does she have to do with all this?'

'She's tutoring Helen. To pass the eleven-plus. She wants her to go to my school.'

My grandmother's lungs burned. She stared at her daughter and realised, with searing frustration, that she'd waited too long to try and get her away. The route she had taken, tutoring my mother for grammar school, was obvious to others and they were catching up. So my grandmother did what any self-respecting middle-class mother would do in such circumstances. She bemoaned the injustice of Ms Rogers's partiality to Helen to the other parents, eventually taking her complaint to Ms Rogers's classroom one afternoon after school. She sat my mother down in a corner of the room and approached Ms Rogers, who was quietly marking, at her desk. 'I'm sorry to interrupt you. Might I have a word?'

Ms Rogers, who had already looked up when they walked in, took off her glasses and narrowed her eyes to see better. 'Yes, of course. You're Katharine Lambton's mother, aren't you?'

'Yes, Jean Lambton. Do you mind if I sit down?'

Ms Rogers simply smiled her assent at the nearest chair and waited.

'I understand you're tutoring Helen Saunders for the eleven-plus. Is that correct?' Ms Rogers put her glasses back on and stopped smiling.

'That's right.'

'Ms Rogers, I haven't come here to cause trouble, but it

strikes me that personally tutoring one child out of a school of many demonstrates a preference that some might regard as . . . unprofessional?'

Ms Rogers swallowed hard and stood up. 'I don't see what this has to do with you. My dealings with another pupil are none of your business.' And then, 'I'm sorry to be so blunt.'

'Don't be. I admire your honesty. And your good intentions. Does the headmaster know what you're doing?'

'Yes,' she lied.

'Very well. I'll raise my concerns with him, in that case.'

The headmaster, Mr Evans, duly discussed the issue with Ms Rogers. He also went on to share the view, that tutoring pupils for the eleven-plus was not a practice to be encouraged in school, with all the teachers in a staff announcement the following Monday morning. Ms Rogers took him at his word and inwardly shrugged at the risk. She found the time and space to continue tutoring Helen by moving the sessions to her own flat, in the early evening. On the day of the eleven-plus, she called in sick to school, arranged to meet Helen at a bus stop near her estate and drove her the short distance into Kingston. Both Helen and my mother found themselves sitting in the large, contained hall. Two rows and many desks apart, they fingered the regulation-issue pencil and paper and waited for the clock, heavy with its own importance, to signal the beginning of the exam. The silence was suddenly stabbed by the leads of hundreds of sharpened pencils. The paper was a passport to another life: a life in this hall. With legs crossed. Waiting for the next instruction. My mother had a view of Helen's head bent down in concentrated submission. She picked up her own pencil and answered her way into more time with Helen.

Three weeks later, Helen's mother received a message from

another world. On paper embossed with the school crest, she read her daughter's name and the words that confirmed she was to have a new life. Helen had not only passed the eleven-plus, she had scored in the top ten per cent of applicants. Helen's success vindicated Ms Rogers's intervention and soured my grandmother's dealings with her daughter's primary school thereafter. But none of that mattered to Helen and my mother. All they looked to was the following September.

My grandmother, counselled by my grandfather, accepted defeat. She knew my grandfather was not prepared to move away. But Helen's admission to the grammar school achieved two things: it gave my mother greater confidence and optimism about going to secondary school in general, so much so that her crippling shyness began to recede and she started speaking more in public. And of course, the fact that Helen had joined the ranks of other middle-class girls. She could now expect to go to university and even attract a suitable husband.

Suitable, that is, by my grandmother's standards. So while my grandmother did not exactly approve of the friendship, she certainly softened to the idea of it.

My mother made no effort with the other girls in her class. And they met her inattention with their own disregard. But Helen was different. Everybody liked her. She was funny, uncompromising and contemptuous of what she called the 'beige' teachers. The ones who were too afraid to teach in a comprehensive school. Their history teacher was a diminutive, round woman called Miss McCabe. She was from the Outer Hebrides and spoke in gentle, self-effacing tones. She dreaded teaching my mother's class because of Helen.

One cold afternoon in November 1973, during a lesson on

Henry VIII, Miss McCabe asked the class what happened to Anne Boleyn. Everybody waited for Helen to clarify matters, and with only one girl willing to answer, Miss McCabe had no alternative but to admit her interlocutor. Helen stood up.

'Helen.'

'Sorry, miss – I'm just not quite sure what you mean. What *happened* to Anne Boleyn is a very general question. Too general, some might say.'

The class giggled. My mother, sitting a few rows behind, crossed her legs uncomfortably. She didn't want Helen to get into trouble. If she got in trouble, my mother would spend break time on her own in the playground.

'How should I rephrase the question, Helen?' Two spots of red had appeared in Miss McCabe's cheeks. They were like little cherries on a Bakewell tart.

'I'm not the teacher here, but it strikes me that you're asking if Anne Boleyn was executed, divorced or died naturally.'

'Yes. And?'

'Wouldn't it be better to ask, "What was Anne Boleyn's fate as the king's wife and why is this significant?"'

'Sit down, Helen. I don't need a lecture on how to do my job from you, thank you very much.'

'But since you ask, he only went and *chopped her bloomin' 'ead off!*' And, hitching her skirt up, she began dancing on the spot in the manner of a naughty cockney, singing: 'I'm 'Enery the Eighth, I am,/'Enery the Eighth I am, I am!' The class erupted in laughter and began clapping in time as she gurned her way through the rest of the verse. The sight was enough to topple my mother's anxiety and she too collapsed into the chorus of hilarity.

My mother remained by Helen's side until the last possible moment of every day. They got the bus home together, but because she was forbidden to visit Helen's flat, they either got off the bus in Kingston and walked around the town centre or travelled on to Surbiton together, where Helen and my mother would sit up in her room or out in the garden if it was warm enough.

The first time they ever kissed was in her bedroom. It was at the end of January, about a week after my mother's thirteenth birthday. My grandparents had bought her a record player and Roberta Flack's 'Killing Me Softly' on seven-inch vinyl. Helen and my mother lay down on her bed and luxuriated in the freedom of filling a room with music. My mother looked at Helen, who lay with her eyes closed, concentrating on the lyrics. Without opening her eyes, she said, 'Do you think *flushed with fever* means she's turned on?'

My mother hadn't listened to the words that closely. 'I don't know.'

'Kiss me. I'll tell you if it flushes me with fever.'

'Why would I do that?' my mother asked.

'Because it might feel nice. And I'll be able to tell you if you've done it right.'

'Sounds a bit dirty.'

Helen opened her eyes and sat up. 'I'm not asking you to wipe my arse. Or even your own, for that matter. Don't you want to just try something out? With me?' As she said the last two words, she looked at my mother's lips. They were full and small, like a little rosebud. Helen knew they'd be soft. She leant in and pressed her own thin lips against my mother's mouth.

My mother pulled back, almost imperceptibly, but like a child that detects sugar in a morsel of food they thought to reject, she came back. The first contact had already begun stimulating the sensory neurons within her lips. As her brain flooded with dopamine and the blood flowed to the vermilion border, my mother kissed. And allowed herself to be kissed.

Helen licked my mother's top lip in gentle invitation to open, but she wouldn't. She'd already gone further than she ever thought possible.

There was no obvious awkwardness the next morning at school, but my mother was even more subdued than usual. She kept stealing glances at Helen and then swiftly return-ing to her books, her face burning at the memory. Sitting on their usual bench at lunchtime, Helen asked her what was wrong.

'Nothing.'

'Is it because of yesterday? At your house?'

My mother flushed red.

'Kath, it was a kiss. That's all.'

'But the tongue thing . . .' Her voice trailed off.

'What about it? It's called *Frenching*. Everybody does it.'

'Do you?'

'Do I what?'

'Do you do it? To other people.'

'No,' she admitted. 'I've never done it before.'

'Never done what?' Two girls from their form group, Karen and Emily, interrupted the quiet conversation. Karen was digging at the corner of a crisp packet, determined to mine the final greasy fragments with her fingernails.

'Don't worry about it,' Helen said dismissively. 'I'll catch up with you in Science.'

But Karen was sucking her foraging finger thoughtfully. Emily stood beside her, bored and impatient for something to happen. Neither girl understood Helen's fascination with my mother.

'What have you never done before?' she repeated, balling up her crisp packet and throwing it at my mother's head.

Helen jumped up, her anger and menace immediate. 'Say sorry right now.'

'Sorry,' Karen smiled as Helen faced her. 'I didn't mean to hurt your girlfriend.'

'What did you say?'

'I said she's your *girlfriend*. I bet that's what they were talking about, Em,' she said, turning to bored Emily. And then in a mocking, high-pitched whine: 'Please can I finger you, Kath? I've never done it before.'

Helen met Karen's smile, staring at her steadily. 'That's right. It is my first time. But I think I'm going to start big. Forget fingers, I'm going with a fist. And the first place I fist will be your face.'

'Oh, fuck off, you pair of lesbians.' Karen's plait whipped round as she turned to stalk back to the school building. Emily followed, slow and spiritless.

My mother stood up, her face red and hot, and shouted at Karen's retreating back. 'She's not my girlfriend!'

'Shut up, Kath,' said Helen.

'I just want her to know—'

'Well, I don't care who knows.'

'She might tell my mum.'

'Tell your mum what?'

'About the *Frenching*.'

'They didn't hear any of that. Anyway, so what if they did? I couldn't give a shit what Karen or Jean or anyone else thinks.' She reached for my mother's hand, but my mother pulled it away.

'Not here,' she said, looking around.

'Where, then?'

'At my house,' my mother said, looking at Helen's hands with fear and excitement. 'We could listen to "Killing Me Softly" again.'

And that's how the title of Roberta Flack's hit song became a euphemism for uncovering something exquisite. The greatest revelation for both of them was that the capacity to experience pleasure was contained within their own bodies. That it had been there all along, and just as they could decide when to set the seven-inch single spinning, they could choose to press their lips together and release something pure and simple. And as yet undiluted.

In the Easter holidays of that same year, Helen's mother took her and her two brothers down to Poole to visit her sister and brother-in-law. During their stay it became clear her mother was in the process of organising a permanent move. They spent several hours in the civic centre, registering for various services, while John went with his uncle to meet people who might be interested in hiring him as a labourer. When Helen asked what was going on, her mother told her she was simply 'looking into things', but as they walked round the perimeter fence of a comprehensive school near her aunt's house, she knew the looking was with a view to joining.

Over the May bank holiday, Helen and her family made another visit to Poole. This time they were shown round a flat on a housing estate a couple of miles from her aunt. She became anxious.

'We're moving here, aren't we?'

'It's for the best. John can work, and I'll be closer to Auntie Debs.'

'But what about school?'

'You'll go to school here.'

'But *my* school. I want to stay at my school.'

'What difference does it make? You're a clever girl – you'll be fine wherever you go.'

'And Kath?'

'Kath? Your little friend? Oh, she'll be all right. I wouldn't worry about her.'

But the thought of my mother did worry Helen. She foresaw her impending isolation and loneliness and dreaded it on my mother's behalf. She felt responsible for her, understanding as she did that my mother only felt strong when she had somebody to stand behind. And that person had to be Helen. Their private communion had made the attachment stronger, deeper in a way that neither girl could articulate.

Helen delayed telling my mother. She hoped the move would not come to pass; that John would do something to irritate his uncle or her mother would fall out with Auntie Debs, but at the beginning of July, Helen's mother gave Kingston Council notice of her intention to leave and began packing boxes.

On the last day of the school year, Helen asked my mother if she could come over after school. She said she had something to tell her. My grandmother had let them in and then disappeared to another part of the house. Though it was only a few roads away from our own, my grandparents' house was much bigger; they lived on a crescent consisting of just nine houses, all with a large garden at the back. It was a warm day and my mother, responding to Helen's request for a drink, poured them both a glass of lemonade. Helen opened the back door and they walked down to the end of the garden, to a little shrubbery my grandmother had cultivated. It was secluded and shaded. They were both in their summer uniforms, light cotton gingham dresses that buttoned up the front. They crossed their legs and sat down on the cool earth, their white ankle socks and scuffed black shoes turned down on their sides. Helen had been picking her fingers; the skin around her cuticles was pink and exposed.

'So what is it, then?' my mother asked.

'We're moving away. To Poole.'

'What's Poole?'

'My aunt lives down there. And my uncle's got John a job.'

'But what about school?'

'My mum says I can go to the local one.'

'You can't go.'

Helen looked down at her ankles. She was trying not to cry. 'It's not up to me. My mum thinks it's a much nicer place to live. And she's sick of John sitting around the flat all day.'

'No,' my mother began to cry, 'you can't leave me. Come and live with me.'

'Oh yeah,' Helen laughed, her voice cracking on the effort. 'Jean would love that, wouldn't she?'

My mother was sobbing, the sound infantile and repetitive. Her nose had started running; she wiped the snot ineffectually across her face with the back of her hand. Helen reached out for her.

'When are you going?'

'Sometime next month. We're going to stay at my aunt's for the first few days.'

'You don't seem very upset.'

'I am. But I can't do anything to change it.'

My mother continued crying, her head bent. Helen reached out to try and hug her but because of their position – cross-legged and facing one another – she couldn't bridge the gap.

'It's only a few years. When I'm sixteen I'll come back. I'll get a job round here. We could get a flat together or something.'

My mother rallied at the thought of living with Helen; she pulled the corner of her mouth to the side in a small smile.

Helen reached out to touch my mother's elbow and gently pulled her sideways, down to the ground. My mother untangled her legs and lay by her side. They turned to face one another for a few seconds before my mother kissed Helen on the mouth. And then she opened her lips for Helen's tongue.

Helen started unbuttoning her own dress, fumbling to go further while the sun and mood was upon them. My mother lay there and watched, wondering where Helen's body might take them. And then there was a third voice. My mother froze as Helen put her gnawed thumb immediately to her teeth in an attitude of absolute terror.

'What on earth are you doing? Put your dress on at once!'

My grandmother's ankles were visible through the shrubs, bent and ready to pounce as she peered down through the foliage.

'Nothing, Mrs Lambton.' Helen was frantically contorting her shoulders in order to pull her dress back upon them. Her fingers were shaking and ineffectual as she tried to do the buttons up.

'Helen Saunders, you are a disgusting girl. And you've tried to make my daughter as disgusting as you are. I want you to get your things and leave this house.'

My mother began to cry. And plead. 'Mum, it was me. It was my idea. Don't blame Helen.'

'Katharine, go up to your room at once. You will wait there until your father gets home. Helen, *you* will do as I ask. Come on! Quickly!'

Helen was marched from my grandparents' house and told never to return. My grandmother didn't know the injunction was unnecessary; that Helen and her family would move to Poole a week later. She didn't know that she'd denied my mother and Helen a proper farewell. The only thing that was evident, immediately, was that my mother withdrew from everyone the day Helen was sent away.

Helen made good on her promise and returned to Kingston, where she did her teacher training. But not until she was twenty. By the time she got back in touch with my mother, in January 1981, she was already pregnant with me and about to be married to my father. Helen was the woman Nicola remembered at the back of the registry office, her head down, as my mother promised herself to a life she didn't want.

The larynx was intact and unremarkable.

She attended their wedding as a mourner would a funeral. And in February 1981, just ten weeks before I was born, Helen went to visit my mother in her new home.

My mother – large and lonely – was delighted to see Helen at her front door. It wasn't the first time they'd met since Helen took up her place at Kingston Poly – but it was the first time they'd been alone since my mother's wedding.

The flat was on the first floor of a neat and tidy modern building. It was set back from the road and skirted by parking and perfect lawns. My mother opened the door to allow Helen inside and hugged her as soon as it was closed. She was warm and urgent in her embrace as Helen tried to maintain balance and some space between her and my mother's bump. I was the foetus that forced distance.

My mother showed her into the sparsely furnished living room. There was just one armchair and a small two-seater sofa. In front of the armchair, in weak improvisation of a footstool, was an upturned cardboard box. On the floor beside the armchair, rising up as a makeshift table, was a pile of books providing precarious balance for a half-drunk cup of tea.

'Where's Richard?'

'Working. He's got a job as a clerk at the National West-minster in Kingston.'

'Well, that's a start,' Helen said, surveying the room.

'Sit down. Let me make you a cup of tea.'

Helen followed my mother into the small kitchen and watched as she filled the kettle, squashing her bump against the sink in an effort to do so.

'How are you feeling?'

'OK,' my mother said, placing the kettle down on the hob and reaching for a box of matches on the windowsill. 'Bit tired, you know.'

'I'm sure.'

'I'm glad you've come,' she said, striking a match and igniting the urgent gas. She turned back to face Helen.

'Me too. It's nice to see you looking . . . so well.' She reached out a hand and touched the bump nestled safely beneath my mother's breasts.

'Why didn't you stay?'

Helen, thinking for a moment my mother was referring to the move to Poole, stared at her blankly.

'At the wedding. Why did you leave so quickly?'

'Oh! I didn't think Jean would be happy to talk to me. Do you?'

'I would have been. Pleased. I've missed you.'

Helen stepped back to lean against the wall. She folded her arms and stared down at the criss-crossed flesh.

'Why did you do it?'

'Do what? Get pregnant?'

'I understand why you're pregnant. Or perhaps that should be how. No, why did you marry him? I presume Jean was involved somewhere along the line?'

My mother reached out to touch the kettle handle though

it was still far off boiling. She was facing away from Helen, her head bent over the stove. 'I had no choice. The baby is due in a couple of months. And Richard is a good man.'

'You always have a choice. You had a choice a few months back.'

My mother turned to face her. 'I didn't.'

'You did,' Helen countered. 'You might not have liked the options, but you had a choice.'

'Listen to me. I can't explain it, not properly, but my body *wants* to have this baby. Can you understand that? She's deep within me. She's part of me. And I felt, even before the accident, that I had to have her.'

'Her?'

'I think so.'

'And what will you tell this girl as she's growing up?'

'What do you mean?' The kettle had started whistling.

'Will you ever explain that you like women? That you loved me?' Helen's voice cracked. 'Will you ever tell her how we loved each other when we were girls? And that here we are in our twenties and that feeling clearly hasn't gone away?'

The whistle was sharp and shrill over the bubbling water. My mother hung her head, her bump rising to meet her heaving chest. Helen walked purposefully over to the stove and turned off the gas.

They took their cups of tea into the living room and sat down together, sipping into the silence. My mother kept glancing up at Helen between sips, as if to check she was really there. They began talking about other things: Helen's shared house in Kingston, the teacher-training course, anything to avoid the direction my mother's life was going in. She stayed on for lunch, helping my mother to make sandwiches in the kitchen, sensing how much she needed her. How much she enjoyed having her near.

At around two o'clock, Helen stood to leave. She walked over to where my mother was sitting in her armchair and put both her hands out. My mother smiled and held her own out. She allowed herself to be pulled up with a heave and they hugged again. 'I better go. Will you be all right here?'

'I'll be fine. Richard will be home in a few hours.'

Helen looked steadily at my mother's face, her lips. She raised a hand to her face and with gentle fingers traced the line of my mother's jawbone. It was a goodbye they both understood: tender and temporary. My mother closed her eyes and reached for Helen's hand, holding it in place against her face. She bent her neck and allowed her head to rest on it. Helen stepped closer, cupping my mother's face, and kissed her softly on the lips. They only stopped when they heard the scratch of an uncertain key in the front door. After several failed attempts, the lock was successfully rotated and someone entered the quiet flat.

'Katharine? Are you home?'

Helen and my mother stood close and still as they heard my grandmother walk into the kitchen and lift bags of shopping onto the work surface.

'I've brought you some bananas. And a few pears. Bought some for myself too – you know how Daddy likes a pear. Here you are,' she said, walking into the living room and pulling her coat from her right arm, squinting as she shook her shoulders at Helen. 'Who's this?'

Helen looked at my mother. Willing her to take control. 'It's me, Mrs Lambton. Helen Saunders.'

My grandmother, to her credit, kept her composure. She pulled her coat back on and drew herself up. 'Helen. I wondered when we'd see you again. And what are you doing here? Have you come to congratulate Katharine?'

'Something like that.'

My grandmother nodded and bit her lower lip. She walked towards my mother and at the last minute reached out to feel the side of her half-empty cup of tea, on top of the tower of books. She picked it up and held it as she said, 'I'd like you to leave, please. Katharine needs her rest.'

'With respect, Mrs Lambton, that's not for you to say.'

My grandmother smiled down at the floating milk skin and returned a look of complete equanimity: 'You are not welcome here. You weren't welcome at the wedding, and you're not welcome now. Please leave.'

'I wanted Helen to come here today.' My mother's voice was quiet. Just about audible.

'And I'm sure I know why! You are a married woman now. And about to have a baby. Have some self-respect and tell her to go.'

'And you have some self-respect and let your daughter live her own life!'

'How dare you speak to me like that.'

'How dare *you*! You've backed her into a horrible corner. Told her the life she wanted was disgusting. Put your middle-class pride above her happiness. The only person who should be ashamed here is you.'

My mother sank down to her armchair in defeat. Helen turned to her in rage and pulled at her right arm, but she wouldn't get up. 'Kath, stand up for yourself! Tell her where to go! This is your home now. Are you going to let her dictate who you can and can't see?'

My grandmother sneered at Helen's bent form, entreating my mother to action. 'You really are a most offensive creature.'

'And you really are a fucking cunt.'

My grandmother opened her mouth in speechless shock. And into this open chasm of dismay came a prolonged and painful shriek. Except the vocal cords coming together, tight and small, to emit the sound, did not belong to my grandmother. They belonged to my heavily pregnant mother, whose loud and inelegant wail suddenly forced attention on her. She put her hands up to her ears and allowed the profound conflict within her to become amplified. The cry deepened and became more guttural as she ran out of breath and pulled for another one to replace the first. The screaming went on and on. It was both alarum and wail until Helen knelt down beside her and cupped her face, gently unseating the hands my mother had clamped there. She was shushing her, just as she had the evening I heard them argue, and slowly the wet notes of reassurance reached my mother, whose deep breaths continued in waves, carrying less and less sound each time. As her breathing returned to normal, Helen got closer. She toppled the tower of books and sat down on the armrest. My mother leant against her instinctively, resting her head and closing her eyes against Helen's strong arm as my grandmother marched to the front door and let herself out with a slam.

I left Twickenham at around three thirty and decided there was still time to drive to St Pancras and meet Andrea off her train. Roadworks and congestion on the A4 meant it took over two hours to get there. The journey through London gave me plenty of time to think. I wasn't shocked by my mother's homosexuality. Her love for Helen made perfect sense. It was suddenly so self-evident: their close intimacy after Christopher's birth, her summary rejection of my father, the intense conversations in the evening. And then I thought of her words to my grandmother that afternoon outside the bathroom, how she'd accused her of making her life 'thoroughly miserable'. By miserable, she meant repressed. She'd been directed by my grandmother's fussy love into a life where she wasn't free to love the only friend she had in the world. I thumped the steering wheel for her; for the life she hadn't been strong enough to own, appalled that she'd gone to such lengths to keep her truth from me. As I stared at the third set of temporary traffic lights I encountered that afternoon, I saw that my grandmother had done a thorough job on her. And, by consequence, on me. I felt the fragment of my mother's dishonesty within me. The piercing shard that led me to seek out David and shred all that was good in my life.

People talk about coming to terms with a person's death. I've heard and accepted the platitude many times. It's always well-meant, and its meaning is that you must accept the permanent and inarguable absence of someone you love. But that's what I raged against that terrible afternoon in the car. The terms. That the revelation she'd loved me but never trusted me with the truth came when there was no more of her to ask. When I was a lost daughter, sifting through her body parts, looking for the woman that was my mother.

I phoned Andrea just after five, when it became clear I wouldn't be there when she arrived.

'I'll head to the champagne bar, in that case. Come and find me when you get here.'

'I won't go into it now but I really don't feel like celebrating.'

'I've had an old man's groin in my face since Market Harborough. And now I don't. I think that's worth celebrating.'

I parked on a side street just after six and ran to the station. I needn't have worried: Andrea was already well into her second glass, the bubbles removing all memory of an uncomfortable journey. I wanted to join her at the top of her tall glass. I wanted to taste the sharp fizz and forget it all. She lifted the bottle from the ice bucket and, grasping it too close to the neck, her fingers whitened as she poured it unsteadily into the glass. 'Cheers, me dears.'

'Thank you. Sorry I'm late.'

'Don't worry. I'm just pleased you're here. I assume we're going to get something to eat?'

'If you want. I'm not massively hungry, but we can.'

'We need to. I've got literally nothing in my fridge.'

'Andrea, do you know what literally means?'

'Yes.'

'It means there's absolutely nothing in your fridge. How can that possibly be true? Are you telling me you don't have butter or mayonnaise?'

'I don't eat butter.'

'But you understand what I'm saying?'

'Everyone says literally now. It doesn't mean what it used to. The man on the train literally had his cock in my face.'

'I didn't think, after the day I've had, that it would be possible for me to laugh again. But there you go,' I said, raising my glass. 'Thank God for the mentally defective.'

'Cheers. So what's happened? What's so awful?'

'Just stuff about my mother. And grandmother, as it happens. I'm still trying to work it all out.'

'Is she still alive?'

'Oh yes. Alive and demented.'

'Was she at the funeral?'

'She was, but only briefly. You wouldn't have even noticed her. The care home arranged for her to attend the ceremony.'

'So what did she do?'

'She was an English teacher.'

'No, what did she do to your mum?'

'I don't know,' I said, sipping champagne. 'Well, I think I do. She was just very rigid in her views on everything. And I'm starting to realise it had more of an effect on my mother than, you know, than I first thought.'

'Can you go and see her? Talk to her?'

'I know where she is. I'm just not sure I have the energy for this,' I said, lowering my forehead to the table. Andrea reached out to rest her hand on the crown of my head.

'I worry about you, Laura. What with all the stuff with Tom. Why don't you just give yourself a break for a little while?'

'Because I just have to know,' I said, looking up at her. 'It's completely mad, but there you go: I come from a long line of crazy women.'

My grandmother and mother were reconciled by the time my father left in 1991. With my mother on her own, my grandparents decided to begin drip-feeding – in modest monthly instalments – my mother her inheritance. This money, together with my father's maintenance payments, allowed her to continue her simple existence. Her relationship with her parents wasn't exactly loving, but it was warm, and she was close enough to notice, several years after losing my grandfather, that my grandmother kept forgetting things, that her movements were slowing down and she was sleeping more. In 2009, before her condition worsened, my grandmother agreed to the sale of her house. A proportion of it was set aside for her care in a residential nursing home in Southborough, an expensive conservation area in Surbiton. The rest of it went to my mother.

The care home was on a wide, tree-lined residential road. It was a wet, slightly chilly Thursday afternoon at the end of September. The Indian summer everyone had been so excited about had given way to a bog-standard autumn; the leaves lay in soggy piles on the pavement. I parked on the road and walked up to the gate. The building had been formed by joining two Victorian houses. The red brick-work, so coveted by the mighty of Surbiton, looked damp and unprotected. I was told to wait in reception while somebody went to tell my grandmother I had arrived. Ten minutes later, a young male orderly in his twenties came to escort me to her room. He had a tattoo on his left fore-arm of a wolf. I tilted my head to the right as I strained to get a good look at it. He glanced at me and smiled: 'It's a grey wolf.'

'Wow. What's the significance?'

'A quote by Virgil. It's just stayed with me: "It never troubles the wolf how many the sheep may be".'

'Why didn't you have that tattooed on?'

'Too many words.'

'Right.'

He tapped lightly on the door of my grandmother's room, waited a few seconds and then opened it wide. She was sit-ting in an armchair by the window. There was a small table at her knees and another armchair opposite, presumably for me. I assumed that during the ten minutes I'd been waiting, somebody – perhaps Wolf man – had placed a tray with a teapot, milk, a bowl of sugar and two cups on the table in front of her. That's what you get in an expensive care home:

service from a tattooed orderly, versed in the classics. Her room was on the ground floor, and commanded a view of the bleak and blown garden.

'Hi Jean!' The orderly filled her small room with manufactured cheer.

'Good afternoon, Neil,' my grandmother said, stiffly.

'Your granddaughter's here!' he shouted.

'Yes, I can see that. Thank you.'

He backed out and smiled at me with an apologetic look, as if to say *you're on your own now*.

I approached the waiting armchair and sat down. My grandmother continued to look out the window.

'Hi, Granny.'

'Good afternoon.'

'I'm Laura. Katharine's daughter.'

'I know who you are.' She turned to me and smiled. 'I remember you from the wedding.'

'Do you mean funeral? I was at the funeral.'

'Yes, the funeral. That's right.' She looked down at her hands, folded neatly in her lap.

'Katharine's funeral. Do you remember?'

'Kathy's dead. Yes, I know. They came and told me.' She began twisting her wedding ring. 'How did she die, if you don't mind my asking?'

'She fell down the stairs.'

'Yes. That's right. I always told her, "Go down on your bottom!" That way if you fall you won't hurt yourself, you see.'

'Yes. But Granny, she was fifty-one. She was an adult when it happened.'

'Oh yes, I know that.' She raised her fingers to her lips, considering what I'd just said. 'How old did you say she was?'

'Fifty-one. She was born in 1961.'

'Yes, exactly. The twentieth of January. They kept me in for a week, I remember! Do you have children?'

'No. I don't have any children.'

'Such a shame for you. It's all I ever wanted, to have children.'

'Yes.'

'But I only had the one. Her name was Katharine. I used to take her for walks in the park. In the pram. She was such a quiet baby, never used to cry.'

'That must have been nice for you.'

'I wanted her to speak.'

'What do you mean? When she was a baby?'

'Babies don't speak, dear. No, when she went to school. I wanted her to speak up for herself. And not let others do it for her.'

I reached out to lift the teapot. 'Do you mind if I pour?'

'What?' And then she remembered the tea. 'Oh, damn. Yes, pour it now, please. Oh, it'll be stewed—'

'That's OK. I don't mind. Look, it's fine, Granny.'

She looked at me warily and sat back in her armchair.

'What did you mean just then, about not letting others speak for her?'

'Speak for whom?'

'For my mother. Sorry, for Katharine.'

'Who is speaking for Katharine?'

'You said that when she went to school, you wanted her to speak more. That you didn't want others doing it for her.'

'I didn't want *Helen* doing it for her.'

I put my cup down on its saucer. 'Did Helen speak for her?'

'All the time! Kathy hardly said a word in infant school. That girl spoke for everyone.'

'They were very good friends, weren't they?'

'Kathy didn't have any friends.'

'But she had Helen?'

'Oh yes, she had Helen. She was always there. I used to say to Paul, if you want to find Katharine, look for Helen.' She nodded at me, as though this were sage advice.

'Is that why you sent her away?'

'I didn't send anyone away!'

'Sorry. I just wondered if you knew why Helen went away, when they were at the grammar school.'

'The grammar school. She should never have been there. Couldn't behave herself like the nice girls.'

'What do you mean?'

'Oh, I don't know.' She raised her hands to her eyes. I could see I'd gone too far. That the effort of remembering was too troubling.

'I'm sorry, I don't mean to upset you. I'm just interested in my mother's life.'

'Kathy. She is your mother.'

'Yes.'

'You're my granddaughter.'

'That's right.'

'Laura.'

'Exactly.'

'When is Kathy going to come to see me?'

'She's dead. She died.'

'How did she die?'

'She fell down the stairs.'

'I always knew that girl would come to no good.'

I always knew that girl would come to no good. My grandmother's words were ringing in my ears as I walked back to my car. She didn't make friends with the nice girls. She got herself pregnant by someone she hardly knew. She didn't go down the stairs on her bottom. My mother. The failed flesh.

I got home around 5 p.m. and, without taking my boots off, lay down on the sofa. The flat was so quiet. And empty. I looked at my phone and thought of Tom, willing him to call. I locked the screen and put it on my chest. I still had a couple of hours before I had to think about food, so I decided to close my eyes. I don't know how long I was asleep for but I was woken by the sound of a phone ringing. It was familiar enough to pull me back into consciousness, but it wasn't my mobile. It was the landline. I never used it – I'd purchased the service purely for the purposes of broadband. And the only person who had ever phoned me on it was my mother. I got up and walked across the room; it was on one of my bookshelves, tucked behind some old batteries I'd taken out of the remote control once and a container of paperclips.

'Hello?'

'Hello. May I speak with Laura Rowan, please?'

'Speaking.'

'Hello, Laura. May I call you Laura?'

'Yes. Who is this, please?'

'Detective Constable Jane Marsh. I'm with the Metropolitan Police. Do you have a moment to talk to me?'

'Yes, of course. What's the matter? What's happened?'

'Nothing's happened, and I don't want you to worry, but I'd like to have a little chat with you if I may. I called round earlier this afternoon but there was nobody home.'

'Yes, I was out. Visiting my grandmother.'

'OK, that's no problem. Will you be around tomorrow morning, say around ten?'

'Yes, I can be. Sorry, what's this regarding?'

'It's regarding the accident your mother had in her home

back in . . .' I heard the sound of papers being shuffled. 'February. Yes. Some new information has come to light.'

'And what's that?'

'It's better if we speak in person, I think. I'll come and see you tomorrow morning at ten. If that's OK.'

'Yes. See you tomorrow.'

Jane was around five foot five inches in height, a little shorter than me, but quite stocky. She looked like she went to the gym a lot – the sort of person who drinks a kale and spinach smoothie before running to work. She was wearing a grey trouser suit with a white shirt underneath. She smiled warmly as I opened the door and lifted her warrant card in greeting. 'Laura?'

'Yes, come in.'

'Thank you. I hope you don't mind me dropping in on you like this. It's just sometimes these things are easier to discuss in person rather than on the phone.'

'Can I make you a cup of tea?' I said, showing her to the sofa.

'No, thank you. I've just had a coffee.'

I pulled a chair over from the dining table. 'What's this all about?' I asked, sitting down.

She sat down as I did, but the sofa cushions were too soft and deep. She nudged herself forward so she could perch on the edge and straighten her back.

'As I said to you last night, we've had some new information come to light.'

'And what's that?'

'Your mother's neighbour, a Mrs . . .' She began flicking through the pages of her notebook. 'A Mrs Harris, got in touch with her local neighbourhood team to say she had reason to believe your mother was not alone in the house the morning she died. She said she tried to get in touch with you herself.'

'Yes! Shit, I never got back to her. It's just that she spoke to the estate agent we appointed. Not to me directly. And then I broke up with my boyfriend.' It all sounded so feeble.

'Listen, don't worry. I'm sure it's nothing to worry about. She's coming in tomorrow to give a written statement, but before she does, I just want to ask you a few questions.'

'OK.'

'Can you think of anyone who might have been with her that morning?'

'No. As far as I'm aware, she was alone.'

'And, I'm sorry to ask, but you're in the process of selling the house. Do you stand to gain financially from the sale?'

'Indirectly, yes. But I'm selling it on behalf of my father.'

'And why can't he do that himself?'

'It's complicated. He lives with his partner and she's pressuring him to move to Guildford. I think he just thought it would be easier if I managed the sale.'

Detective Constable Marsh began writing quickly and then flicked back through her notebook. 'That's Richard Rowan and Jenny Warren. They're not married?'

'No. My parents never divorced.'

'And why was that?'

'I don't know. You'll have to ask my dad about that.'

'OK. I think that's all I need for now. I'll be in touch as soon as I have something more for you. Try not to worry – things like this happen all the time. It doesn't mean anything untoward has happened. We just have to investigate, that's all.'

'Of course.'

'What's the best number to reach you on?'

The spinal cord had been transected by dislocation of the atlanto-occipital joint.

On 12 February 2012, the last morning of my mother's life, I slept late and deeply. I opened my eyes, looking for the terrible thing I'd done the night before, and there beside me was David. Heavier and hairier, his mouth was open, tired and sour from the night before, offering a light snore in his defence. On my bedside table was the opened condom packet, thrown there in an attitude of spontaneous protection.

He had emailed me at the newspaper a week earlier. Seeing his name appear suddenly in my inbox had hit me hard. I stared at the screen in an agony of disbelief. I told myself I didn't have to open it, that I could delete, or read and delete, but my heart gave me away. It was already thumping to a delirious new beat. One with David back in my life.

The email itself was classic cut-and-cover, roofing over the depth of our estrangement with shallow, commonplace enquiries. He congratulated me on my blog and column, and professed himself an admirer of my writing, and, without any reference to his wife and daughter, asked me if I'd like to meet for a drink.

I read it several times before forwarding it to Andrea with the preface: *This is the guy I was telling you about. The one from Cambridge.*

Her reply was swift and to the point: *Isn't he married with a kid?*

Yes. What do you think? I wrote, ignoring the obvious.

Andrea, not one for evasion, forced me to confront the central problem: *I think you should ask him how his wife is.*

I knew Andrea was right, and over the next few days wrote several versions of a suitable response. They varied significantly in length and tone. The first one, stirred by the excitement of first contact, was pleasant and self-consciously humble, loaded with references to my own success and independence. Another draft, written one evening after several glasses of wine, was full of nostalgia and longing. A longing that gave way to a penultimate paragraph full of anger at how our friendship had ended. Finally, a week after receiving his email, I replied with the following: *Hi Dave. It was a surprise to hear from you after such a long time. I understand you and Sarah got married and are now parents. Congratulations. All going well this end – work is busy and I live in Balham now. A drink would be nice – let me know when you're around and hopefully we can catch up properly. Laura.*

He replied within an hour and suggested Saturday night. He even offered to come to Balham. His eagerness vindicated Andrea's caution. I should never have replied, but the thrill of his impatience to see me was intoxicating. It made me feel both frightened and delirious. Every action, every movement, was an indistinct event compared to the one on the horizon. The one I could accept at a moment's notice. His email made me feel wealthy and assured in the most perilous way.

We arranged to meet in a wine bar just off Garrick Street at eight o'clock. As I got on the tube at Balham, I thought of that summer's day back in 2001 when I'd last travelled by underground to see him, full of desire and optimism. I looked up at the map, silently counting down the stops, and felt the dry pain of that afternoon rise up again. I wanted to go back; back to my second year, back to Balham, but the tube hurtled forward, fixed to a black line that led inexorably to a bar near Leicester Square where David waited, suddenly and unaccountably keen to see me.

He was sitting at the bar, his shoulders hunched, his scalp lit mercilessly by the overhead lamps. He was stockier than I remembered, but unmistakably him. I walked up to the bar just as he turned round. He stood up, forcing his feet into the narrow gap between his bar stool and me. We were too close, his chest unnervingly near my eyeline. It was wide and self-consciously heroic. I fought the urge to laugh and instead took a step back. I smiled and he tried to smile back, but I saw the look of panic in his eyes. I made eye contact with the barman behind him and said, 'A glass of white wine, please. Would you like another?'

The question disarmed him, provided an urgency that took the pressure off our reconciliation. He looked at his pint glass and ordered another. 'Please. Sit down,' he said, indicating the stool next to him. 'It's great to see you.'

'And you. Have you been waiting long?'

'No, not at all. Just got here,' he said, looking over at the barman as though he might contradict him.

'How are things?'

'Good, thanks. Living in Buckinghamshire now.'

'Oh, right,' I said, noticing the absence of a pronoun. 'And where do you work?'

'Near Marylebone, so it's really handy. You get a lot more for your money out there.'

'So I hear.'

'How about you? You're in Balham, did you say?'

'Yes, I bought my flat there about three years ago now, 2009. Pretty small, but it's mine. I'm too old for housemates now.'

'I know,' he said, rolling his eyes in understanding.

'How's Sarah?'

He swallowed hard and put his glass down. 'She's fine. Yeah, really well, thanks.'

'And your daughter? How old is she?'

'Bea's seven. She keeps us busy.'

'I bet.'

'How about you?'

'Do I have any kids? No, no kids. I'm not married either.'

The noise of the bar rose up and into the silence, parading itself before our defeated attention. I sipped my wine and looked down at my fingers. Our conversation had grown thick and inert. He asked about my work, what had made me start my blog in the first place and if I was still in touch with people from university. We drank quickly, picking at people from the past, amusing ourselves with stories made funny by wild and careless recollection. As we got away from the reserve that had circled us at the beginning of the evening, I asked him if he still thought Robert Browning was a fucking bellend, and we laughed hard. All that was predictable and mundane fell away as we chewed over our lives, jostling and nudging, renewed to wit and banter by a connection that hadn't waned with time or distance. It was exquisite and without pain. A last chance for both of us. And we took it.

We left the bar and walked to the Lamb and Flag, a small, stuffy pub that promised greater intimacy. The new venue threatened to break the spell, but with a touch, a smile, a story, it was quickly re-established. We avoided any mention of Sarah and his daughter, aware that they would turn our clumsy joy to sordid betrayal. But we both knew what was going to happen.

By ten o'clock we were drunk and hungry. He looked to me for answers and I suggested an Italian restaurant in Soho. He nodded his head and, in answer, grabbed my hand and kissed my palm with his eyes closed. I watched him hold my hand gently, splaying my fingers on the back of his, and knew I would have to make a decision. With the other hand I reached out to stroke his face in silent forgiveness.

Buoyed by agreement, we left the pub and hailed a cab on Long Acre. Our hands entwined on the back seat, we stared straight ahead at the dark road and the driver who couldn't get us back to Balham soon enough.

The following morning I got out of bed quietly and walked down the hallway, into the living room. Too hungover to process emotion, all I could do was survey the wreckage and pick a path of least resistance. I walked into the kitchen and filled the kettle, confident a cup of tea would sort me out, but as I poured the milk onto the tea bag and watched it balloon into the brown water I felt my stomach retract in disgust. I left the cup where it was, put the milk back in the fridge and went to lie down on the sofa.

I must have fallen asleep, because I woke around eleven to the sound of the bathroom door closing and then the shower being turned on. I pushed myself up into a seated position and let my feet drift down to the carpet. My stomach was still horribly empty. I put my head down between my legs and looked at my toenails, hot-pink and indifferent. It had all seemed like such a good idea last night. I sat there with my head hanging for a few minutes before standing up slowly. I walked back towards my bedroom, but as I passed the bathroom door I heard David's voice speak into the wet heat. For a moment I thought he was talking to me, but then I realised he was on the phone: 'All OK here, thanks. Just got out of the shower.

'No, Mark's cooking us breakfast. I'll leave after that.

'Think my train is at one, so should be fine.

'OK. Yep. See you later,' and then, very quietly, 'love you too.'

My brain was faster than my legs – by the time I'd processed that his conversation was with Sarah, it was too late to dash back to the living room. He opened the door and released the pent-up steam of his stolen shower. We stared at each other, defeated by the morning and our divergent realities: I had to drive over to my mother's for lunch, and he had to go home to his family.

He followed me into my bedroom and began the process of dressing and retracting. 'I'm sorry—'

'Don't. Please.' He waited for me to continue. 'It happened. And it shouldn't have. We both drank too much.' He smiled ruefully and, sitting down on the edge of my bed, began to pull an unwilling sock over his damp foot. 'Go home to Sarah.' He stopped and looked up.

'I will. I mean, I am.'

I looked down at the toes I'd painted so optimistically last night.

'It was great to see you, though,' he said.

I pulled at the hem of my nightshirt, holding it away from the contours of my breasts and belly. I wanted him gone. 'I need to have a shower and head over to my mother's house.'

'OK,' he said, looking for his jeans. He stood up to pull them on. 'I'll get my things.' He grabbed his phone and keys from my bedside table, and as he walked past me and into the hallway he reached for my hand. 'I wish things could have been different.' I let him hold my hand, knowing nothing could stop this goodbye. That it had a momentum of its own. I continued staring at his chest until I felt his face descend to mine. He kissed me gently on the lips. I pulled my hand away and opened the front door. He disappeared down the stairs without another word.

I walked back into the kitchen, averting my eyes from the cold and abandoned tea on the work surface and reached for the loaf in the bread bin. I toasted two slices with renewed purpose, buttering them generously, and then took the first bite. There wasn't enough saliva in my mouth to break down the unwieldy toast, but I forced myself to eat it.

I checked my phone and saw that Andrea had texted just two words: *Did you?* I put it down and went to have a shower. The hot water reminded me of normality, but as I lifted my left leg onto the side of the bath in order to shave it, my stomach finally surrendered the chunks of half-chewed toast into the soapy suds that had collected at the plughole.

I got out of the shower, combed through my damp hair and got dressed slowly. I patted some splodges of foundation under my eyes to cover the worst of the darkness there and made my way downstairs and into my car, not knowing my mother would never see my face again. That she was already dead.

I knocked on the front door, rang the bell and eventually searched through my bag to find the spare key. I put the key in the lock and tried to convince myself that she'd popped out. But when I saw the door hadn't been deadlocked and the alarm was off, I knew the heavy silence of the house was ominous. I opened the door slowly and stepped over the threshold, peering into the hallway. I pushed the door further and tried to widen its arc, but something soft and obdurate blocked it on the other side. I looked down and saw that I was standing on strands of my mother's brown hair. I knew what it was. I knew what it must mean. I turned my right shoulder into the hallway and slid along the wall so I could really know. Her head was turned away from me, at a perfect right angle to her body. Her legs were raised, still upon the stairs, but her skirt had risen where she fell, exposing her thighs. It was so sudden and irrevocable. So incontrovertibly true.

I knelt beside her and called her name. At first quietly, and then with panic when I saw her eyes were open. Frozen in terror. I put my hand on her cheek but it was firm and cold to the touch. It reminded me of the weeks before Christopher was born, when her body had pushed me from her. She had grabbed for me then. Tried to pull me closer. But all I could see were her eyes, wide and anxious to explain.

I stood up and reached for my bag, emptying its contents onto the floor to find my phone. I dialled 999 and told the operator my mother was dead. She dispatched an ambulance immediately. I repeated, as though she had misheard me, that she was dead. In a tone of voice both practised and exasperated, the operator informed me a paramedic would still have to attend the scene. I ended the call and phoned Helen. She answered promptly, sharply: 'Laura? Is that you? Is everything OK?' Her voice was so clear and interrogative that I found my own, shrinking and sliding down the stairs to rest on top of my mother's head.

'She's dead.' I swallowed the lump and heard an intake of breath so painful I closed my eyes and braced myself for the exhalation. But it didn't come. Just silence. And then a changed Helen, one seeking to clarify, to ask me, as though I were an overexcited teenager, if I was sure.

'Yes, I'm sure,' and then unwillingly, 'she's lying here in front of me.'

'Laura. Listen to me. Have you phoned for an ambulance?'

'Yes. It's on its way. But Helen, she's gone.' Repeating the announcement opened the floodgates to my own ugly, gulping shock. Gone. I choked on the pain of it. When I found my voice again, Helen was no longer on the other end. I put my phone down on the floor and closed the front door. I sat down beside her, invited by her right hand, flat to the floor, to interlace my fingers with her own. I tried as best I could, but rigor mortis was greedy for her; her hand was already cold and unresponsive.

Some minutes later, I have no idea how many, I heard the siren and saw the blue lights of the ambulance fire intermittently through the stained glass of the front door panels and then onto the wooden floorboards of the hallway. The footsteps on the driveway were abrupt and culminated in loud knocks on the door. I wished then that I hadn't made such a fuss. All I wanted, at that moment, was to sit beside my mother's body for a little while longer. In cold and quiet contemplation. But the people knocking at the door began shouting through the letter box to open up.

My mother's corpse was examined by a paramedic who went about his task with discreet efficiency. He checked her pupils, her pulse, called out lividity and rigor mortis and pronounced her life extinct at 2.16 p.m. I stood and watched this administrative ritual with sombre fascination. He asked his partner to call the police as he guided me out of the hallway and into the living room. I resisted the professional push and asked him about the removal of her body.

'Are you going to take her away?'

'Her body is the property of the Coroner now. They will arrange for removal and, more than likely, a post-mortem.'

'Can't she stay here? With me?' And then, the absurdly irrelevant: 'We were supposed to have lunch together.' I stood with my hands hanging beside me. I must have looked so helpless because he said, kindly, 'Do you have any family you can call? A friend, perhaps?'

Into this stand-off came Helen's voice from the driveway. The front door was open, but not enough to permit a view of my mother's body.

'Laura? Where are you? Can I come in?' There was no time to answer. She marched into the hallway and stood before the paramedic and me expectantly, as if she were waiting for us to explain ourselves. She had not seen the corpse on the floor behind her. I looked down at my mother and she followed my gaze, turning on her heel.

For as long as I can remember, Helen had been strong. Her sheer force of will was enough to hold my mother up at times of great weakness, to pull our family from the mire and encourage us all to keep going. But when she saw my mother's dead body, something broke inside her. She moaned at the pain of it and tried to kneel down beside her head, but the paramedic stopped her, preventing her from this final act of support.

'I must ask you not to touch the body. The police will be here shortly. I need to ask you both to step away from the scene entirely, please.'

We went and sat on the living room sofa, side by side, as though we'd been very naughty. I looked around the room, understanding for the first time that the books on the shelves and pictures on the wall were the possessions of a dead person.

They already wore the dusty, neglected aspect of items that have been forgotten. Left behind.

Helen sat with her head in her hands. She looked as though she were trying to work something out: an equation of such complexity that her head needed her hands as a stand. I was waiting for her to cry. Her tears would be the starter pistol for my own grief; I couldn't have my mother's friend outsprint my own sorrow. But she didn't cry and, consequently, neither did I. I got up and walked over to the bookshelves.

The police arrived around three o'clock and asked me a series of questions: what relation was I to the deceased; what time had I discovered the body; had I touched or moved anything; how long did I wait before calling the emergency services; was anybody else in the house when she died. They were endless and clinical. *The body. The deceased.* My mother's death had already taken on a life of its own, one that would be constructed by stationery and administered by laser printers, held together by staples and sealed in A5 envelopes. Over-whelmed by what she'd become, I told them, fearfully, that I had stepped on her hair and stroked her cheek. The female police officer nodded her head in understanding, as though such bland interference with the scene was to be expected. Helen remained impassive and silent beside me.

They arranged for the body to be removed, suggesting, with practised concern, that I remain in the living room while they wheeled her out. Helen stood by the bay window with her back to us, watching as they loaded my mother's dead body into the private ambulance. Her back was straight and strong.

'When can I see her again?' I asked one of the police of-ficers with rising panic, as I realised they were taking my mother away from me.

'You'll have to deal with the Coroner's office from now on. There's a number you can ring on those papers. You'll need some form of ID.'

I nodded. And then realised I didn't understand. 'For me?'

'For you, yes. You are the next of kin, aren't you?'

I thought of my father and brother for the first time. That I would have to inform them of her death. 'Yes.'

'And what about a funeral? When can we sort that out?' asked Helen. She had turned back to the room, direct and snappy.

'It all depends on the Coroner. They can sometimes issue what's called an Interim Certificate of Fact of Death so you can arrange a funeral. If that happens, the inquest is usually adjourned to a later date. But I don't know. I can't second-guess the Coroner's office.'

I nodded, stunned by all that was suddenly expected of me. Her body was mine but had to be opened up and inspected by a stranger, and then I could dispose of her as I pleased? Just as I'd once been passed to her, here she was being passed back to me. It was confusing.

'Let me drive you home,' Helen said.

'No, I'm OK. I'll drive myself.'

But she wouldn't go. She sat down on an armchair and waited for the police to gather their things and leave.

'I could follow you home, then. Stay with you for a little while. I can't bear the thought of you on your own after this.'

'I want to be on my own. I need time to just understand. I don't understand, Helen. How can it have happened?'

'I don't know. God, I don't know. She must have slipped and gone down the whole lot.'

'Her neck. It looked strange.'

'Don't torture yourself, Laura. They'll be able to tell us what happened after the post-mortem.'

'She was all alone.' I began to cry. 'She must have been so frightened.'

Helen looked down at my feet as her face contorted in time with my own.

'I can't stay here,' I said suddenly. I didn't want to share my grief with Helen. I felt, even in those first moments, an instinctive urge to claim my mother as my own.

She stood up and put her coat on. I locked up and reset the alarm, conscious with every movement that the most valuable thing in my life had already been driven away. Helen hugged me, briefly and without emotion, before she got into her car, a battered Volkswagen Polo. I watched her drive away before beginning my own long and lonely journey home.

We decided her funeral should be a humanist one; my mother was not religious in any way. She cared only for the kind of carefully crafted fiction she could inhabit. Hardy's Wessex, or Eliot's Middlemarch. The implausible vignettes of the New Testament afforded her no foothold and, consequently, she had no time for the landscape of Christ. The service was held at Kingston Crematorium on Tuesday 21 February at twelve thirty in the afternoon. Shrove Tuesday, as Helen pointed out the Saturday before. She drove over to Balham to help me choose the readings and make the final catering arrangements.

'Is that significant?' I asked.

'Not unless you want to make pancakes.'

'I don't remember ever making pancakes at home. So I'm not about to start now.'

'Well, forget pancakes. How many people have come back to you to say they're coming?'

I looked down at my list and counted the names. 'Twenty-four, including Dad and Jenny.'

'And the kid? What's she called?'

'Ellie.'

'Ellie. Is she coming?'

'I don't think so.'

'And where are we with Christopher?'

'His flight lands on Monday evening at Heathrow.'

'Are you going to collect him, or shall I?'

'No, he wants to spend the night in a hotel. Get himself together before the funeral.'

'No Steph, then?'

'Somebody has to feed the dogs.'

Helen rolled her eyes. 'Is there anything else we need to decide?'

'I think that's it for now. Did you have a look at those readings I sent you?'

'I did. I think I'll go with the Khalil Gibran.' She looked around at my dark and messy flat. 'Laura, would you like me to come and stay with you for a few days? At least until after the funeral. This is no time to be on your own.'

'I'll be fine. Thank you. I've just got to get through this bit and I'll be fine.'

I woke around four thirty on the morning of her funeral, and as soon as I began thinking of the day ahead, the flames that would consume her coffin, I knew that sleep was lost to me. I tossed and turned for some time, tried to read and finally gave up, getting out of bed at six thirty. She was everywhere: in the sun rising to tell me today would be replaced by another day and then another until it didn't hurt so much. She was in my bathroom as I looked at my face in the mirror, a trivial version of her own. And at the bottom of the stairs as I pulled the front door open to leave.

I set off around ten thirty and drove myself to the funeral home in Kingston. Christopher was already there, dressed in a dark grey suit with a black tie. His eyes were red and narrow. The sight of my baby brother made me want to weep. He'd been summoned from the other side of the world to say goodbye to a woman he didn't know was leaving. It made me want to howl for him and for me. She'd gone, and left us nothing but her body. And we were about to burn it. I couldn't make any sense of it.

Though we were equals in grief, united by loss, I still wanted to take his away from him. I sat down beside him and put my arm around his shoulders. He bowed his head to the sudden warmth and I felt his shoulders lift with a dry sob. Neither of us could speak into the emotion of that moment.

We were invited to the viewing parlour where she had been laid out. I took Christopher's hand and together we approached and peered over. It felt surreal to suddenly see her, made up and dressed nicely, in a Kingston funeral home. As though she'd spent the last nine days hiding away so she could reinvent herself as a corpse. I bit my lip in muted pain.

Christopher and I were led outside to a funeral car gleaming with grief. It swallowed us easily and gaped expectantly for more mourners. We sat, small and abandoned, on the back seat, lost without our mother. Her coffin had already been placed in the hearse in front of us, and so, with sombre courtesy, the funeral director signalled to his driver to begin the short journey to Kingston Crematorium.

Our modest cortège made its way through Kingston's

one-way system to the cemetery. The chapel was at the end of a long driveway. Helen was waiting outside for us, as were my father and Jenny. She stood speaking-distance apart from them, watching only for my mother, the return of her friend.

My mother's coffin was carried into the chapel and placed on the bier. We took our seats at the front, in uneasy expectation of the flames to come. My grandmother was led to a seat near the front by a middle-aged man in a suit. He whispered something in her ear and gave her an order of service. She nodded her head and began fishing in her bag for her reading glasses. Helen sat behind us, next to the aisle, and as the ceremony began, she stepped forward with her reading. I felt my father shift uncomfortably beside me as she turned to face the congregation. It was a short passage about drinking '. . . from the river of silence', and how a soul shall 'truly dance' when the earth claims them. When the reading came to an end, she didn't move. She just stood before us with her head bowed, as though unconvinced by her own words. And then she walked up to my mother's coffin, slowly and alone. She put both hands down on the lid and looked as though she was trying to decide what to do. Then she bent her head down low to the wood and whispered a final, private communication to the silence within.

I had a meeting with Andy on the morning of Monday, 1 October 2012. I had to be in central London for nine thirty. It was a beautiful bright morning. The air was crisp and cold, acceding to autumn. As I walked to the tube station, my phone rang. It was a number I didn't recognise, and half-hoping it would be Tom, moved by the beginning of another week to try again, I answered it.

'Laura? It's Jane Marsh here. Have I caught you at a bad time?'

'No,' I said, swallowing my disappointment. 'What can I do for you?' I'd reached the mouth of the station entrance. Commuters flowed past me on either side, their irritation sudden and unstoppable.

'I'd really like to have another quick chat with you, if I may. Can you get to Sutton police station?'

'When?' I looked at my watch; it was a quarter to nine.

'Ideally this morning. Some important new information has come to light, and I'd like to discuss it with you. In person, if possible.'

'OK. I have a meeting this morning. Can it wait until after that?'

'I would suggest you try to reschedule your meeting. Would that be OK?'

'Yes. I can do that. I'll have to walk back and collect my car.'

'OK. Just ask for me at the front desk when you get here.'

I phoned Andy as I jogged back to my road. He didn't pick up, but I left a voicemail that was suitably vague yet urgent.

I made my way to Sutton and left my car in a supermarket car park across the road. Jane came down to the waiting area promptly – she wasn't wearing a jacket and her hair was tied back in a ponytail – and invited me upstairs to what looked like a small conference room.

'Would you like a tea or coffee?'

'No, thank you.'

'Cup of water?'

'No, nothing. Thank you.'

'OK,' she said, pulling the chair beside me out and turning it so she was at an angle. I followed her lead and turned my chair away from the table and opposite her. We both crossed our legs. She opened her beige manila folder. 'I think I told you on the phone that some new information has come to light.'

'Yes,' I said, trying not to sound impatient.

'Laura, I just want to reiterate that there's nothing for you to worry about at this stage. I'm here to ask a few questions, and to decide whether we need to involve a different team in the investigation of your mother's death. Is that OK?'

I nodded my head. Speaking felt like an impossibility.

'Are you sure you don't want some water?'

I nodded again and Jane jumped up, pleased I'd finally come to my senses and accepted a beverage. She put a polystyrene cup full of cold water in front of me.

'Last Friday, we interviewed a Mrs Eileen Harris of 119 Crane View Road, Surbiton. Mrs Harris has told us that on the morning of 12 February 2012, she overheard two female voices in the rear garden of 121 Crane View Road. Laura, can you confirm that this was your mother's address?'

'Yes. It was her address, but she didn't live there.'

Jane looked up from her paperwork. 'Can you tell me more about that, please?'

'I've found out, very recently, that she spent most of her time at her friend's house.'

'Her friend. And who would that be?'

'Helen Saunders.'

Jane frowned at the name and looked through some papers at the back of the folder. 'Helen Saunders. She was at the house when you found your mother's body? Her name is included here on the original police paperwork.'

'No, she wasn't there when I found her. I phoned her after calling the ambulance. She came straight over.'

'Yes, yes,' she said, nodding at her paperwork. 'And now you say your mother was living at Helen's. In what capacity were they living together?'

'They were together. They were, you know, they were lovers.'

'And you weren't aware of this until recently? When exactly did you find out?'

'Last month. It was probably two or three weeks ago. I went to see Helen. For other reasons. But during the course of my visit, it became clear that my mother had been living there.'

'You say it became clear. What made it clear?'

'I found something that belonged to her. One of her books.'

'I see,' she noted it down. 'Anything else?'

I thought of my mother's abdomen and the porridge. It felt too fanciful, too self-conscious, to use the contents of my mother's stomach in this conversation. 'Helen was quite happy to tell me the truth. It was my mother who had been trying to hide the fact that she was gay.'

'And was that something that frustrated Helen?'

'I mean, yes. Possibly. I don't know. What does this have to do with my mother's death?'

'Mrs Harris has told us she saw a grey Volkswagen Polo parked outside your mother's house on 12 February 2012. Do you have any idea who that car might belong to?'

'Helen. That's Helen's car. But like I said, I phoned her very soon after finding my mother. She was there for a good while. With me.'

'According to Mrs Harris, her car was there much earlier in the day. For several hours.' Jane pulled a piece of paper from the folder and placed it down on the desk, turning it round so I could read it. 'She believes the Volkswagen Polo was outside your mother's house from nine a.m. until around eleven thirty. It then reappeared later that afternoon, after the arrival of the ambulance. At around two forty-five.'

Part Three

Cause of Death

Cause of Death
1a. Traumatic fracture-dislocation of atlanto-occipital joint with transection of spinal cord.

I phoned Tom as soon as I got out of the station. By the time he answered I was crying, my mouth so contorted I couldn't form the words.

She'd been there. She'd left her at the bottom of the stairs.

'Laura? Is that you? What's going on?'

Several hours. Two voices.

'Laura, answer me. Is everything OK?'

I always knew that girl would come to no good. My grandmother had been talking about Helen. Not my mother.

'Please. Please. I need you.'

'Where are you?'

'Sutton. Police station. Please.'

'I'm on my way. Stay where you are.'

I walked back to the car park, fearful that a passing police officer would see me crying outside and try to take me back inside. The sun had warmed the inside of my car so that it felt hot and unbearably stuffy. I thought of Helen's car parked on the driveway and felt the bile rise up in my throat. I managed to jump out before vomiting. A woman with two small children in a trolley full of shopping returned to the car parked beside mine as I stood there, bent over the mess I'd made.

'Are you OK?'

I nodded my head but didn't look up.

'Here,' she said, holding a wet wipe out to me. I grabbed it from her hand and managed to mumble thanks as she set about opening the boot of her car.

'Something you ate?' she shouted.

'Yes.' I stood up and smoothed my hair away from my face. 'Can I have another one of those, please?'

'Sure.' She pulled another one from her bag. 'I think you need to get yourself home and into bed. You look very pale. Is there somebody you can phone?'

'Yes. Someone's coming. A friend.'

'Do you want me to wait with you?'

'No, no,' I said, looking at her two children. The older one was staring at the puddle of vomit I'd produced. 'I'll be fine. But thank you.' She loaded the shopping into the boot as I leant against the side of my car, my head bent low. She then began the task of strapping her two children into their car seats. As she got in herself, she looked over at me, saying, 'Hope you feel better soon. Take care,' and reversed slowly out of the space.

I went into the supermarket and bought a bottle of sparkling water. I sat on a low wall near my car and gulped at the fresh air. Tom rang thirty minutes later.

'Where are you? I'm outside the police station.'

'I'm in the car park across the road.'

'OK. Coming.'

He joined me on the wall for over an hour. I told him everything. About Helen and my mother. The book. The porridge.

'Is it possible she dropped your mum off and then drove

home herself? Before the accident?'

'Of course it's possible. But why would she lie? Why did she tell me my mother got the bus if not to cover up the fact that she was there?'

'I don't know.' He shook his head. 'I honestly don't know what to say. What happens now?'

'They're going to pass it to the homicide team. Her death is now officially suspicious.'

'Because of what you've told them? About Helen and your mum's relationship?'

'I don't know.'

'Do you want me to take you home?'

'No,' I lied. 'I'll be OK.'

He nodded and walked with me to my car. 'Did you do that?' he asked, pointing to the vomit on the driver's side.

'It was all a bit of a shock. I'm OK now though.'

He took my hand and pulled me round to the passenger side. 'Get in,' he said, opening the door and prising the car key from my hand. 'I'll drive you home.'

We said very little on the journey back to Balham. I fell asleep somewhere around Mitcham and woke up just as he was parking the car. He opened the front door and herded me upstairs to my flat. Once inside, he opened my bedroom door and gently pushed me across the threshold. 'Get some rest. I'll be in the living room.'

I was woken an hour later not by the sound of my phone ringing but his voice answering it. A few seconds later he knocked on the door of my bedroom and came in. He handed me the phone and mouthed the word *police* at me. It was Jane.

'Laura, just a quick call. I thought you should know that the homicide team have asked me to let you know that they'll be handling the case from now on.'

'OK.'

'And you'll probably be assigned a family liaison officer at some point, who will keep you informed.'

'What about Helen?'

'It's no longer my call, but at a guess it's very likely she'll be brought in for questioning in the next forty-eight hours.'

'I see.'

'I know this must be very difficult for you, and it's still early days, but whatever you do, please do not speak to Helen about any of this until they have. Is that OK?'

'Yes. I understand.'

Part Four

Conclusions

Post-mortem examination confirms this woman died as a result of a severed spinal cord. Injuries sustained were consistent with a fall down the stairs.

On 12 February 2012, my mother woke early, as usual. She believed absolutely in the majesty of the morning. That it went unnoticed by the somnolent masses was even more reason to get up and watch the day present itself. She got out of bed quietly and walked down the hallway to the small bathroom at the back of the house, where she washed and dressed.

She went downstairs to the kitchen and set about making a cup of tea. She filled the kettle and switched it on, then opened the cupboard above it to the cracking sound of cold water forced to boil. My mother moved contentedly in the tidy and co-operative kitchen, extracting her favourite cup – made out of bone china with brown flowers on a green background – from the shelf. I'd bought it for her around five years ago in a department store, the flowers still bright and vivid despite near-continuous spells in the dishwasher.

She poured porridge oats into a bowl and then used the sachet to measure the milk that followed. She placed the bowl in the microwave, closed the door and set her final meal in motion. She leant up against the work surface and looked out the window at the small and untidy garden as she sipped her tea. She watched the day grow in confidence and reach out to touch everyone and everything. The microwave pinged to announce her porridge was too hot to eat and then, minutes later, Helen appeared at the doorway. She was still sleepy, her hair tousled.

'What time do you have to be there?' she asked, feeling the side of the kettle and helping herself to a cup from the cupboard above my mother's head.

'I told Laura two o'clock, but I want to head off soon, buy some food and sort the garden out,' she said, looking at Helen.

'Why don't I drive you?'

'I was going to get the bus.'

'But you've just said, you've got to go to the shops. I'll drive you so you won't have to carry the bags.'

'We've talked about this. Not yet.'

'I'll leave before Laura arrives. She doesn't have to see me. What else do I have to do this morning?'

My mother put her cup down and opened the microwave. She extracted her porridge and stirred it in response to Helen's question. She closed her eyes as Helen went upstairs to get dressed.

They left Twickenham at around eight thirty and drove the seven miles to Surbiton. Helen parked her car on the driveway outside my mother's house and together they went inside. Waitrose wouldn't be open for another couple of hours, so Helen made more tea while my mother went upstairs to dust the bedroom she used to share with my father. Against the far wall was a bookcase containing her favourite novels. They were all there: *Jude the Obscure*, *Anna Karenina*, *The Mill on the Floss*. As she wiped the dust that had fallen since her last visit, she ran her index finger along the spines and remembered the many hours she'd spent as a girl, a woman and then as a mother, hosted by men and women long dead who cared nothing for her little life, in a world full of its own desperate glory. She pressed her finger to the creased spine of *Tess of the D'Urbervilles* and, watching her nail bed turn white under the pressure, she longed to fall back in. To recapture the ecstasy of escape. That was all she had ever wanted: to escape from a world her mother had compelled her to join and then, finding her reluctant, had prodded her in the back until she started walking.

'I think there's something you need to see. Downstairs.'

My mother, irritated by the interruption, didn't turn round. She'd been thinking of the first time she'd read *Tess of the D'Urbervilles*. How Hardy, in describing the rape of Tess – however broad the brushstrokes – had held up an artist's impression of what my father had done to her.

'Kathy?'

'What is it?'

'There's a damp patch in the kitchen. I think you'd better come and see it.'

It was about six or seven inches in diameter. Yellowed and dry by the time they craned their necks up at it.

'This is the problem. You're not here to keep an eye on things, and the house is falling apart.'

'The problem is a leaking roof. And it can be fixed.'

At around 11.15 a.m., Eileen Harris heard two female voices in the garden. My mother had taken a pair of secateurs to the bushes that had grown across the French doors at the back of the house. They began to argue quietly.

'Who's going to let a roofer in to fix it?'

'I will. I'll arrange a time and then make sure I'm here. It's really not so difficult.'

'Laura's a woman of the world. She'll understand.'

My mother's voice was quiet and anxious as she snipped. 'This has nothing to do with Laura.'

'What in God's name are you afraid of?'

'I'm not discussing this with you. Out here.' My mother walked back inside and put the secateurs on the dining table. Helen followed, closing the French doors behind her and locking them. She put the key down on the table.

'Where are you going?'

'To get a book.'

My mother walked quickly up the stairs. Helen stood at the bottom of the stairs, looking up at my mother's thighs and swinging skirt.

She put her own foot on the bottom step and looked down at her shoes: one on the wooden floorboards of the hallway and the other on the carpeted stair. She felt beaten by my mother's persistent unwillingness to come out. She walked up the stairs and onto the first-floor landing just as my mother emerged from her bedroom with the copy of *Tess of the D'Urbervilles*: a Penguin English Library edition with the shadow of Stonehenge on the front cover. She was smiling.

'They make you so happy, Kath. Why don't we pack up more of them? I'd like to have them at home. Our home.'

'Laura will know something's not right if my books are gone.'

Helen folded her arms across her chest and stared at the book in my mother's right hand. She'd been here before.

'The book. The bloody garden. Now a leaking roof. Kathy, do you want to be with me or not?'

'Why is it always so black and white with you?'

'Because I'm tired of the grey! You said you'd do it when Christopher left home. Then it was when Laura buys her own place. What next? Shall we wait until Laura has a baby? Perhaps we should let that child reach adulthood before we come clean. I tell you what, Kathy, let's just have it written on our gravestones. Then at least we'll have been honest with everyone.'

'I moved in, didn't I?'

'Quietly. Secretively. I'd hardly call this,' she pointed at the book in my mother's hand, 'living out in the open. Would you?'

'Helen. It's a book. That's all.'

'I couldn't give a shit about the book. Read it at my house if you must. Pretend you still live here. Say you're Lord Bloody Lucan for all I care. You're still hiding. You've always hidden behind me and here we are, in our fifties, and you're still doing it! And I've had enough,' she said and, by way of illustration, tried to pull the book from my mother's hand.

But my mother wouldn't let go. She pulled it back and stared at Helen, surprised. They had engaged in something. A horrible game that required them to participate. Helen grabbed for it again, combative and competitive as my mother's determined tug pulled the book and her body back towards the stairs. Helen wasn't going to be defeated. Not this time. So she allowed my mother to pull at the book, but still she held on. 'What are you doing?' my mother asked, horrified by Helen's grip. 'Let go!'

Helen clenched her teeth and dug her heels in. She wouldn't let go. My mother pulled until her head and neck were jutting over the chasm of the stairs. She saw the look of contemplation in Helen's eyes too late. A decision in the making. She tried to right herself, but Helen's arm was straight and strong. Pulled into position by my mother. Helen did as my mother asked: she let go and the book slipped from her grasp, pulled away down the stairs by my mother's body; a confusing mass of legs, back, head, legs, back, head. It went on and on until an accident of revolution, a grim turn of the wheel, brought the full weight of her body down on the delicate ring bones at the top of her spine. Helen heard the dry crack of the atlanto-occipital joint as her neck was broken, her spinal cord severed by the heavy mass.

She remained on the landing, stunned by how quickly gravity had accepted her final move and declared her the winner. My mother's eyes were open and flickering in neurogenic shock as Helen rushed down the stairs and knelt beside her.

'Kathy! Kathy! I'm sorry.'

My mother was gasping, choking as saliva and bronchial secretions accumulated in her throat.

'Please, Kathy. Don't. Wait. I'm going to call an ambulance.' She ran down the hall to the kitchen table where she'd left her handbag and retrieved her phone. The choking sounds were slowing, and as she dialled 999, she saw the copy of *Tess* that had landed, face down, on the doormat. In that moment she knew the call was impossible. My mother was about to die. And she would have to somehow explain the tussle for the book at the top of the stairs.

She walked back to the foot of the stairs and quickly put the book in her bag. The action – altering the scene of an accident – appalled her. The terrible fact of my mother's fall still so recent it could almost be undone. Deleted. But she knew an urgent consideration of the present was now necessary. Helen reached out, her hand shaking and tentative, to touch my mother's neck. Keeping her fingers away from the hair splayed on the floor, she lightly probed for a beat she suspected had gone. The blood, in silent loyalty to the defeated heart that had pumped it for over half a century, became motionless in lividity. Helen had no knowledge of the changes taking place inside my mother's body – that rigor mortis would soon set in and determine the time of death – but she knew that Katharine, her best friend and lover, had gone. That no ambulance could save her. And with this new certainty, she stood up, walked back into the kitchen and washed and replaced her teacup. She grabbed her coat and all the keys from the table. Then slowly, and with deliberate care, she walked towards the front door and opened it just enough to create an exit. As she stood on the doorstep, her hand poised to pull the front door shut behind her, she hesitated before locking herself out. She knew that I would be the next person to put my key in the lock. That the sight of my mother's broken neck at the bottom of the stairs would begin a search for answers that only she could end.

If you want to find Katharine, look for Helen. My grandmother, for all her confusion, had been spot on. The journalist in me – perhaps in a subconscious attempt to supplant the grief that had felt too normal, too ordinary – had got busy, sifting through the fragments of her life, and in the end it had been a bitter old woman with advanced dementia in a care home who had delivered the truth. Katharine Rowan, 51, had been murdered by her lover in her own home.

Except it wasn't murder. The charge brought against Helen was manslaughter; she hadn't wilfully pushed my mother down the stairs, but her failure to call an ambulance and the action of leaving her where she lay were enough, in the police's eyes, to justify charging her.

The trauma of those days; not just Helen's arrest and the hearing, but the slow trickle of her account of what happened that morning. The only saving grace was Tom. He stood beside me, first as a reluctant friend and then as an even more reluctant boyfriend. We have come back together, slowly, and while his caution pains me, I am grateful for his gradual forgiveness.

But I can't forgive Helen. Despite the police's best efforts, the Crown Prosecution Service decided there was insufficient evidence to provide a realistic prospect of prosecution. The evidence against her was largely circumstantial and, with the absence of any other witness to my mother's fall, there was no real way to challenge her version of events. And in many ways, I don't want to challenge them. Strange as it may sound, I believe her. I believe that in a moment of madness, she let go of my mother. Driven to exasperation by a lifetime of dependence and denial, she gave my mother what she wanted. A way out. The book. I don't know.

She never tried to get in touch with me. She never made any attempt to *really* explain. To me. To the child my mother had wanted and loved despite all it cost her. Her body had been my way into the world, and then the means by which I was able to understand how she lived and died. Passed away. The euphemisms sit more easily now.

On 20 January 2013, almost a year after her death and what would have been her fifty-second birthday, I scattered her ashes in the Isabella Plantation in Richmond Park. It was early in the morning and the sun was just starting to warm the frozen ground. I had informed Christopher of my plan the week before but, unable to justify another expensive flight to the UK, he was content for me to perform this final ceremony alone. And so as I walked past the dormant camellias to the shallow stream that skirted the larger pond, I thought of all that my mother had been before she was an unremarkable body or a weight of incinerated dust in a cardboard box and as I stood on the bridge and tipped her ashes over the side, leaving all that remained of her to the wind and the water, I forced myself to smile, knowing – as I did so – that tears would rise to meet my emotion. I'd given her to a place where I knew she had been happy. The breeze, in an act of unexpected generosity, took some of the fine dust and scattered it on my hair. As I walked to the other side of the bridge to watch her flow downstream and away from me, I was able to say my own goodbye.

My father divided up the money from the sale of the house equally between Christopher, Ellie and me, keeping enough in reserve to pay off his own mortgage and other debts. He and Jenny are currently looking at houses in Guildford.

Christopher and Steph have put a down payment on a bigger house in Melbourne and, perhaps as a result of doing so, finally decided to set a date for their wedding. The ceremony will be in Steph's hometown of Cranbourne, about twenty-five miles from central Melbourne. Tom began researching flights before I'd hung up with Christopher. He's already booked the time off work and is busy devising hikes through the Alpine National Park. The purchase of a cork hat is, I fear, inevitable.

Ellie has disappeared into another busy semester at Kingston University. My father bought her a car so she can commute between New Malden and Kingston. She's already put a deposit down on a house she plans to rent with some uni friends next year.

Andrea is going out with a Polish builder called Aleksander.

He bought the flat above hers in Tooting and quickly set about renovating it. Andrea was on hand to offer tea, biscuits and a curiosity in building materials that even Aleksander – relatively new to the country and with limited English – could see was disingenuous.

'So how did you do it, then?'

'Do what?'

'Get him to take you seriously.'

'I invited him downstairs to see the damp patch.'

'Is that some horrible euphemism?'

'No! You know, the bit behind the sofa, just above the skirting board.'

'OK. And what did he say?'

'He started talking about DPCs. And how he'd have to take the skirting board off to have a look. So I said I'd make him some lunch if he got his tools out.'

'Christ.'

We've been out to dinner – the four of us – and had them over to ours once. Tom spent so much of the preceding afternoon fretting over the state of my flat, nailing cable clips to the walls and resealing the kitchen work surface, all in anticipation of Aleks's judgement, that I vowed never to do it again.

Two weekends ago we drove out to East Grinstead to have lunch at his parents' house. I've met them once before; they stopped by his flat in Wimbledon one Saturday afternoon on their way into London. But this was my first visit to his family home. He was keen to show me his bedroom, a carpeted blue box with single bed (skirted by valance) and a Nirvana poster on the wall.

He sat down and invited me to join him. I closed the door behind me and sank down beside him. The mattress was old and soft with age. He put his arm around me. 'I know what you're thinking.'

'What am I thinking?' I whispered.

'That you never thought you'd make it. Here. To the cave of carnal pleasure.'

I laughed loudly. 'I didn't realise I was about to be pleasured. Don't you want to play with your Transformers first?'

'Are you taking the piss?'

'Not at all. This is a very sexual room. I mean, look at the Bart Simpson pencil case. That's dangerously arousing.'

'Yes, OK. It's a bit adolescent. But in all seriousness, it was the scene of many a great wank.'

'Such history.'

'I know. And it doesn't end there. I'm very happy to announce that you've been selected to perform a quick but rigorous handjob. As a thank you for coming.'

'That's very gracious of you.'

He nodded in agreement. 'I'm a giver. But you do make me happy,' he said.

I looked steadily at him. I knew not to flinch this time. 'And you me. Thank you.'

'For what?'

'For the second chance.'

He smoothed my hair down behind my ear with his right hand and kissed me gently on the mouth. I kissed him back, my mouth open in answer. 'You've missed your chance,' he mumbled as we fell back, the mattress yielding beneath us.

'What?'

'For a handjob. You've missed your chance. I won't accept anything less than full sexual intercourse now.'

'In that case, I think you'd better ask your mum and dad if I can stay.'

*

Last week I covered a student march along the Embankment; they were protesting against government plans to raise tuition fees. As I walked with the crowd, swept along by shouted slogans and chanting, I looked across the river to the South Bank and remembered, in the midst of all that noise and activity, my mother's head bent low over the books under Waterloo Bridge, quietly looking for a title she recognised. And then telling me to do the thing that would make me happy. So I understand, in a way I couldn't before her death, that while nothing is unremarkable and there's plenty that's worth shouting about, there is also a lot to be said for quiet. And I am quieter now.

Acknowledgements

In order to thank people for their involvement in this book I must explain that I wouldn't have had the idea if it weren't for my aunt, Teresa Cummins. I went to visit her in January 2007, eleven months after the death of her mother, my grandmother. Teresa lit the fire and showed me the post-mortem report. And as the flames kindled, so too did the idea that a story about how somebody lived could be just as compelling as how they died. That an unremarkable body does not mean an unremarkable life.

To my mum, Mary Lodato, who listened to my idea with excitement and encouraged me to get writing. I am so grateful for you and your belief in me.

To my dad, Giuseppe Lodato, for promising to buy all the books I ever write. Literally all of them. Your pride in me is a precious gift.

To my brother, Paul Lodato, for his legal knowledge and enthusiasm for my story.

To my sister, Emma Lodato, whose good humour, love and loyalty make me wealthy.

To my uncles, Kevin and Paul Hegarty, and my aunt, Fionnuala Forbes, I know your own stories are closely bound up in the chapter headings of this book. Thank you for lending me pieces of you.

To my husband, Jim Cowell, who made this new life possible for me. You are the very best of men. It was my great fortune to marry you.

To Maddie and Thomas, your arrival in this world helped me find my place in it. This book is for you.

To my mother and father-in-law, Jennifer and Bill Cowell, for cheering me on and helping me find the time to write.

To the teachers in my life: James Orchard, Polly Evernden and Niels Kelsted, for their red pen and reassurance.

To my early readers: Shumon Basar, Rosie Cowell, Donna Dove, Anna Banicevic, Dahlia Basar, Charlotte Morton, Caroline Aird-Mash, Janine Coombes and Sarah Hodges, who encouraged me – in their different ways – to keep going.

To my friends: Louise Patke, Jess Starr, Alex Knights and Alice Thatcher, for their love and support.

To Linda Rothera, for giving her time and expertise so generously.

To Lucy and Simon Jones, Louise Qureshi and Richard Cove, for their medical insights and guidance.

To Rich Coombes, for his photography.

To Kevin Boys, for his inspirational sculpture in Angel tube station.

To Dexter Petley of the Writers' Workshop: my first reader, champion and voice of reason.

To Jane Cobley, Martin Wallis and Kevin Rhoades, for a final steer in the right direction.

To Caroline Ambrose and the Bath Novel Award.

To my agent, Alice Lutyens, whose close eye and perceptive edits turned my dream into a reality. I will never be able to thank you enough.

To my editor, Arzu Tahsin, for writing an email that made me cry with happiness. I know I landed safely with you.

To Jennifer Kerslake, Rebecca Gray, Craig Lye and the rest of the team at Weidenfeld & Nicolson.

And Ursula Hagerty. Always Ursula. Whose life was a lesson in courage and death a lesson in loss. Your absence peoples these pages.

blog and newsletter

For literary discussion, author insight,
book news, exclusive content,
recipes and giveaways, visit the
Weidenfeld & Nicolson blog and
sign up for the newsletter at:

www.wnblog.co.uk

For breaking news, reviews and exclusive competitions
Follow us 🐦 @wnbooks
Find us 📘 facebook.com/WeidenfeldandNicolson